ALMOST CURABLE

ROBERT A. HOYT

TILTED FEDORA MEDIA

CONTENTS

FOREWORD

What can you say about an author who is named after one of the Grand Masters of Science Fiction? The first thought that comes to mind is he has some very big, figuratively if not necessarily literally, shoes to fill. In the case of Robert A. Hoyt, I am pleased to say he has done his namesake, Robert A. Heinlein, proud.

The second thought that comes to mind is that the name of this collection of short stories is very appropriate. As you read the stories, you will learn what many of us have known all along: that Robert is "almost curable". Which begs the question of whether we want to cure him and the answer is a most emphatic "NO!" His stories are the sort that will make you think even as you laugh or cry. They entertain at the same time you shake your head and wonder how his parents managed to survive his sort of imagination during his formative years.

I won't say Robert has a "unique" voice. That phrase has been overused in publishing circles and now tends to signal a publisher stretching for ways to lure in readers without realizing that unique isn't the first thing readers want, especially not in genre fiction.

I could say Robert's writing is "fresh." It is, but not in the "fresh like a daisy" meaning. No, Robert's writing is fresh like the strong wind that blows through, sweeping out the tired literature and stories we leave on the shelves, reading maybe once but never picking them up for a second time. His stories are fun and thoughtful even as they are thought-provoking.

His writing is also unique.

Vampire shopping carts. Need I say more? (Bite One, Get One Free)

Almost Curable contains 14 short stories that will take you on a journey of flight and fantasy, dreams and nightmares. Even as he entertains, Robert challenges you to think and ask yourself questions. More importantly, at least from this reader's point of view, you will imagine yourself in his character's shoes, asking yourself if you would react to the situation as they did.

Would you, if given the opportunity to determine your own fate for the right price, do so? Would you take that shortcut to fame and riches or would you step away and follow your heart?

What would you do when faced with the Devil and his attorneys? Would you try to beat him at his own game or would you fold? Now, throw in a guardian angel of law and learning – who also happens to fight like a ninja. Would that be enough to convince you to stand up to the Devil?

There's more, much more.

What makes Almost Curable such an intriguing collection is the way Robert can take every day items or actions and turn them into something completely different. I've touched on a few of the stories already. Add in others that deal with dreamcatchers, or a house AI that starts acting on its own, or even a heart-wrenching story like The Baby. Robert takes you on a journey through many of the sub-genres of science fiction and fantasy. As I read it, a quote from Wizard of Oz kept running through my mind.

But instead of it being "Lions and tigers and bears, oh my!" it was "Aliens and vampires and weres, oh my!" And so much more.

Robert A. Hoyt may be "Almost Curable" but I hope he never finds the cure, not as long as he continues writing stories like the ones included in this collection.

Amanda S. Green, author of the Honor & Duty Series and the Nocturnal Lives Series, among others

Dallas, Texas 2022.

FATE DOGS

He was a somber gentleman, of the sort who might be a CEO, and as it happened that afternoon, he was manning one of the many roach coaches in New York on my lunch break. He had in his hands a copy of the *Times*, but for some reason the picture on the front page wasn't quite visible. As I walked by, he lifted his head, and in the practiced voice of a street salesman said, "Fate in a bun, sir?"

I paused in midstep, and turned to look at him.

"What?"

"Fate in a bun, sir. I can add mustard, if you like. No extra charge."

I looked up at his sign, which sure enough said, clear as day, "Fate" in big bold letters, printed on gaudy yellow and red stripes.

The man behind the cart, clean-cut and wearing an expensive designer suit, was as out of place as a cabbie speaking Oxford English. Part of the act?

I had to admit, it was original. After a moment, I reached discreetly for my wallet.

"What the heck. I admire the gimmick. How much for a 'fate?'" I asked, a crisp five-dollar bill between my fingers.

"Five dollars even will get you a Business fate, sir. Would you like anything with that?" His expression didn't seem to contain even a hint of irony. I guessed it was for the believability.

"Do you have any relish?"

"Always, sir." He reached behind the mysterious semi-counter that all of the hot dog vendors have on their cart.

A couple of moments later, he handed me a steaming hot dog. At least I imagined it was a hot dog, although I couldn't really tell through the steam.

"And, as ever, all of our fates are guaranteed, or your money back," he said, while carefully filing my bill away in a cash register that I didn't remember seeing before.

I decided that it would be prudent not to attempt to interfere with his business approach, and took a bite of my hot dog.

For a second, I didn't taste anything. There was a sort of faint, watered-down impression of a sensation, as if I were remembering eating a hot dog before.

And then, through the mists of my mind, came things that I had only half-heard.

The grain company that my boss was about to drop all of the stock on due to a twenty-point decrease in the last few days. The market analysis that I glanced over briefly on the subject.

And the twelve years of market investment experience coming into sharp focus between the two.

A sweet taste flooded my mouth, like dollar bills dipped in honey.

Success.

Laboring with the weight of my sudden realization on my shoulders, I wolfed down the remainder of the hot dog, taking off in a running sprint for my office.

The lobby of the building was empty, as it always was on the lunch hour. The air felt heavy with the scent of fresh coffee in twelve stories of offices, and the faint muffled tone of groundbreaking meetings being held in the remote reaches of the building.

Briefly, I paused by the elevator. But the instructions in my mind burned like a poker inserted into my forehead, and I couldn't wait.

Half-crazed, I charged through the door to the stairs, and pushed my legs to their limits as I ran the seven flights separating me and my office.

I burst out into the silent office, and frantically greeted the secretary.

She was a stunning blonde named Sophie, who had surprisingly not developed a junkyard dog personality in so many years of playing mother hen for a little over a hundred disgruntled employees.

She was beyond beautiful to me, but then if I had to tell the truth, I was in love with her. But I knew she was out of my league.

"Sophes, will you buzz me in, please? I forgot something on the computer." My voice wavered a little. She smiled.

I would have smiled, too, but it was all I could do not to rip down the door. I had to get to my computer.

She took my keycard and buzzed me in.

The screen saver lazily taunted me, a glaringly colored, bouncy ball striking the edges of the screen and bouncing through the middle again. I moved the mouse, and with a speed that I had never had before, struck keys in rapid succession, first bringing up the stock reports, and then the information for buying the stocks.

The stock was running at a lowly twelve dollars a share.

I paused as I decided where to find crazy investors. Finally, I bought a large block of stock from my own account, but not before I called up a few friendly clients who liked taking risks.

As my own little gift to her, I sent Sophie an e-mail with my hot tip.

With a final sort of fortitude, I pressed the enter key to accept the transaction.

Three days later, the grain company announced a major breakthrough in genetic engineering. At the press conference, the representative revealed that their long-awaited zero-carb flour – called "Puff" – was finally developed, tested and slated for rapid approval. With luck, it would be hitting the shelves within the year.

The ticker price skyrocketed. In less than a week, the company was running strong high seventies, and was expected to continue to increase.

In the meantime, the adrenaline rush of investing my life savings on a whim had caught up with me. I even considered confessing to the boss.

And I did, when the timing was correct.

I hadn't had time to eat lunch for a while, and I hadn't gotten another fate dog since the first. But when the ticker price on the grains company went through the ceiling, I did tell my boss about my little personal venture.

There was a silence that lasted about two minutes, as he seemed to ponder the situation in a serious manner. Finally he looked up, put his fingers around the cigar that wreathed his face in smoke, and said, "You took a risk...you followed your gut. And it seems one of your tip buddies told a friend at one of our biggest clients, so they're mighty happy with us, too. Far be it for me to criticize one of the few workers around here with balls."

I thought I had just barely survived, until a week later a promotion came through. I was suddenly a whole new level of business broker, and my paycheck rescued my bleeding savings account from the incident.

Even Sophie pulled out a tidy little sum...her somewhat shy smile as I walked past in the mornings an ever-present reward.

And the more I considered this unimaginable and unforeseeable run of good luck, the more trouble I had with telling myself it was all a coincidence.

But the extra wad of money in my wallet wasn't enough to justify it as true for my subconscious. And the more I thought, the more I realized that only one thing would satisfy my curiosity on the subject.

I had to get another fate dog.

So when my lunch period came around that Thursday, I used the elevator, and walked out on the street to find the vendor.

I laughed at myself when I saw him in the same place as before. I was almost afraid that he had left.

As I walked up, he carefully put down his newspaper, folding it down the middle and without yet having made eye contact said, "Fate in a bun, sir?"

"Yes," my mouth said, before my brain could attend to the matter. Wrestling for control, I added, "But could you tell me the menu first?"

"Business for five, Gambling and Dispute for ten, twenty for Love, and of course, our famous fifty-dollar Chance, sir. Chance covers what the others don't," he said dryly. His businessman's tone could have fit in without a single turned head at a meeting of the board. "Difficult to get prepared, though, sir. That's why it's more expensive."

I thought about it for a second. In the end, Chance seemed the most likely prospect. But something about his tone put me off the idea. I wasn't really sure what he meant, but it didn't seem entirely pleasant. As for Dispute, that was something that the newly rich do well to avoid.

But if Chance and Dispute were out, then the most likely one would be...

"Gambling. I'll have a Gambling dog, please."

Once again, the same complicated technique with reaching behind the counter, and a steaming bun whose contents were just barely obscured emerged.

I stared down at it. For a second I felt somewhat apprehensive.

"No...it's just a silly urge. A lucky strike. Nothing to be afraid of," I told myself.

I rammed the hot dog in my mouth quickly, before I could think of a rebuttal and let my good sense get in the way.

Once more the watered-down hot dog taste, like eating something extremely far away. And then, without warning, I knew more than I had ever realized about the world around me.

I could taste the things around me happening, and I knew at once where the money was being made and lost.

"No!" This was in my best Telling-A-Dog-It's-Done-Something-Wrong voice, and aloud, which fortunately didn't make me exceptional from all the street crazies around.

But I had to interject some willpower.

Too little, too late. My legs were off on their own. Like a deranged maverick, I cut through the crowd of lunchtime commuters.

I would have felt some sort of fatigue, I suppose, after the first mile, if I had paid attention, but I was more concerned with this urge to keep going.

Finally, my legs drew me to a halt in front of a local gambler's haven. It was a grand and exceptionally notorious establishment in my circles, hidden behind a grubby iron door in a back alley, ignored by police who didn't want to get certain people angry.

My legs took me through the front door. The floor of the gambling den bristled in my senses. And then, I saw the roulette table.

I couldn't hold myself back. I ran past the bouncer, who vouched for me to the boss with a nod, and entered the game with ten thousand dollars.

The wheel spun hypnotically and the whirl drew me in. A man standing next to me took me for a tourist, snickering under his breath.

He didn't expect my money to last too long.

But my brain screamed at me. Red 32.

With no choice but to obey, I placed all of my cash on Red 32. The wheel whirled, the little white ball clicking along rhythmically.

Time slowed down for a moment as the ball came to a stop balanced between two numbers, finally landing on Red 32 with a little plunk that took up the majority of my consciousness.

Three spins later, a couple of men came up to me and ominously requested that I retire for the evening. I knew better than to say no.

I cashed out, getting a standard tin suitcase to hold my phenomenal winnings—less my original stake, which I pocketed for ready cash—hailed a cab, and took it home.

But as I stepped out of the cab, I heard a click behind my head.

My thoughts cleared as only a cocked hammer on a powerful handgun can make them.

"And now, sir, if you would be so kind as to hand over the suitcase, then I believe that we can both call it a night." The barrel pressed into my neck.

I tried to calculate my chances in my head, and realized that my ability to gauge odds had deserted me, like my heightened ability to sense the air around me.

"Very interesting," I said, to no one in particular, as I handed the suitcase to the man who had come up behind me. "Disappears under high duress."

By this time, my cab driver had taken the opportunity to get far away from us both.

"Much obliged. And now, as I can see I have made you uneasy, I shall be glad to repay you by helping you sleep."

A gun handle clocked me like a cavalry charge, and I fell to the ground.

The early morning sun shone on my face. I was in the suit that I had been wearing the day before, slumped over on my front doorstep.

The quick run over my senses acknowledged that I had the sort of deep-seated headache that seeps into your brain and permeates every single nerve with pain.

I looked at my watch, which luckily I still had. Then again, in my state, I didn't look like the sort of person who would own a watch, anyway.

My spine went as straight as a rod. I was an hour late for work.

Not even bothering to dress in fresh clothes, I stood up and felt in my inside pocket. A sheaf containing ten thousand dollars—less last night's cab fare—came to hand.

I hailed a taxi. Ten minutes later, I was standing in the reception lobby of the seventh floor, where my promotion had booted me.

Of course, it looked like the same lobby as the seventh, and more importantly, Sophie was at her desk.

She looked at me in surprise. "Are you all right? You look horrible." She seemed genuinely concerned.

"Fine, fine. Could you just check me in, Sophes, and hold my calls for a while? My head hurts a little. Nothing more."

A little being horribly, I added to myself.

"Normally, I would, but the boss asked to see you as soon as you came in. You didn't check back in yesterday."

Damn. I had forgotten to come back to work in my starstruck haze.

I would lay even money now that the boss was not about to offer me a CEO position. If I was lucky, he might offer me references after he fired me.

I should be so hopeful.

"Good luck," she said, as she buzzed the private elevator with the button under the desk.

My humiliation was complete. I would be fired after showing up to the office and attempting to get the girl that I loved—I supposed it was high time I admitted it—to check me in, immediately after I disappeared randomly...all the while looking like a bum.

Gambling fate. Lovely.

I stepped into the elevator. The doors shut with a ding and it began to whir along quietly, passing floor after floor.

Finally, the moment to face the music came. The elevator doors opened, revealing the boss, looking stern behind the thick, smelly cigar smoke.

"Take a seat," he said, hand gesturing towards the leather guest chair.

I did so, the red carpet thick like molasses on my steps.

"I hear that you disappeared yesterday. Care to elaborate?" he asked, with a sort of trap taunting me in his voice. You could almost hear a sort of half-hearted chuckle in his question, as if he were enjoying a fine irony at my expense.

I considered telling him about the fate dogs, and the inexplicable urge to go and gamble impossibly large amounts of money, and the whole shebang.

And then I asked myself why I felt it necessary to get into therapy, and the loony bin, when I was already getting fired.

"I ran into a client," I said, my mind spinning an elaborate yarn. His eyebrows rose. "Who?"

"I don't remember. We went out for drinks, and then I came back around. But a man mugged me, and clocked me on the head, so I don't feel so well, as you may imagine."

A complicated alibi needed more memory than I had.

He stared at me for a moment.

"I see," he said, and then after a minute asked, "Can I get you a drink?"

Why was he toying with me?

"No, thank you."

"I didn't think so." He shook his head and leaned forward. The desk creaked under his weight.

"How about you just tell the truth, kid? You met some blonde piece whom you helped invest, and you have a hangover from drinking enough alcohol to stock an infirmary. I was young once, too."

He got up, poured himself a gin, and downed it in a single shot.

"Look, just don't let it happen again. We can't have you disappearing in the middle of an important deal. Now go on. Use the executive gym and get yourself cleaned up."

I couldn't believe it. I walked over to the door of the elevator. It made a little ding, and opened. The boss stopped me by the door.

"Remember, kid, I have hopes for you. Do me and yourself a favor and don't piss it away."

I just nodded.

After the ride down, I was greeted with Sophie's face. She was waiting expectantly.

"Which way to the hotshot's gym, Sophes? I need to freshen up a little."

I handed her my access card, and she swiped it for mods with a smile I hoped was because I had not been fired.

"Down the hall and to the left. Congratulations on surviving!" she called after me as an afterthought.

I just smiled half-heartedly, and headed for the shower.

For a day or two, I was too scared to think about the hot dog stand.

But hope springs eternal.

The more I thought about it, the more I fell for Sophie. I even occasionally toyed with the idea that she might feel the same way about me.

If there was anything that might give me the fortitude to charm her, I had to try it. And then I thought of the Love option the man had mentioned.

It was insanity, I knew. I was throwing good money after bad, I knew.

But...I knew I would regret it if I never tried.

I waited carefully, biding my time until Friday came.

That way, if something went wrong, then at least it wouldn't interfere with work. I wasn't taking any chances. I waited until the day ended to find the hot dog vendor, sitting in the usual place.

"May I ask you something?" I asked the man in the booth, and waiting only long enough for him to glance up at me, plowed ahead. "I know this is a crazy question, but will a 'Love' make me able to charm a girl whom I already love?"

He stared at me blankly. "Yes," he replied flatly, without thought.

I forked over a twenty-dollar bill.

"One Love, please. Mind you, remember the ketchup." I was half-deranged with precautions.

Seconds later, I held in my hand a Love dog. I didn't even think about it. There was no argument. I just ate it.

And even as I bit into it, I realized that I had only asked if I would be *able* to charm her. And it struck me very hard that I likely wouldn't.

However, I could already feel the beginning of the craziest night of my life pressing itself into my mind.

I knew where to go, and I knew what to do for the night.

My first stop was a local nightclub.

Almost involuntarily, I greased the doorman with a hundred dollar bill, and slipped through the door.

I was there for half an hour. In that time I got two drinks and two girls who had had far too many drinks.

I don't recall their names.

I don't even recall offhand whose place we went to.

Two hours later, I woke up in whomever's bed we had gone to, in between the two girls.

I resisted the urge to peek beneath the covers, even though I knew that if they were in the same state I was in, I would regret that for the rest of my life.

I got dressed hurriedly, took a quiet shower, and left the apartment with the other two still sleeping.

It was early in the morning. The majority of the city was undoubtedly still asleep.

I walked beneath the city lamps, the early morning chill clearing my head. It was a quiet part of the city, and there were no people on the streets.

Well, so much for saving myself for marriage. Or, somewhat more urgently, just facing Sophie. The worst part was that I remembered everything because I kept thinking about Sophie. I had had a night that other men only dreamed of, and I had actually hated every minute of it.

Congratulations, I thought. *You have officially gone crazy.*

But who cared? I had pretty much blown it, anyway. My last chance to get Sophie was gone. I had used the fate dogs, and they had reacted perfectly.

But not the right person for my purposes.

I was ready to cry. I saw worst-case scenarios rain down, each one with her finding out in more and more uncomfortable ways.

It would take a miracle.

The man said Chance dogs handled "everything else."

"Forget it," I said aloud. "It isn't going to happen."

I wasn't worried about looking insane. There was no one around, and besides, I might well be insane, anyway.

But that prying little voice that had gotten me into this situation in the first place persisted.

And little by little, I broke down, until I found myself standing on the street where the vendor normally was, in spite of my better judgment.

For a moment, I peered into the night. I told myself that I wouldn't see him.

For a second I believed it. But I knew what I wanted.

And then, even in the fog of the predawn glow, I could see the gaudy yellow and red stripes.

They wrapped around me like a blanket, and I took a step forward.

I would just buy a Chance dog, and then I could have Sophie.

That was how the world worked, I knew it.

I walked forward, and came to a stop in front of the vendor.

He looked up in anticipation. The air grew heavy and thick, as if he were simply waiting for me to give a request that he already knew.

Even in the city that never slept, there was a lag in pedestrian traffic at five in the morning on this street.

Looking around, I suddenly realized that I was standing alone on an empty street. Not even a car in the road.

"Can I help you?" he said. His slate grey eyes fixed cold and unfeeling on mine.

My skin crawled.

It didn't feel right.

It wasn't right. But I needed to do it. It was my only chance with Sophie.

But that wasn't right, either. Even I knew that.

Even before, we had always talked. We knew each other. Maybe I could have a chance, anyway.

A chance at a little more than a one-night stand. That was really what I had been after, even if I hadn't admitted it.

I felt my hand go to the money in my pocket.

I was about to spend fifty dollars. I was about to lose control of my decisions again.

Could I really afford that?

I paused. The tiny little itch in my mind suddenly had a megaphone, and was screaming in my ear, in none-too-diplomatic terms.

I never really could control the fates these dogs gave me, and telling myself I could was madness. I knew in my heart that another fate dog would just make me lose control again.

And at the same instant, I realized that none of them could possibly act as I would. It was like becoming someone else, someone who loved other people, knew other things.

Wanted other things.

And none of them were Sophie.

Finally, defiantly, I seized the reigns of my own willpower.

I stared the man at the stall in the eyes.

"Good morning," I said, with a slightly ironic smile on my lips, and walked away.

The man in the stall went back to reading his paper. The sun peeked over the horizon, showering the streets with gold.

After all, if I still had a chance, then I wanted to make the most of it.

I thought about where she lived.

It wasn't a long walk, really.

"Besides," I chuckled to myself, "I feel lucky."

THE MAGE IN THE MOON

I did something stupid, but it saved our lives.

You couldn't judge scale, out here. The scrying array was designed for our approach to the moon. Yet, instinct told me the purple fireball flying towards us was big, bigger than the ship.

Automatic reflexes took over. The spacelev for the moon trip was basically an orbiter, but with a beefier main resonator to increase outgoing thrust and some extra seating. So I did as I had been trained for orbital missions, if a slab of undocumented debris blindsided you. I popped open the aether skimmers, goosed the resonator to keep them driving, and tried to roll.

Roll, the ship did. But unthinkingly, I tapered the throttle before retracting the skimmers, as you should in orbit. Here, there was an accompanying explosion from the aft that shook my teeth even in the pilot's cabin. At least we avoided the fireball, by a hair's breadth.

Venna looked at me.

"That sounded like the aetheric drive."

I pinched the bridge of my nose.

"Close enough. I'd bet that was the main resonator. Though given how close it is to the drive, it may be a distinction without a difference."

She looked at my left hand, guiltily drawing down the skimmer controls, and her eyes widened.

"You let the skimmers draw negative aether!"

I winced.

"Got rattled by the fireball." I ground my teeth in frustration. My form had been good, for Earth orbit. Skimmers drew when they weren't pushed, so that spacelevs

wouldn't need a "fuel source." Earth's aetheric field was strong enough to be trans-
duced actively into motion. A less-tentative veteran pilot would have done worse,
since you got maximum thrust by riding the line and drawing aether at exactly the
rate it burned. If I'd done that, the resonator would have exploded immediately.

I cursed the thaumic engineers for not putting a failsafe in. But then, negative
aether was so volatile it was difficult to safely detect. And the skimmers were needed
to slow the ship for descent. You couldn't just disable them when you left orbit. So
it was up to us to keep the skimmers under thrust any time we had them open in
negative aether. Unfortunately, a lifetime of contrary training came to the fore, under
fire.

"Canceling the aether waves liberated the stored energy of both. But that could
mean—" she said, with dawning horror. She immediately began to undo her buckles.

"No! Don't go back there. I need a co-pilot if I'm going to pull an emergency
landing."

"Don't you understand? We've got who-knows-what in our hold now," she said,
pulling down her staff-helm from its hook. "Someone has to go kill it."

I started to say that I doubted the energy had taken any form more coherent than
an explosion when an unholy shriek came from the back of the cabin. I twisted in my
seat to see a terrifying chimera of terrier, squid, and lobster burst through the door.

Venna flipped backwards over her seat, tucking her legs to stop herself from hitting
the ceiling. She grabbed her battle staff off the wall and slipped its carry strap over
her shoulder. In one smooth movement, one hand went to the slanted grip inset at
the base of the handle, the other to the casing of the resonator array, steadying her
shot. Perfect range form. A sheen ran over the surface of the helm. The thaumic fork
at the end of the battlestaff sizzled, and a fireball shot across the cabin and caught
the creature center mass.

Johnson climbed out of his straps. Recruited from an urban ghetto with a "vibrant"
goblin community, he'd come with impressive scars, and an amazing proficiency with
blades. He turned his combat knife on the struggling creature. The claws came off
first. Then, in a blink, the entrails were cracked, and he was pulling out great viscous
black blobs of unrecognizable offal.

Major Brumly turned to me. He counterbalanced his rough dwarven features with
crew-cut red hair and a neatly trimmed beard, which made him look stern in the dim
light. I thought he might rib me, but we had bigger problems.

"Keep your eyes on the sky, Palder!" he shouted, and turned to the seated men.
"Johnson, Hogness, Ditri, Wauler! Grab your gear and get under. Slougham, Campbell, follow and assess engine damage. Dress for vacuum—we don't know if the

wards on the hull paneling held. Everyone else, except Rhines and Venna, follow and secure a hall. Rhines, you and I will watch the door. Venna, get to the fore and help Palder."

I heard all this over my shoulder, while desperately working to read the dials. The demons in them were never wrong. Their whole existence was tied to knowing the attribute they were bound to. Unfortunately, they were never wrong. The dials were moving too fast to read. The moon loomed ahead, filling the viewport. Our angle of approach was negative. The force of the explosion had us coming in fast, steep, and upside down.

Venna sat down reluctantly and confronted the dials with similar bewilderment. I turned to her.

"Okay, unless the engine compartment is destroyed, in which case we're all dead, anyway, as soon as our men get to the emergency switch they'll cut to the backup resonator in the fore. And if it survived, there's a good chance the steering drive did, too."

She looked at me like I was insane.

"You want to slow the ship down using the steering drive? Its thrust is laughable in comparison!"

I nodded. From below decks came shouting, and a symphony of bangs and cracks. I tried to concentrate.

"That's true. We're not going to get down to a stop with it. But with constant controlled thrust, we can slow her considerably and nudge her into a shallow trajectory. Since we're coming in upside-down, our best bet is to drop our nose far under the edge of the moon before flipping over or thrusting. If we don't mitigate the downward vector, we'll bury in the moon like a nail in a plank."

I toggled switches. If you could see arcane energy flow, the ship would have been a great web of thaumic entanglements. Lay-lines in the aether were bent, intersected and twisted by runes in the auto-circle mechanism, allowing effortless control. Now they formed a channel of magic that coupled the steering drive to the main engines, when extra impulse was needed for a turn of speed or evasive maneuvers. Not all the time, or the ship's smaller steering drive would be unbelievably sensitive and probably slowly burn out from sheer aetheric load. But with the main resonator down, it was perfect.

"Don't draw negative aether again," Venna warned. A sharp <u>thump</u> against the deck below punctuated her statement, and she looked back up at me. "It would kill everyone down there."

"I know. Once we've got our tack, we'll modify the procedure for a negative aether landing. I'm going to hold the throttle before opening the skimmers, and drain the resonator until we're close to out of juice. Then I'll retract before I pull the throttle. "

Behind us, the floorboard dented so sharply that a claw poked through. Rhines stomped on it with a combat boot. Someone dragged it back under.

"So, to get to tack, you'll want to stutter the skimmers. Do the same thing in short bursts to nudge us onto course. It'll wrench the mechanism, mind you. But this ship isn't going to come down without some chipped paint, anyway," she said, thoughtfully.

"That's the idea."

A magical flame flashed to life in a red bulb on the console. The team downstairs had activated the backup power.

I looked over at Venna, who nodded.

"Major Brumly! As soon as they're able, the team should assume crash positions, sir!" I called over my shoulder. I rested my hand on the controls.

"Let's do this."

We still came in hot—but we came in *survivably* hot. Skimmers out, drive wailing, we seared a trench across the surface of the moon. The plates scraped right off the lower hull and the nose buried in the rough lunar sand.

But we survived.

The lev came to a juddering, wrenching halt. I forced myself to keep my grip on the yoke. It kept me grounded and conscious. I hadn't yet gotten my vacuum-wear. I had to stay awake. Had to move quickly.

I hauled myself up. It was dark, but I knew where my vacuum-wear was. I'd done this enough in training, I could do it now by feel. Dizzily, I donned the Seven League boots, the gloves, and the high-collared, quilt-like robe. The suit was topped with a staff-helm. Unlike normal helms, used just to translate thoughts into patterns of magical energy, these had built in features to integrate with the robe, and full visors, warded against the blinding lunar sun. Along the top of each was a magic mirror for communication.

Last was the backpack. It was mostly a portable resonator array to power the suit, except for the most important part, my air supply, an inconspicuous tube on one edge. Difficulty in supporting time-accelerated plants on early suits had led thaumic engineers to use an air-filled pocket dimension. As it shrank, the air's pressure increased, keeping the suit supplied. A system of valves routed the CO_2 into another pocket dimension, which the energy from the shrinking dimension expanded, buffered by the resonator array.

I got my battlestaff, and holding it in one hand, thought the activation code. The robe reacted instantly. Its thick material gripped my body and spread itself over the surface. Within seconds, the suit was a contiguous piece of impermeable, skintight white fabric, marked only by pockets, patches, and American flag badging. The hoses rose off the backpack like snakes and plugged themselves into the helmet. All ambient noise was cut off. The welcome hiss of flowing air began.

Lights, I thought. Bright magical fire, white and heatless, rose on the bar mounted above my visor. A curved mirror directed the light wherever I pointed my head.

Now I was ready. No. Almost ready. One final detail.

I turned around, and went to my personal belongings. The straps were hard to operate in gloves, but at last I got access, and pulled out my allotted keepsake.

"What in the seven hells is *that*?" said a familiar face, popping suddenly into my mirror. I turned around.

Venna was standing up, looking totally unmoved by the crash while my head was *still* ringing. She had clearly finished putting on her own gear a moment earlier, but she'd had a slight headstart with the helmet, so to speak.

"An enchanted Samurai sword. My grandfather thought it was lucky. Picked it up in the Pacific theater. Or at least, so he said, though he always refused to explain how."

Not that he'd said much about the war. We'd only found out he'd made sergeant first class in World War II when they buried him in the uniform. Most of my memories of him were watching baseball, on a magic mirror he'd enchanted himself.

"A *sword* was your personal item?"

I laughed, as I belted the weapon onto my back. I had *just* enough flexibility to draw it out of the sheath.

"I'd intended to use it for fencing practice. But after seeing the beasties that pop up when negative aether is mishandled, I want an extra blade. And if it really *is* lucky, brother, could I ever use that, too."

I moved aft. All hands had successfully suited up and taken their seats. They looked badly rattled, but were fully present and accounted for. Major Brumly flashed in my mirror, looking winded.

"Well done, Palder, Venna. We seem to be in one piece."

I nodded.

"Thank you, sir. Sorry about the ship, sir."

He tilted his head dismissively.

"Don't worry about it, for now. I definitely expected better piloting out of you, Palder, but the trip was only meant to be one way, anyway. The last lev sent up is just docked, gathering dust. Or at least," he looked up, thoughtfully, "it was, last we checked. How far are we from the base?"

Venna came up in the mirror.

"The scrying array was destroyed in the crash, sir. We can't say for sure. Probably a walkable distance. We were on course until that fireball came at us."

He frowned.

"I heard you mention that. You say this fireball came close to the ship? Did you see the origin?"

"I was watching the sky carefully at the time, sir," Venna replied. In fact, she'd looked downright apprehensive, but I hesitated to mention it. I'd never have seen the fireball without her. "It looked like it came from the moon base, or close to it," she said.

The major looked grave.

"That's bad news, although it does put our crash in context, at least. We've got to get our bearings as quickly as we can."

A tidbit from pathfinding, back in basic, nudged me.

"A battlestaff can do routine scrying, sir. Depending on how far away the target is, it can be energy expensive. But that's mitigated by how *unique* the target is."

"Go on."

"Detection of surface features, Fourier transform to separate the aetheric waves, is only necessary if you need a map. But with a distinctive target, like the main resonator of the previous spacelev, we can scry for far less energy."

There was a pause. Venna came up, nodding approvingly.

"That's actually a pretty good plan. With ours destroyed, the only resonator of comparable scale within thousands of kilometers is on the old spacelev."

Johnson flashed up, unexpectedly. Everyone was listening to this.

"Why not scry for the base itself?"

I shrugged.

"Have you ever seen it? Without a clear mental picture, scrying won't work."

Major Brumly raised his hands for attention.

"It sounds worth a try to me. Any further objections? No? Excellent. Slougham and Campbell, you're the experts on engine design. Do you two know how to scry?"

They both affirmed.

"Then concentrate on that resonator and give us a direction. I want agreement between you before we head out. Once we have a heading, set 7Ls to 1 kilometer until the base is in sight. No need to wear ourselves out when we still don't know what to expect in the base. However, you will *stop* and confirm everyone is together before each additional step. Clear?"

A chorus of agreement.

"All right. We march in five. Get going."

Leaving the wreckage of the spacelev behind us, we set out westward. From outside you could tell how badly the ship had been beat. The abrasive moon dust had sanded the flag nearly away.

For reasons I couldn't explain, I was drawn to look at the crash during each roll call between steps. On the fifth step it was just a tiny dot in the distance, in danger of being eaten by a steeply curved horizon.

By seven league we proceeded across giant craters and a featureless plane of rough particulate. There were mutters and grumbles, and one or two comments about my flying skills from anyone who thought the major was distracted.

Part of me, the part that watched the ship, was likewise grousing and chewing over our predicament. But another larger part was thrilled. Never mind the circumstances. Here I was on the moon, at last. I'd dreamed of this for years. As a kid, I'd spent hours staring through a telescope at the "mage in the moon," revealed up close as a chance collection of craters on her face. Unromantic as that was, as a teen I'd spared her many a glance that belonged rightfully to my earthbound sweethearts. I'd joined the Air Force entirely in hopes that someday, I could be here. Granted, my fantasies had had more stars and fewer grousing soldiers. But those were details. I was no longer looking at the mage in the moon. I was sitting on his doorstep.

At last, the major called a halt. On the horizon, I could make out a squat, grey building, crouching furtively on the edge of a crater like a boy sneaking into a forbidden swimming pool.

"From here, we walk," the major said, sizing it up. "Keep your eyes and ears open. Assume nowhere is safe. And especially note any potential sources of giant fireballs," he added.

I closed my eyes and toggled my boots off. Walking after using them usually felt unbearably slow, but as we got closer to the base, I began to feel grateful for the controlled approach. Something about it felt dangerous. It had the feel of a ruin—like it belonged to someone else, and our trespass had been noted.

I realized it was slowly getting darker, too. The sun peeking over the horizon behind us, untempered by atmosphere, was no longer as intense as a blowtorch. Which, on the upside, saved the energy our enchanted multiweave used to move heat to the ground beneath us.

But darkness surrounded the base. It pressed in on the peripheral vision insistently and unnaturally. For a while, I thought I was having some delayed effect from the crash. Then helm lights started coming on.

They did nothing. The darkness was like fog.

The major came up on the mirror, swearing. He was not a dwarf given to swearing.

"I've never seen anything like this. I've heard black magic is associated with darkness, but I'm used to the mines and even I can't see in this."

Johnson stepped forward.

"I've seen something like this before, sir. Goblins had a few cults in the neighborhood, you know? Worshipped the *old* gods."

"With respect, sir, what darkness are you talking about?" said Venna. Everyone looked at her in surprise. Her helm light wasn't on.

There were a few minutes of confused discussion. Apparently, the blindness affecting everyone else wasn't affecting Venna. Johnson did a little test in which he threw a spare knife (of course he had one), into the darkness behind her. With no difficulty whatsoever, she walked into the gloom and returned bearing the knife.

Her body language indicated some complicated internal conflict. Whatever it was, she'd resolved it when she came back on the mirror. She addressed the major.

"If everyone else is blinded, it may be best for me to take point, sir. I think I have an innate resistance, for...some reason. Which means that I may be the only one qualified for pathfinding. For example, the entrance to the moon base is over there."

She pointed into what was now just impenetrable black mist, at about ten o'clock relative to our current heading. "I was about to ask why we weren't heading for it when we stopped, sir."

The major looked unsettled.

"Hmm. Staff sergeant, you know that I trust you implicitly. Nevertheless, that seems—"

Johnson cut in.

"Seems like you're strangely unbothered by dark magic. You got any stories we ought to hear, Venna?"

She came up, looking affronted.

"No. I don't. Why?"

The major stepped between them, surprisingly imposing for a man barely over three feet tall.

"None of that. Venna, to the front. Johnson, back in formation. We won't look a gift horse in the mouth just now. Staff Sergeant Venna has an impeccable record of service that I'm not going to ignore over an arcane magical phenomenon."

"But sir, she might be in the control of some dark—"

"Well, then it's very polite of them to show us in. I gave you an order, staff sergeant!"

Johnson muttered something about necromancers, but obeyed. We proceeded, headed up by Venna, until at last we came to a large square door. Ordinarily, entering would have required a magical key, or password. Now, you could just step through the gaping, human-sized hole.

"Oh, this just gets better and better," said Murrey, scowling.

The major looked grave. He pointed out two men. "You two, you're with Venna. Advance."

We secured the airlock, and headed inside. The darkness had settled to a four-me-ter radius, which was plenty short enough. After seven years of construction and three years of habitation, the building was labyrinthine. Most of it was laboratories. There was a barracks, too, somewhere in the distance, but the hallways were flooded with hard vacuum. Search and rescue seemed unlikely. The major came up on the mirror.

"Our primary objective is the so-called 'Great Arc,' the super-circle that controls this building. The lay-focuser for secure communications to Earth is directly con-nected to it. But it also stores information collected in these labs and personnel data. If a foreign interest staged an attack, odds are good that they came for it. I'm raising the building map on my LaF now; tune to ignis, argentum, plumbi, and spin it onto your pack's autocircle."

I waved my hand in the air. Three interlocked concentric circles appeared, which I turned to the aspects. As I finished, they spun like a gimbal ring, representing their true orientation in the lay-focuser. The auto-circler whirred as it imprinted the pattern of the map. A thought brought it up on my mirror.

"We'll proceed West to the Eastern hub," said the major, as I studied the map. "Then turn North and advance towards the Great Arc. Johnson and Slougham, take the flank."

We advanced. The hallways were a mess. Piles of paper drifted before our feet like heavy, square smoke in the low gravity. Streaks of brownish crystals spread across the wall. It looked like blood, dried to crystalline in the vacuum. But where were the bodies?

When we reached the Eastern hub, I noticed a trace of movement, in a thin spot in the darkness. It was just out of my sight. As I hailed Venna to check it out, the thing suddenly leapt.

Adrenaline surged in my veins. I pointed the battlestaff. Golden fire erupted from the end, hitting the thing in mid-leap. By that point, the rest of the unit had seen it. Fire poured through the room and hammered the creature into submission. As it died, the aura of non-darkness around it was subsumed.

I crept over, and prodded it with my foot, battlestaff poised in case it needed another dose. It looked very similar to the things that had manifested on the spacelev, but it was larger, and slimmer, like a jungle cat. It also had thick scales, which were no match for a battlestaff, but would have given Johnson's knives some trouble. It somehow still looked half-squid.

"Well, if our experience is anything to go by, there's been a serious accident with negative aether," Svedkos said. You could tell him immediately by the protrusions in his helm for his horns, and the short, saucer-bottomed boots for his hooves. Most people considered him odd. Satyrs traditionally preferred to tend farms, but Svedkos's family had lived in New York City for three generations. His father was an architect.

"No, that was different," said Winechord. "We had air. That thing didn't seem bothered by hard vacuum."

I pointed out the thinning of the darkness around the creature.

"Maybe it was somehow absorbing this stuff, rather than breathing?" I suggested.

The major shrugged. "Our objective hasn't changed. Just watch the shadows. Sergeant Venna only has one pair of eyes."

Sure enough, we got jumped as we headed North. Not just once, but half a dozen times, by increasingly large contingents of strange, tentacled creatures. There were more armored cat-like ones, but also hulking monstrosities with no visible head and six bulky arms ending in three long, pointed claws. Blowing chunks out of them with fireballs didn't stop them. You had to hit them in the circular mouth set between the arms. But the worst creature was spotted by Venna, who was checking our flank occasionally, and tagged it before it came out of the dark.

It tagged back. No sooner had she fired into the darkness than a returning volley of purple fire came rocketing back down the hall. It passed within an inch of my face. For a moment, it looked like one would hit Venna, but she moved her staff at the last second and raised a small shield. The fireball ricocheted into the ceiling.

The rest of us fired blindly into the dark, and charged forward. Purple fireballs flew around us. Slougham, furthest back, was slower with his shield. He went down, shoulder burning in the darkness. I heard him scream in the mirror, with a wine-glass overtone as the sound overloaded it.

The aggressor was a floating eye. It was about the size of a basketball and trailing tentacles like a man-o-war. Direct hits of magical fire dissipated inches away from it.

So. Between Venna and the eyeball, we knew that spells cast in negative aether could interact with spells from positive aether without ramification. Which made sense, since the energy of an aetheric wave was lost when a spell was formed. It also opened some interesting opportunities.

I reached up, pulled the sword, and leapt over the creature, giving it the best slice I could. It wasn't textbook, but the sword was enchanted and the blade was sharp, so the density of the magic at the edge was high. The thing burst, spilling vitreous fluid across the floor.

"Nicely done with that sword," said Johnson, giving me a hand up. From him, this was the highest praise.

I looked back.

"Did Slougham make it?"

Johnson shook his head.

"No. Burned a hole right into his lungs. Couldn't keep air in. The major is stowing his body away from the creatures."

The major came up to us.

"Think that's where your fireball came from, Palder?"

I shook my head.

"No chance, sir. Too small."

"Maybe that thing has a big brother?" said Ditri.

"Hm. Duly noted. The door to the Great Arc seems intact. Can someone get us through?"

Rhines and Svedkos advanced. Their battlestaffs spit white-hot cutting flames, and they burned a hole in the door large enough to walk through. Air flooded through the hole, water precipitating out as ice.

For a moment, I worried that there might be survivors in there. But then the pressure popped the plate open like a soda can, and a black apparition leapt directly for Rhines' helmet. Svedkos brought the flame of the battlestaff around and expertly cut the thing in two.

Instantly, they were pouring from the door. We pulled back, and regrouped. The creatures looked like pixies conjured from liquid ink. Fortunately, they weren't bright.

It took minimal marksmanship to take them down. But there were a lot of them, and the darkness made them almost impossible to see until they were on top of us. I switched to concussive fireballs, which burst among the running stream in an iris of flame, expanding and contracting in a heartbeat. The walls flashed with golden light, which attracted yet more creatures from the darkness behind us. Thankfully, no floating eyeballs. I turned to defend our flank. Tagging two six-arms with targeted fireballs, I turned to find Johnson dodging a panther-squid. As it leapt, I too side-stepped, and cut its head off with a quick stroke of my sword.

Then, as I watched, one of the final black pixies leapt at Venna's back. She couldn't have seen it. But she turned around, and grabbed it out of midair with one hand.

And then it vanished. It expanded in a cloud of black smoke, wrapped into a ball within her grasp, and was gone.

A few final fireballs dispatched the remaining imps. It was over. The building shook distressingly. The ground vibrated. Dust crumbled from the roof. Seismic activity? Did the moon have that?

Johnson wasn't letting it distract him. He had seen Venna's trick, too. He cornered her.

"Okay. No more games. You going to tell me that imp disappeared by itself?"

"Perhaps this is not the time to—"

"I disagree. Now is *exactly* the time!" Johnson roared.

At that point the major broke them up. But once Johnson had said his piece you could tell Major Brumly was equally concerned. He turned to Venna.

"Is this true?"

She looked off to the side for a long, tense moment. When she spoke, she sounded angry. At herself, as much as at Johnson.

"Yes, okay, fine. But it's not what it looks like."

"It never is, is it?" Johnson scoffed.

"I can't help it! I'm... I'm..." Her voice dwindled, and when it came back, she sounded defeated. "My grandmother was a night-elf."

There was a collective in-drawing of breath.

"A night-elf," said Brumly, flatly.

"Yes. *Believe me*, I'm not proud of it. My grandfather got little choice in the matter. You know what they're like with the glamour."

"You hear stories, yes," said Wauler.

"Why did you come on this mission, staff sergeant? Surely you know night-elves were born before the aether inverted. You could be as susceptible to the influence of negative aether as an orc, or a goblin. *Any* of the races born under the old gods."

Major Brumly's voice was tense. Night elves lived underground, and Dwarves had had a century-long war with them.

"With respect, sir, I'm three-quarters human." She hung her head. "You're going to say that gave me something to prove?"

"Do you think you're proving it?" said Brumly.

Venna came back, in slow, deliberate tones.

"Right now, sir, I'm here to kill these creatures. Yes, I have certain advantages at it. But I'm still a soldier of the United States. I came to hold our moonbase, against any threat foreign, demonic, or alien." She drew herself up. "I didn't choose who I was born to, but I chose who I fight for. And I'm far more dangerous to the enemy than I am to you. I can influence their magic, not ours."

Brumly considered this.

"But the imp—"

"I didn't know I could do it until I'd done it. I just wanted it to go away. And then it—"

"Don't do it again. Negative aether is not to be toyed with. Do you understand, staff sergeant?"

Venna nodded.

"Very well. Let's go and look at the Great Arc."

But there was no longer a Great Arc to look at. Sure, all the mechanisms were there. There was a modern interface ring out front, made up of sleek grey stones. Towering behind it, around it, under it, were thousands of arcane circles in all sizes, inscribed with runes. I walked around the walls, watching them creep in and out of the darkness. It was probably very impressive when you could see it all at once. But there were supposed to be consigned demons to make the circles spin. They'd vanished. Murrey was the first to put two and two together.

"Bet you a nickel that those imps we killed were the demons that ran the Great Arc?"

This met with skepticism.

"A demon's task defines its existence," Campbell pointed out. "To make them *creatures*, not just constructs, would take overcoming that bond with enough free, unpatterned magic to form independent will. A shift in aetheric potential of MegaAmbres, if not more."

Granted, that would explain the other creatures. Enough flux to break the bonds on demons would be comparable to the shift that created magical creatures on Earth.

"Any chance of getting a clue about what happened from this thing?" Svedkos said to Campbell. The thaumic engineer looked thoughtful.

"Without the demons to spin it, we can't manipulate the positions of the circles, so we can't access most of the stored information. But the runes should be holding the aetheric potentials in place. If the Arc's resonator were working we could project them into the ring right now. Reading, without editing, just translates existing potentials into a comprehensible form."

Unfortunately, the entire base was dark. The resonators had all been destroyed, somehow. I was increasingly surprised that scrying for the ship resonator had worked, in fact. But perhaps it was offline.

"But we *could* see the last thing they worked on?" the major said.

"Probably. We'd need a spare resonator of some kind. Even a small one would run it, if only for a few seconds. I'd raid a battlestaff and do it now, but I don't fancy taking one out of circulation, given what we've seen already."

"I know a guy who can donate one." Johnson ran out, and came back holding Slougham's battlestaff.

Campbell did some back-of-the-napkin work and figured out how to couple the resonator to the ring. He pulled the resonator array, and placed it meticulously. Then, taking his own battlestaff, he bent the ley-lines. For a moment you could see the golden traceries spinning through the room. They cut through the darkness, illuminating, dimly, the myriad machines. A complex ring of light surrounded the resonator array, and matched the twisting of another larger ring as it passed overhead, seemingly inset in an even bigger circle that was only partly visible. Then the whole disappeared, and the stones shimmered. The major stepped into the ring, and spread his hands to open the interface.

Diagrams came up, floating in midair—mostly schematics, with some pages of supplemental mathematics off to one side.

We all looked over the major's shoulder. After a few seconds, the battlestaff's core petered out, and the light winked off.

"Interesting," said Campbell. "Those were plans for a resonator. But did you see the math?"

Venna nodded. She had a knack for mathematics. "Circular wave vectors. But not a junior-level proof. They flipped the signs on the matrix's starting parameters before trying to solve for a stable wave. Although—"

"English, please?" said Johnson.

Campbell shook his head.

"They wanted to build a resonator to hold negative aether."

"I don't think it worked," Svedkos volunteered, after a while.

"You're damned right it didn't," the major growled. He turned to Campbell. "Did you see where they were building it?"

"I can lead the way, yes."

"Right. Unit, in positions. We're going over there right now, before whatever is over there comes to—"

Everyone looked up. The darkness had suddenly thinned, as though blown away by a sharp wind. Then the dragon burst through the roof, and cooked the major on the spot.

It wasn't like dragons I'd seen. All the malevolent dragons, born when negative aether ruled the Earth, had died out in the middle ages. The accounts that passed down always concentrated more on the brave knight who vanquished the beast. Dragons were just a thesaurus list of synonyms for "horrific."

But it wasn't horrific. It *was* unpleasantly organic. Its face, silhouetted against the Earth, was an asymmetric mass inset with six flaming blue eyes. A jaw of gnarled teeth was decked, beneath, with writhing tentacles, extending down either side of its long throat. It had huge wings, filled with chaotically striated webbing and punctuated by spikes and tentacles. You could actually see the darkness pouring into it, swirling like a whirlpool. It reached down a claw like a tangled tree root, and crushed Rhines, Ditri, and Winechord shockingly fast. Their corpses were thrown high in the air and swallowed right in front of us.

The rest of us scattered. I dodged, turned in midair, and fired my battlestaff at the dragon's claws. The fireballs bounced right off.

But I certainly got its attention. It looked at me, and reared back its head. A massive fireball rocketed towards me. For a moment I thought it was over. The conflagration would hit my shield like a waterfall on an umbrella.

But Johnson came out of nowhere, rocketing across the room. He slammed into me, and the fireball exploded behind us, sending us tumbling.

I rebounded off the wall, slid backwards, scrambled to my feet.

"How did you—"

"Dumped the remainder of my staff's power, that's how," he said. I helped him up.

"Wish we had air. Would've made a helluva bang." A shadow fell across us.

"Look out!"

The dragon's jaw snapped closed on Johnson, inches from me.

And that was it. Another man down, before I'd even managed to thank him. I wanted to be shocked, or angry, but there wasn't time. If you find yourself on a battlefield, trust me, find time for those once you survive. My subconscious asked just one question.

How do I hurt it back?

Instinctively, I latched onto the tentacles on the dragon's jaw. It reared back again, and I gripped as tightly as I could. Without air resistance, the hardest part was when its head *stopped*. I flew back across its brow. An eye meters in diameter swiveled to look at me.

I closed my eyes, switched spells, raised my battlestaff. I'd give it something to look at, all right. A volley of tiny steel bearings materialized in the air and blasted across the eye. The dragon shook its head sideways. I slammed into the mane of tentacles behind its head, grabbing a new handhold.

I looked down from my perch. Far below, the dragon sat astride a resonator. Its surface was tarnished and rough. Skimmers, like the ones on a ship, spun furiously in a track on the floor. Beyond the dragon's aura, darkness roiled across the room like smoke. A flying eyeball surfaced lazily, then vanished again.

Wait. Skimmers like the ones on a ship. In a flash, everything clicked into place.

"Campbell!" I shouted, in the mirror.

"Listening!" he responded.

"I've found the resonator from the old ship. I think they used it for their experiment. And the dragon looks to be hoarding it."

The dragon shook, trying to get me to fall off. But it wasn't getting the momentum, and I held on.

"Copy. Me and the remaining men are on it. Where are you? Is Johnson with you?"

I slung my battlestaff across my back and began to climb, even as the tentacles pulled against me.

"He ate it," I grunted. My head felt light. "Or vice versa. So I took the opportunity to get on top of the problem. Watch yourselves. I see more flying eyeballs from up here."

"You're on its head?" said Campbell, surprised.

"Harder to bite me up here." I crested the edge of the skull, threw my legs up and over, and straddled its complicated brow ridge.

Far below, I could just barely see the team enter through the darkness. The eyes immediately started attacking.

"We're in position, but pinned down. By all the hells, this thing is massive!"

"You don't say." I gritted my teeth as I wrestled tentacles. "Listen. There're skimmers spinning down there. Do you see them?"

There was an eternal pause. Finally, Venna flashed in the mirror.

"I do. The darkness is too thick for anyone else to."

"Sounds like a jury-rigged power plant," said Campbell. "That must be the darkness. The resonator is over capacity, but the skimmers are still drawing in magic. Negative aether is getting concentrated here." I saw a volley of steel spikes destroy a floating eye. Creating solid objects was more energy expensive, but eyes had a lot more trouble deflecting them.

"Do you know how to shut it down?" The dragon's arm reached up. It was coming for me.

"Destroying the skimmers isn't going to be enough. I think the aether is sustaining the dragon. The resonator itself is going to need to be destroyed."

I pointed myself down the dragon's back. There were sharp, irregular spikes, but they were meters apart, as the dragon was so massive. A shadow fell across me as the claw loomed overhead.

"Well, we got a nice lesson on how to do that this morning," I said, and let go.

The dragon's scales were surprisingly smooth. Not polished, like a dragon out of positive aether, but a cohesive surface of plates. If you were desperate, and I was, you could treat the dragon as a giant slide.

Mind you, steering would have been difficult even in full gravity. I dodged the first few spikes on sheer adrenaline. Then my weight tipped dangerously sideways and I grabbed wildly to stop myself falling the several hundred feet to the ground. I caught a spike full in the stomach. Fortunately I was going the wrong way to be impaled, but I folded like a newspaper.

"You're thinking we flood positive aether into the system?" said Campbell, in my mirror.

I wheezed. Apparently he took this as affirmation.

"We need a source, though. All we've got are battlestaffs and backpacks. I'd love to volunteer our fallen comrades' gear the way we did Slougham's, but unfortunately they're in the dragon."

I wrapped myself around the dragon's spike and tried to think. Campbell was right. The only source of positive aether untouched by the negative resonator was currently in the safest place it could be.

Or so I thought. Venna came up on the mirror again. She had a cold expression in her eyes which frightened even me, the dragon cowboy.

"We can still use them. If the positive aether can't be brought to the resonator, we'll bring the resonator to it."

"What do you mean?" said Wauler.

"The waves just need to superimpose, right? The waveform is currently highest at the resonator, and its amplitude is maxed. So suppose the peak was depressed, sharply?"

"Normally the energy would redistribute into two peaks equidistant from the center, with half the integrated energy," said Campbell. "A simple magic circle."

Light dawned.

"Which, given how close the dragon is, could cause significant overlap with the positive resonator arrays it ate. But you still need a way to control negative aether. These researchers didn't have much luck."

When Venna spoke again, her eyes were glowing the same blue as the dragon's.

"Maybe. But they weren't me."

Staffs were a tool for magic, not a necessity. Humans used them, because we were born almost exactly in the middle of the aether's flip, and had limited ability to store positive or negative aether. So we *studied* thaumaturgy, until a quiet man in overalls could wield TerraAmbres of magical energy using nothing but a slide-rule. Conversely, elf and elemental, orc and goblin, had significant natural reservoirs, as fundamental to their survival as a bear's tooth and claw.

Venna was mostly human. But night elves had once held the world in terror of their magic. Somewhere deep down, the blood *remembered*.

From above, I watched the darkness coalesce. It fled from the corners of the room, and spun into a swarming, frothing ring of midnight, running right through the dragon's entrails.

Venna stood behind the resonator array, arms outstretched, blue light shining from her helm's glass. The others provided cover from the flying eyeballs.

The dragon reared back, and though I couldn't see it, I felt the explosion rock the dragon as raw energy filled its belly. The resonator cracked in a complex pattern of circles and lines. Its pieces shot into every corner of the room. The darkness dissipated, ceasing to pile into inky fog.

The dragon tumbled sideways. Feeling as though the gravity were conspiring against me, I bounced, headlong, across the tumbling surface of scales, up a flailing arm, and leapt off the end of the claws as they approached the ground.

Landing near the remaining men, I came to a complicated halt.

I turned around. Venna was crumpled, on the floor, unmoving. I began to creep over, to check on her. And then we all felt the thump. I looked up. Another thump ran through the still ground.

"Its heart is still beating," said Svedkos. "With a massive hole in its stomach."

His voice was tinged with disbelief.

The negative aether was thinned, but it still poured into the dragon. Flesh crawled at the ragged edges of the hole. The dragon was healing.

Why so surprised? said the voice of subconscious. *A dragon can only be killed when its heart is pierced, dontchaknow. The brave knight must get up close, find the weak point and—*

But this wasn't some old story. We weren't in it for glory—we'd come to win. We didn't find weak points. We made them. If a man who came in his own serving tin could pierce this thing's heart, I could.

I drew my grandfather's sword, and ran towards the dragon. I leapt into the festering, verminous mess exposed by the hole. I expected heat. Instead, I found a cold so severe it made space seem tropical. My suit's backpack fizzed, desperately working to keep me from freezing.

I followed the sound of the thumping, cutting my way through entrails until at last I found the heart, beating like a giant's war-drum in its sac. I held the sword over my head, and with freezing hands plunged it deep, severing valves and coating me in a gushing flood of frigid jet-black gore.

The dragon roared, a roar so strong that even without air, it made the walls shake. Then, at last, it lay still.

The brave knight felt a strong need for a bath.

That took time to negotiate. It took the better part of a day, hauling equipment back from the ship, to even jury-rig air. Venna and Campbell oversaw the installation while looking over the remaining notes scrounged around the base, whispering conspiratorially. Then we needed food. We'd taken up shop in the barracks at the far end. It was breached, but fixable. We patched it as best as we could using the remainder of the ship's resources. The first few days were rough, but bit by bit we hewed together the necessities.

When we were stable, I went out and dug graves. Only one of them, Slougham's, had a body, but in the reflected light of the Earth above, I dug six graves, just the same. Some would call it a waste. If they say it to me, I'll punch them. I knew every mage in the moon. I'd put them there myself.

A couple of days later, we were ready to raise a low-power lay-focuser.

It took hours for Earth to get our signal, but when they did, they were eager to talk. They debriefed all of us, wanting to know what had happened, what state the moonbase was in, how everyone was.

"If the whole network of positive resonators was destroyed by adding negative aether, how are you running your systems?"

"Staff Sergeant Venna has the details, colonel. Suffice to say that the experimental negative aether plant was built wrong. We've found a workaround that seems, so far, to be safe."

She leaned into the mirror I'd thrown together. Those summers with my grandfather had not been wasted.

"It was engineered around a wave that wasn't constrained to proper bounds. It's a shame. They *had* made breakthroughs in stabilizing the wave. If they'd inverted the signs on the starting parameters *correctly*, it would have worked." The colonel looked blank. She smiled. "Let's say that in an n-dimensional sense, they forgot to carry the two, sir."

"We'll need more supplies," I pointed out. "The resonator we're using is the backup resonator from our ship. It will keep our hidey-hole lit, but we can't get the base fully operational."

The colonel grinned.

"Son, when they hear you've stabilized negative aether, our engineers will be up in droves. They'll be tripping over each other to explain to you what's wrong with the design and tell you you've got aetheric dynamics all backwards."

"If they bring materials for repair, sir, I'll loan them a red pen," said Campbell, from the back of the room.

"Point taken," said the colonel. "Shall I ask your address for postage?" he joked.

"Send it care of the mage in the moon, sir," I said. "We'll get it."

Afterlife 2.0

The man died with a gasp, and Ian flipped a switch on the machine. The cold, sterile light of the hospital room glinted oddly off its surface. There were a lot of doctors and nurses around the bed, but whatever they were doing, it didn't seem to be helping. The machine made a small whirr, as the fans in the back came on to handle the processing load. Ian squinted at the screen.

"That one definitely registered. I think we've got him."

I nodded. Beneath Ian's mop of ash-blond hair lay the mind of a technical wizard. Whether that meant he was actually capturing the souls, or just better equipped to fake the mumbo-jumbo, I didn't know. Since we got paid either way, I also didn't care.

One of the elderly female relatives of the recently deceased was glaring disapprovingly at the machine as though it was going to explode. I'd worried about this. Most of our clients were not exceptionally religious—that was rather the point, usually—but there were the families to contend with. Responses ranged from the standoffish and skeptical to the downright hostile, not that I couldn't understand why. At best, they simply considered us fly-by-nights.

She walked over to us, harrumphed sharply, and drew herself up to her full height, although it wasn't much.

"If you *gentlemen* don't mind..." pronouncing the word the same way one might say "animals," "you might notice that Uncle Ward has had another relapse. They are trying to save his life, and you are in the way."

It was a testament to Ward Graflander's age, and by proxy, survival chances, that even his niece had already taken to the permed white hair and floral patterned dresses that most women eventually succumb to in old age. Adding to that that she'd had to walk most of the way across an unused portion of the room to deliver this accusation, I had to stifle a giggle. But I couldn't resist glancing at the machine, just for a moment.

She pursed her lips. I could practically hear it coming.

"Oh, yes. I know all about you two and your little 'private Afterlife.' I suppose you think you're clever, cheating my uncle out of all that money. When the doctors patch him up again, you can be sure we'll have some words about it."

Ian spoke up. "Ma'am, I assure you, we will provide the services he bought. The interference from the monitoring machines made it a little difficult to calibrate, but once you stabilize on that person's particular energy pattern..."

She held up a hand to cut him off.

"I didn't ask for a lecture on how you conned him. If you wish, you can give it to our lawyers at the McMorning firm later. Until then, you will leave."

"But..." Ian began. I cut in.

"Now, now, Ian. Mrs. Graflander needs some privacy to mourn her uncle," I said, smoothly. "That's only fair."

And before she could restate the opinion that the doctors would have her uncle up and running triathlons in a matter of moments, I grabbed Ian and steered him out the door, the man's soul in hand.

Damn. That was, what, the fiftieth person who had called their lawyer on us, now? Especially the McMorning firm, which had a reputation for hiring the biggest, most brass-plated bastards available. It was quite impressive for a firm I hadn't heard of a month ago. Unfortunately, the sort of client we tended to attract also tended to have that kind of lawyer.

"Hold on, Sam, are you going to just let her throw us out like that?" Ian protested. I nodded.

"We contracted to collect a soul. We collected the soul. Now we take it back to storage, Ian. Technically speaking, we don't need to be there."

"But there's so much noise in there, the capture was pretty fragmented. I mean, we got most of it, but there's probably still a considerable echo left behind."

I rubbed my temples. Of all the jobs to be a perfectionist in, Ian had to choose this one.

"Remember back when we were hunting, Ian? Always deal with the big stuff. Don't waste time tracking energy anomalies in microjoules when you can find one that delivers in megavolts, right? Well, we've dealt with the big stuff. We've got, say, 99.9% of Mr. Graflander? His niece is probably going to sue us either way, Ian, so does the other tenth of a percent really matter?"

Ian hung his head.

"I see your point. What we're leaving behind is still definitely going to have his signature, though." After a moment, he brightened up. "Then again, I *have* been working on some promising algorithms to reconstruct the overtones on a soul from the main signature. This might be a good time to try them."

Oh, dear. That was Ian to the core. Mr. Graflander was probably going to end up spending eternity thinking he should have three arms, and that was if he was lucky. Someone who didn't know the kind of businessman he'd been in life might even feel sorry for him. Nevertheless, I managed to smile. We'd been called out here so late it was early. Now I could see through the window that the sun was rising, and it had already been a very productive morning.

"Good boy. Now, let's get back to Heaven. Collection runs always make me thirsty."

Heaven wasn't much to look at. It was our playful name for the office, since that was where we kept the Afterlife. We'd moved once since we'd begun, and it was, well, Hell on our Afterlife, because we needed to keep it powered at all times. Although in the end, not much had changed. Even in our new building, the Afterlife took up the majority of the room.

It had been built in a retrofitted mainframe shell, though to say that the devices for storing souls were computers would be stretching the term to the breaking point. Souls weren't exactly made of electricity. On the other hand, once they left a body they also weren't self-powered, so it was still necessary to *provide* them with electricity. Any number of "wild" hauntings were dependent on ambient sources of energy, like electrical outlets, fires, even devices for detecting their existence.

The Afterlife also glowed an eerie blue. This served no mechanical function, but it certainly impressed potential clients.

Our secretary, Diane, was sitting at a desk near the front of the room, filing large portions of the day's mail stack in the trash. She had short, neat blonde hair, blue eyes, and a cheerful-but-businesslike expression at all times. She didn't seem to mind working in Heaven, which put her instantly ahead. She even showed up early, and never once went home before we did. That was more than we could have hoped for, considering most secretaries had taken one look at the amount of hate mail we got on a daily basis, turned around, and walked right back out the door.

I was not, therefore, especially surprised to see her busily sorting paper at 6:45 AM, even though she didn't actually need to arrive until eight. She nodded pleasantly at us as we came in.

"Hello, boys. Get another one for the Afterlife?" I nodded.

"Old Mr. Graflander finally bit it. The guys down at Williamson and Baker are probably popping Champagne right now. Him and his lawyers have had them on the ropes for years now." I shook my head. "Now it looks like we'll get to deal with them instead."

She nodded, as if this didn't especially surprise her.

"I bet the girls down on Macy Street will be happier knowing he won't be coming around again, too."

Ah, yes. Diane was very good at picking up obscure bits of dirt like that. I hadn't heard about Mr. Graflander showing down at the local red-light district, but I'd believe it. The only attractive thing about him was his pocketbook, and his personality had been so abrasive even the gold-diggers gave him a wide berth.

Ian pulled out the transfer cord and attached the collector to the Afterlife. It was a little crude. He said that the machine siphoned the energy from the soul into the Afterlife, and then post-correctional devices induced the same oscillations as those measured at the source when it arrived. It was like copying a file would be if, for some reason, the file had to be composed of the same electricity at the other end as it was before moving it.

While Mr. Graflander transferred, I walked to the mini-fridge and grabbed a beer, then sat down at my computer. When you worked the kind of hours we did, five o'clock was a state of mind. The SimplyHeaven Company logo flashed on the login screen. I typed in my password and logged on.

I glanced quickly at the health of the Afterlife. We had so many souls in there, I worried about the system all the time. It probably wasn't warranted. Ian had upgraded the cooling system last month, and now it was so strong that we could probably have overvolted the system many times over without it even creaking. I checked a couple of the more esoteric stats as well, and shut down the monitoring program.

My wallpaper was a cartoon haunted house. I kept it there for sheer nostalgic value, because it reminded me of the ghost-hunting days. It had been a few years, so maybe there was a rose-tint on my memories, but it seemed like it was a lot less stressful. For one thing, although people generally thought we were crazy then, too, they didn't call in the lawyers over it. It was like a mania, these days. I was genuinely surprised that we didn't get sued for walking down the street.

Almost without knowing what I was doing, I found my mouse cursor straying to the internet browser. I really wanted to research the McMorning firm. Everything about them bothered me, but I couldn't put my finger on why. That they had suddenly become the go-to firm for suing us, in particular, was a little disturbing. I kept expecting to see billboards posted in town.

"Do you have a problem with the SimplyHeaven company? Come to the McMorning agency. We already file most of the suits against them."

A Google search didn't produce anything interesting beyond the company website. It was a standard site, with a strange crest featuring a five pointed star in a shield, which I assumed was the morning star, superimposed over a line of flame, which probably represented their deep passion, or something. Otherwise, it was just several pages of dark red backgrounds with bright red accents, albeit very professional. It didn't really look like anything very special.

Diana gasped. I turned around.

"What's up?" I said. She shook her head.

"We've gotten a request by Luke McMorning, the head of the McMorning Firm, to speak with us personally."

I rubbed my eyes, and took a swig of beer.

"Lucky us. Maybe he's coming to thank us for all the business we got him. So, when is he supposed to come by?"

Diana bit her lip. For a moment it seemed like she felt the question I'd asked was a lot more complicated than it seemed at face value. But the hesitation only lasted a moment.

"It says here that he plans to come by at 7:06 AM."

I raised an eyebrow.

"That's an awfully odd time to come around. What sort of person has their schedule plotted out to the minute?"

Again, Diana got a complicated expression on her face, like she didn't properly know how to answer that question. I glanced at the computer clock, and smiled.

"Anyway, he must have gotten delayed at a light. In about five seconds, he's going to be late."

I barely had four seconds to take another swig of beer before the knock came.

Diana narrowed her eyes, and turned to the door.

"Come in," she said, without a hint of enthusiasm.

What stepped through the door, it struck me later, resembled a medieval mural more than an arriving law firm. First, the lower-level lawyers, all dressed in black with white shirts, opened the door and fanned out on both sides. Then the higher rank, probably the partners, who dressed all in black and had white hairs, stood by the door like heralds. And finally, from the suddenly oddly-shadowed hallway emerged a figure clad in an impeccably-tailored black suit, black shirt, and blood red tie. His face seemed locked in a permanent sneer, and his face was deeply creased, as though he was much older than he looked, somehow. His eyes were black, but they seemed to reflect light strangely, like a predator looking from the darkness. His hair was flame-red and neatly trimmed.

"Mr. Sam Procher and Mr. Ian Waggel? Pleased to meet you. I hope you can guess my name?"

The phrase bumped a memory, but it didn't make much sense. Diana put her head in her hands and shook it. Ian piped up.

"You would be Luke McMorning, right?"

McMorning nodded. "That would appear to be the case, Mr. Waggel. Ah, Diana. I hadn't expected to see you here." He had pronounced Diana oddly, eating the "a." The man's accent was unplacable to begin with, so I couldn't tell whether it was intentional.

Diana didn't say anything. She just leaned back in her chair and sized up McMorning. There was a tense silence. Against my better judgment, I broke it.

"Mr. McMorning, not to be rude, but we're very busy and I somehow feel like you didn't come around just for a meet-and-greet."

Both Diana and Luke seemed so surprised at this that they turned to face me at once.

"But Mr. Procher, this is..." Diana began.

McMorning tutted her.

"Ah, ah, Diana. I'm sure you can explain it to them after we leave. Mr. Procher is indeed correct. I like a man who's not afraid to violate a few social taboos in getting what he's after. They're so much more fun to deal with in court." He smiled mirthlessly, and continued, "Mr. Procher, my firm and I have a little business proposition for you."

Diana faded behind him, shaking her head and drawing her finger across her neck urgently.

"Now, Diana, that's impolite," McMorning said, exasperated. That was strange, since he couldn't possibly have seen her. "At least let them hear it first. Gentlemen, as you may be aware, several people are bringing suit against you over your little... business."

"You should know, Mr. McMorning. Your firm is contracted by most of them," I said bluntly.

He not-quite-smiled again. "Quite. And you may also know, Mr. Procher, that we have the *best* lawyers at our firm. That's very important to us. I can think of no firm you could probably hire to successfully fight even one of our suits."

"Sorry, did you just come over to brag?" Ian asked, grimacing from the back of the room.

"Oh, no. On the contrary, Mr. Waggel. You see, and this is strictly off the record, of course, I rather admire you. Bold entrepreneurs, striking out into an untapped section of the market. And the idea of an alternative Afterlife, well... I couldn't have done it better myself." The spin he put on this phrase made a chill run up my spine. The thought from earlier went and got friends, and came back to gang up on me. Even in the morning light, the shadows seemed to lengthen, and he seemed to grow slightly.

"Oh, you wouldn't have the necessary experience, sir. We spent a lot of time as ghost hunters in order to find out what makes them work," Ian said hesitantly, but with a hint of professional pride.

McMorning turned on him.

"Really? You may find I have hidden aspects. I know, for example, that just about anyone can store a soul. But I'm curious, Mr. Waggel. How did you solve the problem of creating a personal reality relative to the souls that you store?"

Ian looked impressed. For a moment, he forgot his obvious trepidation in the face of a technical question.

"Well done! Well done! You're quite right, that was the hard part. Well, I can't divulge the exact mechanism, but we just used the observational property. Since the observer influences the observed, if you provide a client with excess energy, they mold a personal reality from it that can be whatever they imagine. I have yet to find out how much energy a single soul can mold, but so far the amount of additional input that conforms to the client's personal signature scales to amounts that are hundreds of times larger."

This time it was McMorning's turn to look impressed.

"Fascinating. I really *couldn't* have done it better myself. I must congratulate you, Mr. Waggel, on your insight." He turned back to me.

"With that in mind, although it's rather unorthodox, I have a proposition that will allow you two to walk away from this without getting all of your assets removed by serial suits. Having consulted with my clients, they've agreed that they'll drop the suits against you if you allow the firm to buy your enterprise, and dispose of it as those filing suit decide to."

I stared at him. Unbidden, thoughts arose in my head about how hard it had been to run the company. We could go back to ghost-hunting. Heck, with some of the stuff we'd developed for SimplyHeaven, we could probably go into it in a more literal manner.

Are you crazy? came the voice that had tweaked when Luke McMorning had introduced himself. *You can't sell these people's souls to...*him.

"How many clients do you have, Mr. Procher?" McMorning said, smoothly.

"Two-thousand, four hundred, and seventy-six," I responded, automatically. It was a common question for people considering an Afterlife to ask, and it was practically hardwired into my brain. Most of them, I'd noticed, were like Mr. Graflander, the irredeemable and rich who bought an Afterlife like a retirement home in a country with looser laws. Some were atheists, of course, who weren't bad people but wanted to hedge their bets without spending a lifetime praying. A few were even the religious equivalent of anorexics, who couldn't ever be holy enough to match their ideal self-image and wanted a third option.

"Seventy-seven, actually, as of this morning." I said, having remembered Mr. Graflander.

"My word, that is a lot, isn't it?" he said. "And you realize that almost every one of them that had a living family is now filing suit? Believe me, if any part of you is thinking the company can weather this, my professional advice is to ignore it. Even if you could successfully fight the suits, legal fees for the sheer volume will bankrupt you. And, of course, my clients will demand custody of the Afterlife in court, anyway, so the result will be the same, no matter what happens. But in only one scenario do you walk away with enough money to retire."

I suddenly wanted to accept very badly. His voice was so inviting. When he said something, you could see why it was better for everyone, and besides, it was what you wanted to do, anyway, wasn't it?

"I think we'll take it," I started to say.

The voice in the back of my head, however, managed to hold out just enough to keep me from taking the plunge. You could write books about how he wasn't quite right. So what I actually said was, "I think...we need some time to think about it."

The room felt a little smaller as McMorning glared at me. There was a flicker, like reality was just a mask, and the face underneath had a lot more teeth. McMorning seemed swathed in a dark cloud, and I felt very hot. Then, as quickly as it had come, it was gone. His sneer returned so fast it seemed it had never gone.

"Very well. Diana, file my card for these gentlemen, would you?"

Diana looked fit to be tied as she took McMorning's card.

McMorning glanced over his shoulder as he left. "Think carefully about what I said, Mr. Procher. You may not get a second chance."

And with that, he swept out the door. His band of under-lawyers imploded behind him, the last one pulling the door shut in one smooth motion.

I realized I had been holding my breath, and took an opportunity to inhale. The conversation seemed as though it had taken a century. I glanced at the clock, and gasped. It was just a few seconds after 7:07.

Diana stood up, and crossed her arms.

"Did something about him seem strange to you?" I asked her, directly.

"Something? *Something?*" Her secretary demeanor was evaporating like fine morning mist. Suddenly, she seemed to pull back, and take a deep breath. When she seemed reasonably calm again, she spoke. "All right. I'll admit that not many people do very well with it their first time. And you, silly thing that you are, haven't really been taking religion seriously. Sam, think about it for a moment. I know you know it, somewhere deep down. Who did you really just have a conversation with?"

I glanced at the door.

"Luke McMorning?"

"No." The reply came like a slap.

"*Think*, Sam. Sometimes, I really wonder why He bothered giving you brains when you never *use* them."

The voice was screaming the answer from the back of my mind, but it was Ian who got the courage to say it first.

"We just had a conversation with the Devil, didn't we?"

Diana nodded.

"Well done, Ian. And you two are in so much deeper than you know."

It was a couple of hours later. Diana had done a lot of explaining.

The short version was that Hell was not happy with our little operation. Most of the people in our Afterlife had been bound for the bottom, as it were, and Hell took the view that we were robbing them.

"And you're a guardian angel?"

"My real name's Dina. I was assigned to guard the law and learning. You two seemed to be doing serious damage to the first in the act of furthering the second, so it was judged that I'd be the best to send. I'm used to being male, but I'm more attached to my name than my gender."

"But so far, all he's done is threaten to bleed us dry in court."

"So far, yes. Sam, he's the *Devil*. You think he'll deal square? He'll send some of the lesser demons to try to steal the Afterlife—you can depend on it. Besides, I'm not really here to protect *you*."

This surprised me a little.

"Well, then, why *are* you here?"

"To protect *them*." She pointed at the Afterlife. "This is a rare opportunity for Luke to pick up a few good, or at least redeemable, souls, in addition to his usual. You don't even want to know what he would do with those."

"So, what, are you going to represent us in court?"

Diana snorted.

"I could, but we never got the hang of the bloody-mindedness needed for a proper court defense. Most of what he says is lies, but what he said about their prowess in court was true enough. No, here's the problem. You two have contracted to keep the Afterlife running for all eternity. Insofar as I'm an angel, I really can't encourage you to violate that. But I'm assuming you have some kind of exit clause?"

Ian nodded.

"That's true. We've got backups of the signature patterns for each soul and we've got backup generators, but we still have a clause saying that serious, unavoidable natural disasters, like meteors, earthquakes, that sort of thing, that destroy the equipment irretrievably, are not our responsibility."

"Most of our clients prefer the mild possibility that they may end up as ghosts to the certainty that they'll end up as toast," I said, half-joking.

In response, Diana half-smiled.

"That's not going to be much help. No, the souls will have to stay in the system. Unfortunately, I'm afraid I just don't see how we're going to save them."

Suddenly, Ian piped up.

"I...*might* have an idea."

Both Diana and I looked at him. Ian had the strange expression of an engineer working on an especially difficult logic problem in his head.

"What if we *did* sell him the Afterlife?" Ian continued, carefully.

Now Diana and I looked at him like he'd gone insane.

He held up a finger.

"There's more to it than that."

Luke and his lawyers didn't show up until the strike of midnight. That was fine by us, because we had a lot of work to do getting ready for him. I was a little sleep-deprived, but it was nothing compared to ghost-hunting. Besides, it was nice to see that evil had a sense of drama, if not a sense of humor. Once more, I couldn't help but note that time seemed to freeze solid as he entered the room.

"So, you gentlemen have reconsidered?" He had to speak up to make himself heard over the fans, which were a lot louder. That was the one disadvantage of our plan. The systems were running hot.

I nodded mutely. *Don't tell any lies,* Diana had said. That was very important. He wasn't called the father of lies for nothing. *He* would *notice,* she'd said.

"Where's Diana?" he asked, his eyes narrowing. "I would have expected her to be around."

"Diana said she didn't want to watch us sell the souls," I said, truthfully. Actually, Diana had carefully recited a long list of helpful expressions before the meeting. I could have said with equal truth, for example, that Diana had said she was turning into a giant teddy bear, because Ian chose the strangest times to express his sense of humor.

"What a pity. I'd have rather liked to have seen her expression. Very well, gentlemen. I took the liberty of drawing up a contract for the transfer of the souls, if you'd just care to read it."

I cut him off.

"With all due respect, Mr. McMorning, we're both familiar with your firm's reputation. We took the precaution, therefore, of producing a contract of our own. For our own peace of mind, you understand."

That one toed the line, but he didn't seem to catch it. He did look at the contract suspiciously.

"Tell me, did Diana say anything about me?" he said slowly.

Ian and I looked at each other in seeming incomprehension. We'd practiced this a lot before the meeting. Diana had coached us. As she put it, "You have a natural talent for being uncomprehending, you just need to learn when to use it."

I paused. "She did say that you weren't to be trusted, but that's generally true with lawyers. As I said, your firm has a reputation."

He stayed very still, like a cat listening for a mouse squeak.

He's trying to taste a lie, said the voice in the back of my head, *but he can't, and it bothers him.*

I waved the contract Diana had written up to distract him. She may not have been able to face him in court, but you didn't become the guardian angel of knowledge and law without learning something. It looked as ironclad as anything, although the wording had had to be very careful to allow for Ian's little trick.

He read it over. Then, since it was so short, he read it over again. Finally, he raised his gaze and fixed it on me.

"I notice that this only grants me the rights to the main Afterlife system. Can you explain why? I...that is, my clients...want those souls, Mr. Procher," he said, with a menacing air.

Damn. I had hoped he wouldn't notice that one. This had to be stated very carefully indeed.

I smiled and spread my hands.

"Mr. McMorning, the backup servers represent a significant investment, and are essentially the first working model of the technology. This being our invention, I would sincerely hate to part with them. Yes, they do contain the signatures for the souls, but as you may or may not know, without the essential energy that comprises a soul, that information is useless. A bit like sheet music without an orchestra. However, if you have any doubts about the presence of the souls, Ian will be happy to show you the Afterlife system." That one barely passed, but it passed nonetheless.

McMorning tilted his head to the side.

"Yes, I think I would like to see them."

I gestured expansively towards Ian, who walked over to the upload computer and logged in. McMorning stalked behind him, watching all of his movements carefully. I made a mental note to remind Ian to change his password.

He opened up the Afterlife management app, and showed Luke the stats. You could clearly track the signatures of each of the souls on the screen. If you wanted to, you could scan through the whole system of nearly 2,500 souls and check in the individual status of the oscillations in all of them. And evidently, Luke wanted to.

After a long pause, Ian said, "I can bring up some of the archives if you want to ensure that the readings are consistent."

Luke waved a hand in distaste at the implication.

"No, no, I can clearly see that everything is in order. There was one other strange piece of wording in your contract, however...now where was it...ah!" He acted like a cat pouncing. "Gentlemen, would you be so good as to explain why this contract specifically disallows future transactions regarding these souls?"

I froze. I had read over that like it was typical boilerplate, although now that I thought about it, it was critical to the plan.

"I believe it's just a standard for contracts," I said slowly.

Luke shook his head.

"Speaking as a legal professional, I rather think not. If there are no objections, I believe that can be marked out." He pulled out a red pen from his inside pocket and uncapped it with one hand. My mind raced.

Just before the pen touched the paper, however, Ian won a gold medal for clear thinking.

"Wait!" he said. Startled, Luke's hand stopped moving.

"Mr. McMorning," Ian said, hurriedly, "I think we can agree that when souls are involved in a deal, there's a lot more on the line than, say, when people sell a crate of herring at less than market value."

Luke gave a grudging nod, and Ian, encouraged, continued.

"With that in mind, it's important that we do everything possible to ensure not just the short-term, but the long-term safety of the souls, as well. Can you imagine what might happen if they fell into the wrong hands? That would be a terrible thing to have on your conscience. So in this case, the clause is necessary to ensure that the souls remain in dependable hands."

You could practically feel Luke searching through what Ian had said for a lie. He had said it well enough, and it even took me a moment to realize that he hadn't, by the barest of margins, actually said anything untruthful.

Luke seemed to be thinking very hard. Without moving the pen, he glanced again at the computer. Then, slowly, as if going over all the facts in his head again to make sure they lined up, he raised his head and asked one last question.

"Before I sign, boys, tell me honestly: are you trying to trick me? Yes or no?"

I gave it a moment's thought. He'd probably sense a no, but would he sense...

"Yes," I said, finally. As his expression began to change, I added quickly, "Well, Mr. McMorning, if you consider attempting to ensure the long-term well-being of our clients to be tricking you, then yes, I suppose we are. We have explained everything you've asked about, haven't we? Do you have any further questions?"

He really strained to catch anything on that one, but once more it was ever so carefully not there. Thank heavens for the qualified yes.

After a long moment in which the whole world seemed to be holding its breath, he finally said, "No. I suppose not. I sign...let me see...right on this dotted line, here?" And he put a dark red signature on the paper. I watched his hand carefully, because Diana had mentioned that he might try to add his own elaborations to it, but he didn't seem to be inclined.

"Good," he said, after a moment. "My clients will be very happy. Especially because, boys, you seem to have forgotten to put in any stipulation that they not sue you. Now, however, you cannot continue to fund yourself with revenues from your little private Afterlife. I look forward to seeing you in court."

I was stunned. Damn. We got so tied up in running the trick, we totally forgot to cover our own asses. I couldn't think. And because I couldn't think, I went with the cliché. "I thought we had a deal," I said.

"Oh, we do, boys. And I'll abide by it. To the letter."

Ian had a dreamy expression on his face. "Really? There's nothing we could do to convince you to deviate from them, Mr. McMorning?" he said.

"Oh, no," Luke said nastily. "No matter what you do."

"Well, in that case," said Ian, looking Luke squarely in the eye, " I sincerely hope you enjoy the Afterlife system. Why, you could even put some souls in it."

Luke growled. "I *knew* it. What did you do?"

Ian laughed, quite a feat in the circumstances.

"Well, Mr. McMorning, we already had an algorithm I've been working on for synthesizing overtones out of a main soul's signature. But since overtones are distinctive reflections of an individual soul, I realized that I could simply run the algorithm in the reverse direction to make a nearly indistinguishable replica of the main soul's oscillation...albeit from highly unstable electricity. Since souls can make quite large amounts of additional energy conform to their oscillation patterns, we simply harvested the overtones from the souls, transferred the main souls to our backup server, and overvolted Afterlife to allow the smaller amounts of energy on it to look like the whole thing." Luke was looking at Ian with murder in his eye.

"Of course, we had to harvest a bit of spare energy for souls like Mr. Graflander for which we couldn't get decent overtones, but that was fine, because it gave us a chance to run the reverse synthesis on totally synthesized overtones to check the fidelity of the algorithm. Oh, you'll be pleased to know that it's very good, by the way. Enough to fool even an expert eye. Unfortunately for you, since the overtones are indeed sufficient to symbolize the souls themselves, the stipulation that no further deals may occur regarding these souls keeps you from ever getting your hands on the real things."

Luke drew himself up to his full height. That seemed to be slightly larger than physically possible, somehow. His eyes were now truly glowing.

"I see. Very clever. What a pity, boys, that you will not get to live to enjoy your success. It might have been a good idea, you see, to state that the contract is still binding after your death. Many such transactions aren't. I wonder, whom does Afterlife go to? We shall see if your next-of-kin are as clever."

I panicked. We had a plan, didn't we, if he turned violent? But suddenly it seemed, somehow, inadequate. Where the hell was Diana?

"But boys, rest assured...even if I can't find a hole in your contract, it won't matter to you. With no one around to collect your souls, I suppose it shall have to be me. But don't worry. I'm looking forward to an eternity with two boys as clever as you."

"Before you start thinking about eternity, Luke, you'd better make sure you can survive the next couple of minutes with me," said a voice from behind us.

Finally, Diana showed up. She was dressed like a guardian angel, but apparently things had changed a little. She was wearing a skin-tight white suit that looked like a cross between a combat uniform and a ninja's outfit. In her hand, she was holding a metal briefcase, which she dropped with a clang on the table beside me.

"Diana. So nice of you to join us," Luke said, with venom in his voice.

Diana wordlessly snapped the clasps of her briefcase, without taking her eyes off Luke, reached in, and pulled out a shining golden circlet, which looked like the edge had been sharpened. Carefully, as if balancing it on something we couldn't see, she placed it two inches above her head. It stayed there.

"Oh, my word, the Mark Two Battle Halo, I see. We did come prepared," Luke taunted.

Diana shut the briefcase, and reached behind her back. When her hands returned, they were holding two flaming katanas, with golden blades and ornate pearl handles. There was a flicker of motion behind her in the air, and her feet rose off the ground. If you looked at her out the corner of your eye, I realized, you could almost believe she was being supported by a pair of giant, ethereal wings.

She glared at Luke.

"Well, what are you waiting for, Lucy?" she said as he met her gaze. "Come and get it."

Possibly it was the fact that Diana had come up with the most insulting possible diminutive of Lucifer imaginable and the Devil has no sense of humor. Or perhaps it was that he, by definition, does not deal in self-control. Whatever the reason, in response to Diana's taunt, he leapt like an animal. Reality seemed to stretch around us. The feeling that the mask of the world was slipping returned. Time and space distorted, as though both fighters were trying to stretch reality to their advantage. It seemed, suddenly, that Diana was everywhere, in all places around the room, parrying a thrust from an under-demon here, deflecting a blow aimed at us, and hacking violently at Luke while beating back a barrage of attacks.

Gradually, it became clear that outnumbered as she was, Diana was still winning. Demons fell, left and right, usually decorporializing at the same instant. She ran through them like a withering flame, chopping limbs, heads, and torsos, while somehow at the same time protecting us.

In an instant, all the demons had fallen save for Luke, who was taken aback but not beaten. The two lunged at one another, Luke holding and deflecting the flaming swords with his hands alone.

Finally, he spotted a weakness. Diana moved just the tiniest bit too slowly for one moment, and in that moment, Luke grabbed a sword by the blade and wrenched it out of her hand.

She moved the other instinctively to the handle of the remaining Katana, but now Luke had the advantage. Every time she tried to grab her halo to use it as an auxiliary weapon, he forced her to parry again. His blows came from every direction.

But Luke seemed to have forgotten the discarded blade. I pointed at it, then at myself. Then I gestured to Ian, then pointed at the Devil. Ian nodded. Trembling, I picked up the sword.

Diana desperately fought to make the remaining blade do the work of the both blades, but the fight had turned against her. Again, and again, Luke's hands managed to break through her defense, finding a mark and leaving deep gashes. They didn't look like cuts so much as blackened burns in her flesh.

Yet, if she felt the pain, she didn't show it. She fought on valiantly, until Luke had her pinned against what seemed, in our little pocket of space, to have been the far wall.

"I've waited a long time for this, Diana," he panted, his voice more animal than human, now. "Back to Heaven with you."

But before he could deal the final blow, a voice cut in from beside him.

"Hey, Lucy! You got 'splainin' to do!" Ian shouted, so loudly it filled up even the strangely distorted space. Yep. That was Ian all right.

But it did the job. The Devil wheeled around in a bloodlust.

That was all the distraction I needed. While his attention was focused on Diana, I had snuck up behind him with the katana. Now I struck, with all my might, right at his torso.

He gave the sort of scream that nightmares are made of.

I twisted the blade and yanked it violently sideways, cutting through half his torso like butter. Then, with a speed that didn't seem entirely my own, I brought the blade back around, and cut off his head.

Reality snapped back. The demon carcasses remained in the strange distorted space, however, including the Devil's body.

"Back to Hell with *you*," I said, and dropped the sword beside Diana. She picked it up, the flames went out, and she slipped it back into the sheath on her back.

"He'll be back," she observed, dryly.

I nodded. I had figured as much. But for now, he was gone. And it was important always to deal with the big stuff.

It was a long while later. The papers had commented on the mysterious implosion of the McMorning firm. A company that had had a meteoric rise ended with an equally meteoric fall.

It became clear, in the midst of all this, that the McMorning firm had largely catalyzed the vast preponderance of suits against us. And while people still didn't like us, without the technical expertise of Hell on their side they were finding it a lot harder to sue us.

Meanwhile, I was sorting out the other details with Heaven, with Diana acting as the mediator.

"So, wait, Heaven doesn't mind if we continue running our Afterlife?"

Diana dithered a little bit.

"Well, it's a dreadful security risk, but as long as you boys don't mind donating a significant portion of your proceeds to charity, we don't mind dropping by to keep an eye on you. With some of your clients, it's the only way the money will ever go to charity, I'm afraid. Apparently, that's enough for it to do more good than ill. And it's not like it's really changing anything, in the long run."

"I'm sorry? But what about all the people who are escaping Hell? You don't mind?" I said, looking askance.

She laughed. "Oh, dear. Back to incomprehension, I see. Look, if Hell was that easy to escape, it probably wouldn't even exist."

"Come again?"

She sighed, and rolled her eyes.

"Think about it, boys. Do you really think Luke set out with the intention of making Hell horrible? What would be the point? He wanted to make it just like Heaven, only his own. Only, you see, you can't do it. By taking all the people Heaven wouldn't touch, he guaranteed only *their* influence shaped Hell."

Ian glanced up at the ceiling as though he'd had an epiphany.

"I wondered about that. We could guarantee that the observers had the spare energy to mold whatever they wanted, but insofar as the observer influences the observed..."

"What happens when the observer is unspeakably evil?" Diana finished.

"Precisely. But I was afraid that if we found the answer, it would ruin the company," Ian said.

I thought about it. Then, I rubbed my temples.

"Oh, swizzlesticks, Ian, it probably will. All of our marketing is based on the idea that people might be able to escape Hell. Now it turns out that, as much as were developing Heaven 2.0, we were developing digital Hell. "

Diana put a hand on my shoulder.

"Don't think I'll let you get away with anything when I say this, but don't sweat it too much. Just tell people that you cannot guarantee anything specific about the actual state of their Afterlife. It's absolutely true, and there's nothing wrong with admitting it."

I started to grin, and she wagged a finger at me. "Not going to let you get away with anything, remember? I don't just have to answer to a higher standard—I have to answer to the highest standard." She added, sternly, "Also, you don't have to, but you may prefer to let me vet your charity list. Let's just say I may be privy to information that you aren't."

I sobered up a bit, and nodded.

"I'm starting to feel like we're a wholly-owned subsidiary of Heaven, Diana," Ian said, protesting.

Her eyes twinkled. "Sooner or later, everything is," she replied with a grin, and left.

Bite One, Get One Free

It was noon, and the sun was shining tauntingly through the "skylight" at the top of the store, where the foliage was thin enough that a green-tinted light filtered down lazily through a huge flower bloom. I watched the shopping carts crawling lethargically, took a sip of my soda, and looked over the store reports.

The tanker still hadn't come by. You'd think that if you'd invested several millions of dollars in developing a biological store, you'd do your best to ensure that it got the proper growth material. You couldn't grow a plant this big on the basic minerals in the dirt.

Sure, you were cutting your overhead. Heck, it was environmentally friendly, to boot. The simple, cheap solution for keeping your store alive was to put a tank underground for the root system to tap into. It was just like building a gas station. But if the shipment of gas didn't come through, then you closed the gas station. It didn't start crumbling to pieces. The store, on the other hand...

A cart crawled up to me, dragging its tentacles and desperately looking for food. I patted it on the head, and it sucked empty air through its proboscis and nudged me in a heartbreaking way.

Normally, they just tapped into the feeding wall and sucked sap right out of the phloem of the store. After all, they had to move around, so they couldn't put down roots like normal plants. But while the store was still doing okay, since it wasn't using the nutrients for any real growth at this point, the sap in the feeding tank had dried up. Thus, the poor carts were starving. I wished I could do something about it. I was the store manager, damn it.

It wouldn't have surprised me to know that someone was doing it intentionally, of course. Heaven knew, the carts weren't pretty to look at. How the GreenTech

Company decided that people would get used to looking at these things, I didn't know. I pitied our marketing team.

Biologically, they were nothing more than a form of ripened fruit from the store-plant. But what they looked like was the unholy offspring of a squid, a mosquito, and a snail with a basket-shaped shell.

They slid around behind shoppers on monopods, using their tentacles to fetch items into their baskets. When they weren't doing that, they stocked shelves. But the function they performed full-time was scaring the hell out of people. Soccer moms from the nearby neighborhoods would come through the door, take one look at a cart lumbering towards them helpfully, waving its tentacles to get their attention, and run screaming back out the store doors. And those were the ones brave enough to enter something that looked like a fifty-foot-tall hedge in the first place.

But then, my job wasn't to make aesthetic judgments. My job was to manage the store. Since it handled all of its own ordering and directed the carts for stocking, that position was usually only a title.

Unfortunately, I was also responsible for fixing anything that went wrong. Right now, that meant finding some way to feed the carts, because clearly corporate wasn't going to.

Just then, for a brief, confusing moment, it seemed the sheer force of this revelation had caused my hand to wet itself. Worried about what this boded for my anatomy, I turned to see, with very temporary relief, that the cart was slobbering on it, trying to get a proboscis at the soda I had been waving in the absentminded motions of determined thought.

I shook my head. The poor things were getting desperate enough to drink anything that smelled sugary. If it weren't for the fact that they had a pathological fear of destroying shop stock (which was actually an understandable aversion to give them), they'd probably eat just about...

And suddenly it occurred to me that I was staring my answer right in the face. But would the carts actually go for it?

Experimentally, I tipped my soda up for the cart.

It was as though someone had turned on a very strong vacuum. The liquid swiveled ninety degrees in midair and disappeared into the cart's proboscis.

I'd take that as a yes. I put the soda on the ground for the cart. It greedily jammed its proboscis into it while I thought.

I could probably use the contents of the food court. The cook had quit after seeing the carts, and we couldn't get customers in past the checking lines, let alone to the food court at the back of the store. And while it was bad for business, it was good for me. The soda machines were still loaded with syrup, and the carts were hungry enough to drink it.

First, I was going to wash my hand.

I was busily running soda into a kiddy pool for the starving carts to suck up, when the most boring person in the world walked into the store. He wore an offensively unadorned grey suit and an expression of eternal dissatisfaction that indicated his job was telling other people how to do theirs. He was the sort of person I had always wanted to paint purple while they were asleep, just to see their reaction. His eyes caught me from across the room, despite the herd of carts huddling around the first nutrients they had gotten in over a week. He made a beeline for me.

From the look on his face, I could tell that he was calculating price per second of the soda I was streaming into the pool.

But he looked up as soon as he had gotten close enough to address me. The carts did not seem to concern him at all.

"Gavin Shlen?" he said, coldly.

I nodded. He was clearly trying not to break a gasket, watching me pour soda into the pool. I wondered, privately, if anything about him could get any drier.

"May I ask, Mr. Shlen, why it is that you have not received any tanker shipments in the past month?" he said in a reedy grey voice, cocking a grey clipboard like a shotgun, and digging into me with the gaze from his steely-grey eyes. I could see him composing the note to his superiors now. It used the word "inappropriate" a lot.

I wiped my forehead, and struggled through the carts around the pool.

"Well, I could ask corporate the same question, Mister..."

"Grey," he replied flatly. *How shocking*, I thought.

He continued. "The company, Mr. Shlen, is expecting sales receipts on the tankers of nutrients. Insofar as repeated cancellations have occurred in excess of what this store can survive, we have reason to believe you are failing to file them. I am here to see that those receipts get filed."

"Believe me, I'd love to get some. But since I don't have any authentic ones, you'll have to make do with whatever I can fake," I said, grinning manically, then added, "Have you considered checking with the shipping department?"

"Naturally, Mr. Shlen, we did that first," he said, with an edge in his tone. "But there is a clear record of orders being made. And an equally clear supposed cancellation of the orders on each occasion, despite the fact that the nutrient tank must certainly be empty. That problem is on your end."

"Could there be something wrong in the store's ordering ability? Have you checked the connections it has grown into the phone lines?"

The man gave a contemptuous shake of his head. "Mr. Shlen, the status reports from the store have been completely normal. It doesn't reason, and it certainly doesn't file cancellations on its own. You are the only one capable of being at fault in this building."

"That's interesting. Yes, I can certainly see your point. Could you just look behind me, Mr. Grey?" I said, this time with vicious politeness. You had to deal with this sort of bureaucrat a certain way, if you wanted to drill through their thick heads. Which I wanted to do both metaphorically and physically right now, come to that.

"Do you see those carts, there? The ones around that pool? Do you know why I've gone through all this trouble to get them fed? Would you *like* to know why?" I was starting to lean closer then was socially acceptable. I figured I looked a little crazy, at this point.

"Because, Mr. Grey, that's what I'm paid to do. I was hired to keep these little fruitbaskets...or in this case, basketfruits...alive by any means necessary. Believe it or not, I didn't just fill a swimming pool with soda because I enjoy taking a nice Cola bath in the food court," I said, an inch from his face. "I do it because my carts are starving to death. Because the store doesn't have any sap for them. Because the store isn't processing any material. Because your blessed tanker hasn't come within ten miles of this place. Because someone on *your* end screwed up. Now, Mr. Grey, I'm sure you're a busy man, so let me save you a little time in your schedule. Whatever theory you have to explain why I'm attempting to kill my own carts, specifically to endanger my own job, is undoubtedly quite amusing, but ultimately wrong. So rather than waste your time telling it to me, why don't you go back to those lying bastards in shipping, and get me a load of nutrients for the store. Or..." I added, glancing backwards at the carts, "...if nothing else, you could get me some more Coke. We're starting to run low. Can't think why."

What happened next did not surprise me. Bureaucrats do not run. No bully does. Bureaucrats try to maintain what little dignity they have when they leave a place. Mr. Grey did not run. He did not suddenly break out in a fit of rage. He did not shout something dramatic about not seeing the last of him. He did not let his expression change one iota.

He was not interesting enough to do any of these things. What he did do was make a little mark on his clipboard, turn around, and walk quickly and crisply out the door.

And he didn't need to scream obscenities or make threats for me to know that I had just gotten myself into a lot of trouble.

It soon became clear that Mr. Grey was the least of my worries. Something was very wrong with the carts.

For the first half-hour, I had thought that they were simply trying to get over the prolonged starvation.

Two hours later I was worried. We were a small, suburban store. We were the next best thing to a prototype. We only had thirty carts. Between them, they had emptied the pool seventeen times.

I had observed the carts. I oversaw all operations in the store, and the difficulty in attracting customers meant that that was all I had to do. Your average cart approached the feeding wall a maximum of five times a day and fed for between five and ten minutes. The rate at which they were consuming soda was not normal. It was not even technically possible, as far as I knew. Their metabolisms had to be racing like a juiced-up hotrod on a drag strip.

I had emptied the shelves of everything including Mountain Dew, the only flavor of which they really liked was, for some odd reason, "Code Red." After that, I went through the generic energy drinks. Now they were in storebrand sodas, and at this rate would soon be forcing me to pour sugar into water.

I stood by as the carts gunned for eighteen pools.

It occurred to me that you could overfeed certain animals. Horses would drink themselves to death, if you let them. It stood to reason that carts might do the same.

Except that didn't make any sense. They had unlimited access to the feeding wall at all times. And the more I gave them, the more desperately ravenous they seemed to become. It seemed as though I was only making the problem worse.

I crossed my arms. When the pool got too crowded, carts went and buzzed around in the sunlight that the store filtered. They were very dark, to allow photosynthesis in green light, but it was more of a side benefit, not a desperate full-time occupation. Now I could have sworn I could actually feel the air becoming more oxygenated as I sat there.

But what was in soda that wasn't in sap? They both had sugar, water, and I imagined some flavor. But there weren't preservatives in sap. And of course there was no caffeine.

My eyes widened. Caffeine! No wonder the carts were hyper-metabolizing. They were hopped up like twelve-year-olds at a sleepover.

I held my head and sat down.

All right, I told myself, *stay calm*. The carts didn't seem very ill, yet. All I needed to do now was find a way to slow them down.

I couldn't use sleep aids, or lemon. Heaven only knew what those would do, but I suspected they would kill the carts. Ditto for tranquilizers, and I didn't even want to mess with the effects of the chemicals in teas. They might get mad cart disease.What *could* I do, then?

An unpleasant voice in the back of my head told me something I didn't want to hear. It was terrible, but it was true.

Caffeine wore off. My carts had been fed. I knew not to do this again, and tomorrow, I would use sugar water. But in the meantime, there wasn't much I could do except stay in my office. It was relatively quiet, and since I couldn't afford to shell out for dinner like this again, I could use the door to help shield me from puppy-dog eyes. Or at least puppy-dog heat sensors, which was the best the bioengineers could muster.

Unfortunately, the best laid plans of mice and men...

The longer I watched the store cameras, the clearer it became that it was not going to be so simple.

The carts emptied the pool. Then they waited for more. They began to swarm impatiently. When food didn't come, they started roving. Then, they started searching for any open pool of liquid in the store and drinking it. There was a brief convergence on the toilets in the men's restroom, which would have been highly disgusting if anyone had ever been in it. But the lack of nutrients made them increasingly desperate.

I locked the door to the office as the passing scratches became more aggressive. Carts had weak reasoning skills. They didn't know for sure where I was, but they knew that they wanted food and they were going to look for me until they got it.

Then a fight broke out between one pair of carts, then another. Desperation overcame the reluctance to destroy store stock. The juice section turned into a warzone, as carts burned the last of their calories and fought to find more.

I continued waiting for things to calm down. At this point, I was seriously in doubt for my safety if I tried to intervene. It was going to take a while. The caffeine high was going to wear off, and it was not going to be a pretty sight.

It was at the point I resolved to sit through this that five people walked into the store, apparently in hopes of making my afternoon more interesting.

The cameras in the store were also biological, as were the screens, so sometimes you had to think about the pattern the chameleon-like screen took on before you could interpret it.

Now, in bad light, with them standing as far as possible from the camera, I might just as well have tried to read Sanskrit behind my back while blindfolded.

I hesitated for a moment. It could be dangerous out there.

But I was the manager, wasn't I? I was responsible for what happened in my store. By reason of that alone, I had no choice but to do something.

I grimaced, stood, walked to the door, undid the latch and prepared to open it. I took a deep breath. Then, with more agility then I thought I had, I bounded out the door, sprinting as hard as I could along the shortest line to the front entrance.

And nearly had a heart attack as a cart darted past an aisle away, missing me by at most half a second. I thanked my lucky stars and put on an extra burst of speed.

Within moments, I could see the family a mere twenty yards away.

More importantly, I could see that they were not a family. I halted in the middle of calling out to them. Not that I had much choice in getting their attention, since I was wheezing like a bellows and standing in plain sight.

Mr. Grey looked directly into my eyes from the immense distance. He was accompanied by four men with arms the size of my torso and torsos the size of an economy car.

"Mr. Shlen? I suggest you come with us. It is time that GreenTech found a new manager for its…"

Except that Mr. Grey did not manage to finish his sentence. He did, however, handily finish his life.

Attracted by the noise, twelve carts had leapt out of nowhere and, crazed by starvation, with metabolisms still going insanely fast, actually drilled their proboscises into his skin to get at the blood underneath.

Apparently I had been wrong. He *could* get drier.

But how dry, precisely, I did not stick around to see. I was already running full tilt in the opposite direction, along with Mr. Grey's muscle-bound accomplices.

Unfortunately, that direction was not my office. The store was radially symmetrical, with eight divisions of shelves radiating from the center, broken by two concentric circles of aisles. My office was halfway between the food court and the doors. But I had cut up along the shelves towards the center, rather than going around the rim, which was the path that the men took to get to my office. Their path was probably shorter, in the long run, but walking around the rim was less efficient in the vast majority of cases, so I never did.

That may have saved my life. When I turned the corner on the shelf, I had seen the men standing in the next aisle over, and one circle out. But rather than running through the center, where carts were gathering, I ran the circumference of the inner-most circle. When the carts basking in the light sensed me moving as I passed the third shelf, I bolted. As the famished shopping carts gave chase, I desperately tried to think of an escape.

If I was running perpendicular to my office, then...

I had to make it to the loading docks. They were the delivery point, and like the store parking lot, they had the cheap answer to the question of how to keep the carts from leaving. After all, doors like mine were expensive, since they had to be custom-installed depending on the store's growth, and were less practical in places where high daily traffic was expected.

They needed something simple and cheap to keep the carts in line. So it had been decided that "X" would mark those spots, and some very smart people had devoted a lot of energy to making sure that the X-shape scared carts like hell. So at the loading docks, in case any carts came out, there were X-shapes in the security gates.

If I could get past those, I would be safe. I slammed through the door to the loading dock, the carts gliding along as fast as they could behind me. I leapt and rolled off the dock more gracefully then I thought I could, wincing as the harsh sunlight outdoors caught me. As I came out of my roll, my fingers found the bottom of the gate.I ducked under and slammed it hard, right as the leader of the pack leaped over the dock and jammed its proboscis where I had been a second before.

And then, without warning, it began writhing in pain. Sunlight shone on its sensitive skin, and normal photosynthetic processes got overloaded. This, in and of itself, was not a problem.

Unless, like the cart, you already had a speeding metabolism. Its body began very quickly trying to digest nutrients that it didn't have, like the cellular equivalent of the snake eating its own tail. Within a few seconds, the cart disintegrated in a puff of confused and nutritionally-depleted powder.

I put my hands on my knees, and breathed out. The other carts sat on the edge of the loading dock, circling menacingly and watching me with their heat sensors.

Well, that was new.

On the plus side, I was outside, and the carts were still afraid of X-shapes, so I was safe for now.

On the other hand, I was also alone, and night would fall soon, so the sun wasn't going to protect me much. The Xs surrounding the parking lot had a weak point at the gate, where the Xs were actually just printed on the ground in heat-absorbent material so the carts could see them. Anything else would have impeded the flow of cars, and the carts, like most plants, were supposed to be dormant at night.

I had a sneaking suspicion that would no longer be the case. When the Xs cooled off, they'd look the same as the surroundings for the carts' heat sensors, which meant that the carts would just roll right over them.

What I needed was help. I needed weapons, and warrants, and a really good spin-doctor to make this disappear from my résumé afterwards.

But what did I *have*? If I called the police and told them my shopping carts were trying to kill me, I'd have to assume they knew about my store. If they didn't, I would end up in a padded room with no sharp objects.

I could go and tell people to leave, but they'd probably think I was an end-of-the-world nut.

In fact, what very quickly became apparent was that the only person even vaguely qualified to deal with this crisis was me. This did not make me feel better.

I took a breath. Someone had to do something. I had determined I was the someone. What was the something?

Well, the carts were clearly susceptible to sunlight. The skylight at the top of the store looked like a perfect opportunity to take advantage of that.

But I still needed to keep them out of the city all night. I could close the doors, but then they'd be all over me if I tried to get in the following morning. No, if I wanted to stop them, I needed to get them in the sun. Preferably at the earliest possible moment, because being stuck in there with ravenous shopping carts any longer than I had to was not appealing.

I looked at the setting sun in dismay. The only way was staying the night. Climbing the outside wasn't an option. I was just an amateur climber, but the interior of the store had the advantage of radially-symmetrical access tunnels, designed for when the time came to install fluorescent lighting and add a nightshift, or other such projects. The tunnels converged on and led right to the skylight, although that would not be an easy climb.

That left me just one question. How on earth was I going to survive the night with a whole cohort of shopping carts out for my blood?

As it turned out, it was a matter of careful path-finding. The store had a deli next to the food court, which I knew had one access tunnel behind it, and that looked like the best ground-level access available. If I crawled through the tunnels up to the top of the store, then I could get to the skylight and destroy it. It was essentially the underside of the flower blossom on the store, but it was several feet in diameter and required access from each tunnel to saw the edge, so I wasn't going to have time to cut it down. Instead, I had brought a lighter, a packet of matches, and a backpack reservoir squirt-gun loaded with gasoline.

I'd also found the most resilient material in the way of clothing, in my hasty trip home. It probably wasn't going to do me any good, but the image of being sucked dry like a cheap smoothie tended to stick in the brain.

The temptation to simply burn down the store was great. Unfortunately, I didn't have enough gasoline for that. The *gas station* didn't have enough gasoline for that.

Now the biggest issue was timing. Sunrise at this time of year was exactly 5:33. I was going to have to time this very carefully in order to catch the carts at the right time. And that meant that I was going to need a place to stay the night.

After extensive deliberation, I'd chosen my car. Cars are known for being huge hunks of metal that are remarkably resilient to being punctured, whereas I, by contrast, was an under-exercised store manager who could be very easily perforated. By placing the latter in the former, I figured the latter gained all of the protective traits of the prior, with the most major trade-off being a future in which an insurance claim for "proboscis damage" would almost certainly be denied.

The last rays of the sun were waning, and soon there would be nothing to stop the carts from coming out through the doors and sucking all the fun out of the neighborhood. They were milling about near the open store door, waiting. They'd been waiting since I'd arrived in my car, though they didn't seem to have spotted me. I hovered my foot over the accelerator.

The last sunlight gave a final twinkling on the horizon. I took off the parking brake and put the car in gear. The carts began to inch out the door, little by little.

But at the sound of the engine, they paused. Whatever they had in the way of senses told them that something was not right.

As the sun disappeared for good, I mashed the accelerator and rammed through the main doors. In a shower of carts and coupons, I turned sharply and applied the brakes. To a cart, it must have looked like a bat out of hell. The car was hot, noisy, coming right at them, and filled their world enough that they tripped over their monopods trying to slide out of the way.

Now came the hard part. I turned the wheel sharply and hit the emergency brake. I burst from the driver's side door like a cannonball, and leapt for the open door that I'd chased the carts from. As quickly as I could, I grabbed the handle and hauled the door shut.

With a satisfying slam, the three Xs on the doors barred the exit out. I ducked back into my car, a dozen enraged proboscises slamming into the door vengefully behind me.

Now, to the only other place in the store that had a lockable door. This time, I did follow along the rim. I didn't see the corpse of the lamented Mr. Grey anywhere near the door, so I assumed that the carts had taken him and his companions somewhere else. At least I was marginally safer. The carts tried to catch the car, but they were never designed to match six screaming cylinders.

I shed half the tire on the floor coming to a halt in front of my office. I had a couple of seconds on the carts.

I could pull out my secret weapon. I ran to the back of the car, lifted out a giant, hastily made wooden X, and dragged it in front of the office door, binding it tightly with a piece of heavy rope.

I dragged the door closed, and heard the sound of the carts screeching to a halt, and in one case colliding with the office door. I had found a place to weather the night.

Or at least, I thought I had, until I turned on the lights to see the pallid, disapproving face of the late Mr. Grey.

I had had a meager and unappetizing dinner, although thankfully I didn't have to split it with my companions. The conversation had been dead, but one of the walking walls had had a pocket flask filled with the sort of strong liquor a man wanted when he was trapped by murderous shopping carts in a room with several corpses. I drank and stared at the clock. I didn't dare sleep.

It didn't help that the carts had been making noise all night. Apparently they had found something to take out their frustration on. Hour after hour, there were crashing and scraping sounds outside the door.

It was 5:10 AM, according to my watch. It was time to bid adieu to my grave companions. As quietly and swiftly as I could, I opened the door, and held the lighter at the ready in front of my gasoline-filled gun.

Opening the door did not make the space beyond any more accessible. I was looking at the underside of my compact, which had been carefully and efficiently propped against the door.

Beyond trapping me, in conjunction with Mr. Grey and Company, this showed that the carts were strategizing. I was positive that they hadn't been designed to do so. How much strategy did it take to find the shampoo aisle, after all?

Had I been Superman, this would have posed no problem. Unfortunately, my alter ego was a store manager, I had a schedule to hold to, and failing to do so would result in my being late in all senses of the term.

Then it occurred to me that I was in a really good position relative to my gas tank. The carts had propped up the car with the undercarriage towards me.

So, supposing I didn't get killed in the process, I had a way to get out. But first, I needed to make a hole.

I looked at my companions. It occurred to me that if I were a henchman, I probably wouldn't come with just my muscles.

I felt around in the inside jacket pocket of one of the larger guys.

Bingo. There was a knife in there that could have cut a ribcage in two. These gentlemen were full of surprises, if not blood. The knife made short work of the connection to the fuel.

Then, as the pool of gasoline gathered, I ran to the other end of the office. I tilted up my desk. Then I added my file cabinets.

I pumped the air pressure on the water gun to the absolute maximum. Then I flipped open the lighter, peeked over the desk, and took aim.

The good news was, the explosion didn't kill me. The bad news is, it didn't kill the carts, either. But it certainly got their attention. Heck, it probably caught the attention of the whole state. But by the time the carts came to investigate, I was already moving towards the deli at top speed. It didn't take more than a couple of seconds for the carts to give chase.

Ten miles per hour may not seem very fast by car. For running, it's a heck of a minimum pace. The carts were starting to catch up.

The deli was in sight when I realized that I could only have about half of them behind me. I was certain, because the other half were in front of me. But it was too late for me to stop, and with carts nipping at my heels I certainly wasn't about to slow down.

So I did the only thing I could do. I sped up. I leaped over the counter, and slid across the smooth glass top. A cart bore down on me, proboscis at the ready. Without thinking, I grabbed the nearest thing at hand. In this case, it was a frozen steak in an icebox. I was the one who had decided to put the entire deli counter in deep freeze, since our rate of actual customers meant that our premium aged steaks were halfway to fermentation.

I brought down the sharp T-Bone end through the primitive brain center of the cart with both hands, denting the tile with the sheer force. The cart dropped where it stood.

Imagine that, I thought. *All it takes is a steak through the cart.*

I flicked open the lighter again, and sprayed in a semi-circle to get the other carts to move back. The bark-like shell of the largest caught fire, and its pinched screams chased me as I crawled into the technician's access.

I looked at my watch. 5:30. I had to fly. Below me, the agitated carts tried to crawl into the ducts after me. Thankfully, however, they were much too large. I could not imagine how desperate one would have to be actually reach me.

I found out in about ten seconds. I felt a sharp pain, and looked down to see a proboscis in my leg, and one of the smaller carts crammed into the tunnel, its shell cracking in the small quarters, its monopod sticking to the wall like glue.

I went up the duct so fast, the walls blurred. Turning the strange crawling motion the tight quarters forced me into to my advantage, I pumped the gun with every motion. At the summit of the store, I glanced downwards. The carts had evidentially used their newfound logic skills. They had given up on chasing me in favor of swarming beneath the place where I would land if I fell. The feeling of air being drawn into the proboscis of the ravenous cart on my heels, however, was a more immediate issue.

I snapped the lighter. The flame didn't click on. Cursing, as the cart inched close behind me, I pushed the igniter once, twice, three times. Finally, just as the sun was beginning to touch the canopy, the lighter came to life, and I sprayed desperately at the thin skylight. A burning ribbon of gasoline splashed across it. The blossom caught like kindling.

I looked at the center of the store below me filled with writhing carts. There was no way I was going to survive that. On the other hand, I didn't have any options left.

Nevertheless, what I did next can probably be attributed to the henchman's delightful little hip flask. With a surreal sense of freedom, I grabbed the cart that had been chasing me as it reared up over the edge, relaxed, and tilted backwards out of the shaft window.

When falling from a height of fifty feet, if you choose to use a biological shopping cart as your cushion for landing, you should always completely remove the shell first. Also, be certain that said cart will not come under enough sunlight that it will completely self-metabolize into dust ten feet from impact.

From where I lay on the floor, having cleverly decided to land on my back, I saw the flames licking the harder-to-burn edges of the skylight and letting pure, unfiltered sunlight down to destroy the carts. On the plus side, my belated parachute had hardly been the fastest to react. The morning air was filled with screeches and clouds of starved dust.

And then, first blurry, then more distinct as they fell, the giant seeds came down. They were like helicopters seeds, but they were as large as tennis rackets.

As the sunlight crept into every corner of the store, one landed across my chest, feeling heavier than it had a right to be. I lifted it, and stared at it for a moment. Distant sirens wailed in response to the smoke from the store, and my sleep-deprived brain wasn't processing.

A horrible revelation hit me.

Normally, it took forever to get through Greentech's internal service, but they set new speed records once it became clear that I had just destroyed large portions of their multi-million dollar store. *That* got their attention.

What quickly became clear, as I had suspected, was that the store wasn't supposed to reproduce at all. The scientists were at a loss for why it was producing seeds. Or at least they were until I related the fact that it had been blocking sap delivery.

Apparently, the design of the store shunted sap through the main tap root, so the feeding wall processed directly from the root in the refillable tank. It also appeared that the store had been surviving off peripheral roots, instead. A nearly insignificant dip in the status reports just after a delivery some time ago turned out to be the point when the store had finally switched. The store had thusly detected that the tank was full, and interestingly, it was completely correct by that logic in canceling shipments by itself. Although that was no excuse for inflicting Mr. Grey on someone.

That had been a flaw in the design. True, the stores were environmentally friendly and self-sufficient, but they were still plants. It is very difficult to kill the reproductive urge, so instead scientists had merely bypassed it. They thought that feeding carts via the tap root would leave the store without the necessary nutrients for seed production. They were right, in a way.

As a paramedic patched my arm, I asked the question I had been thinking in the back of my head since Mr. Grey had told me about the cancellations. "It sounds, sir, like you mean to say it was self-aware?"

"I would not be that hasty," the geneticist said, in a tone that sounded as though privately, he was planning to be as hasty as anything later. "We merely made some ...miscalculations regarding the store's biology."

I leaned forward.

"All right, listen closely. If that thing dispersed seeds, that means we're going to see more. Care to give me a figure on how prevalent you think that miscalculation is?"

The scientist scoffed over the phone.

"I assure you we won't see any more, Mr. Shlen. Seeds need to germinate, you know. The seed coat must be removed, somehow. Washed off, or ground off, or for some plants, burned off. Especially considering the size of the seeds, it is hardly likely that will happen."

There was one of those silences you get in comedy routines where one person says something so frighteningly naive that the other person has no response. Finally, I managed to find words.

"Did you say burned off?"

Somewhere far away, evolution was occurring. Experimental genes unsilenced and arose from DNA that had never been activated. A seed had taken root in the middle of some fertile soil, and had been growing steadily, choking the roots of the trees around it. Eventually, it absorbed and pulped the trees around it, grinding them into its ever-expanding bulk.

And then, for a few weeks, silence reigned again.

Until one day, a small bloom opened at the top, letting a thousand rough paper leaflets fly out. The first plant to engage in littering was following the instructions of nature.

Unfortunately, the instructions of nature were dyslexic. What the store had painstakingly produced, in biodegradable dye on the papers that flew away, was a sad little epigram that only forest creatures enjoyed.

A piece of paper caught in a nook, and stuck there, flashing its cheap slogan, again, and again.

"Bite One, Get One Free."

THE BABY

I did not, in fact, when I first entered the humane society offices of Maine, Oregon, intend to acquire a pet. I was not a man hankering for companionship, nor was I an animal lover.

The thought on my mind was protection. Guard dogs have become thoroughly expensive to the point where it would in fact be much cheaper to hire armed militia. I would save boatloads training one myself. So in I went, being guided around by a volunteer, to look among the cages of abandoned creatures, stacked like children's blocks pell-mell on top of one another.

That being said, I *certainly* did not originally intend to walk out with the dopey, slightly cross-eyed mutt after roughly one hour of searching and two hours of extreme frustration later.

It whimpered, it hummed, it barked, it wet its carrier, and by the time I got home I was about ready to drive it back. Thus my appearance and general scent would have put a sane man off solids for months by the time I had battled the thing into the small dark room with newspapers on the floor, where it was intended to sleep.

It was two nights before the full moon of the month, as I recall. I made my best attempt to sleep that night and ended up failing miserably, repeatedly. That horrible dog made such whimpering from down the hall that I eventually stuffed cotton in both ears, and swallowed the four remaining capsules in my bottle of sleeping pills.

Thus I retired to my stone-hard mattress in a near-coma state. When I woke up in the morning, rather late, it was silent. I pulled the cotton out of my ears. Nothing. I clapped, to make sure my obscene dosage the night before had not resulted in deafness. It hadn't.

Now worried about my investment in a guard dog, I crept down the hall in my slippers, stopping in front of the pink-tinged door to the room the dog was in. I opened it, and the dog looked up from the corner it had been sleeping in. Inane blue eyes fully open, and tongue lolling, it pattered toward me, sitting down expectantly at my feet. Figuring it was hungry, I made my way to the kitchen to open the dog food I had bought it.

But so finicky a beast I had never in all my life seen! I fed it every brand of dog food on the market, and it wouldn't touch a single one. "Fine!" I said, giving up. "You can decide which one you want to eat. I…"

I picked up a box of cereal. "…Am eating breakfast now." However, no sooner had I poured the milk into the cereal than the phone rang. I went to answer it, only to find that it was a telemarketer. I was walking back to the kitchen when I saw the dog on the table. It was rather happily munching my cereal.

I went over and lifted my hand as though to strike it away, then thought better of it. Frustrated beyond description, I slumped into a chair and held my head.

"You frustrating animal," I murmured, now well in anger beyond the point of yelling. "What in the world, was I thinking, getting you?" The dog stopped lapping, cocked its head at me, and then eagerly trotted down to me and licked my hand. I stared into its inane blue eyes, and they stared back at me. Finally I gave in and gave it a pat on the head. "Very well," I said, "do you like marshmallows?"

The next two days after went something like that. With fetching, with chasing, with barking at suspicious characters, it didn't matter. In the end the dog won its way. Then came the night that will haunt me until Judgment Day.

It was the night of the full moon and I was settling down to rest, when I again heard the dog whimpering. This whimper was different from the first time, though.

It was closer to the whimpering of a baby. Curious, I crept down the hall to the room. I nearly had a heart attack when I opened the door. Staring at me from where the dog had been was a stark naked baby with huge blue eyes and teeth protruding just beyond its lips. I slammed the door in a hurried rush and crossed myself.

That night, between the unholy whimpering of the THING now occupying the room down the hall, and my internal urge to continue praying until sunup, I got no sleep.

As the sun rose, I finally got the courage to go to the room down the hall, and rid myself of the thing once and for all. Sleep-sogged and stumbling, I made my way to the room one final time. Cautiously I opened the door, and looked in. There, sleeping peacefully on the floor, was the dog. I picked it up and hurried the confused creature down the hall and out the front door.

I yelled just to have somewhere to put my feelings. " Go away!" I screamed, in tears. "I never asked for one bit of this, and never paid for it. You were a stray before and I'm certain you can be one again!" Than I slammed the door to scare it away.

The morning after next the deed caught up with me. It seemed a small baby had been washed up on the shore, drowned by a small sneaker wave. According to the forensic reports, it had big blue eyes, and slightly longer than normal canines, precocious in a child that young.

Every Sunday I go to mourn at the grave of the mysterious baby. No one has claimed it yet and I have a funny feeling that no one ever will. I have adopted many animals since and make generous annual donations to the shelter. But somehow I know that I will never again find a dopey blue-eyed dog. I just vainly hope day to day. But the thing is, he's gone, and you don't know how much you need something until it is.

THE PRICE OF DREAMS

The spray of the ocean was invigorating, touched with sweetness and salt, hissing over the prow of the boat like sand over a dozing man's eyes. Sleepgulls cried as they flew over the waters, looking for choice morsels. The sun of enlightenment rose above the ocean of the collective subconscious, casting its light into the crystal waters. It made you glad that Carl Jung had been born.

Pat's father came tromping over the creaking deck of the *Hypnos*, holding a freshly strung dreamcatcher on a line. He spoke in gruff tones, patched over here and there with accents he'd picked up traveling...mostly Australian and American Indian, but they were having a barfight with American Fisherman.

"Now, you gotta remember, son, that these ain't quite the same as the dreamcatchers out 'in the world.' You've still gotta switch out the feathers they come with, so's they're baited properly."

Pat's brow furrowed.

"But if we change them, won't the connection be broken?"

His father waved a hand.

"Nope. Don't matter, son, don't matter. These here are the *essence* of our dreamcatchers. Remember... I can stir salt into the glass of water, right? The glass don't change. Never changes. It's important to remember, 'cause it's why this little 'catcher can trap a fish of any size. Maybe here the fish is just caught by a fin or tooth. Its essence is stuck all the same. Out in 'the world' we can take it and sell it, just the same."

Pat nodded. His father took out a bucket of feathers. They wriggled when he touched them. Sleepgull feathers kept a spark of life in them, no matter what. The sleepgulls were people, Pat's father said, or at least they were the essence, like the dreamcatchers. They were the part of people that could normally get in here. They flew, all night, over the surface of the endless ocean, searching for little dreamfish to pick up. And as they did, feathers would molt, which attracted the dreamfish to the surface, and so the cycle went.

But the real scores, the dreamfish that a very rich or troubled man might pay for, were the big dreams that carved through the deep, subsisting on little dreams, becoming complex and fascinating. Usually they only came up once in a very great while. If a person could get, say, a fishing boat in here, he could catch lots of them. And today, finally, Pat was going to get a chance to hold the reel himself. He was going to pull his first dream from the depths of the subconscious. He'd been waiting a long time. He'd started apprenticing on the *Hypnos* when he was in second grade. Now he was a sophomore in high school.

His father handed him the reel.

"Now, I know I've never explained to you what these feathers really are, son." He picked one up and dangled it between his fingers as it squirmed.

"But you're old enough to understand now that it's 'cause you can't really know. They could be anything a dream needs...mostly I figure they're hopes and possibilities, the stuff you think could happen and want to see come true. But not always."

"You mean like nightmares?"

Pat's father looked grave, and shook his head.

"No. Nightmares, they're another kinda thing entirely. You gotta watch out for them, they likes the same kinda little dreams and hopes as the big dreams do. But a nightmare grows different from a dream. They comes up to the surface sometimes. You'll see the sleepgull try to grab 'em, and they'll grab back." His hand made a claw, which he raised up like a fist and snatched his other hand with. "They'll take 'em under and drown 'em, which is when the person wakes up. The nightmare gets the whole gull. All them hopes and dreams at once...nightmares grow fast, son, remember that."

He patted his son on the shoulder.

"But don't worry. They dies fast, too. I figures they swim into the backmind where they comes from. Deep, deep down. Never been down there and never plan to. I got an idea somethin' nasty lives down there, that lives off the nightmares and spawns 'em, too."

He pointed at the dreamcatcher on the pole.

"Besides, whether good or bad dreams gets caught in the 'catcher is all in the weave, so as long as you don't go tampering with the weave you're fine."

He knelt down, and proceeded to show Pat how to string the sleepgull feathers onto the dangling hooks below the dream-catcher.

"You wants to be careful to use the freshest ones you got. Dreams ain't grown on yesterday's hopes. Hold 'em like this, and see how much they move. The ones that are most alive'll be the ones the dreamfish like best."

Then he let Pat select feathers from the bucket and hook them on the dreamcatcher. He nodded with approval at his work.

"Well done! That's the hard part done. Now we just puts the reel in the holder here, like so, right? And then it'll mostly be waiting, so sit in the chair there and wait. I'll go and grab fresh feathers. Drop the line in and give a shout when you've got a bite."

Pat took a moment to admire the dreamcatcher he'd strung before dropping it in. The sun sparkled on the strings and beads, the feathers twisted slightly on their hooks, the wooden hoop rocked gently as the sea swayed. He wanted to remember every detail of it. It was, after all, the first dreamcatcher he'd made himself. Okay, granted, it had been bent and woven by someone else, but he'd baited it to catch actual dreams.

But worried that his father might look over and remark on his slowness, at last he relented and let the reel spin. The dreamcatcher plopped into the water and sank majestically deep, deep into the ocean.

Pat sat back in his chair, relaxing, watching the dreamfish jump and the sleepgulls dive, but keeping one eye on the reel. It was a fine, brass-plated double-handed reel, in case the big score was a bit bigger than expected. It was perfect. And so far as he knew, the line run through the reel was perfect. It probably would drag the boat down before it would break. He sipped a beer his dad had let him have from the boat's fridge. It was perfect, too. Everything was perfect. His dad had made sure of it.

He'd never quite understood how his dad's technique got them into the dream as people rather than gulls. But he knew the seeds of his business venture had been planted a long, long time ago, when his father was about his age and took a trip to Australia. There he'd begun to take an interest in aboriginal legend, specifically the concept of the dreamtime...which, as best as Pat could understand, had a completely different meaning for both dream and time than "the world," what most people knew as reality proper.

Whatever he'd learned, it wasn't enough for him. The son of a not-particularly-wealthy fishing family, he'd nevertheless spent every moment and dollar he could scrape for the next twenty-odd years traveling, asking questions, and reading books of myth and science, trying to understand what he was sure was the deeper truth behind the dreamtime. And then, when at last he found it, he realized he could make a lot of money from it.

Pat had once asked, early in his apprenticeship, whether the place they were in was the dreamtime. His father had shrugged and said "yes and no." And that was all the explanation he'd ever been able to get from him.

He glanced idly over at the bucket of feathers next to the seat. His father had laid a couple more dreamcatchers there too, in what seemed to Pat to be the increasingly optimistic hope that Pat would catch multiple dreams.

But something about the dreamcatchers was troubling. He picked one up, and examined it thoughtfully. That was odd.

He got up, and carrying the unbaited dreamcatcher with him, walked over to his father. The man looked up at the sound of his footsteps. He was using a long net like the ones people used to clean swimming pools to lift feathers out of the water, and putting them on angled banks of shelves to dry in the sun.

"What's the matter, Pat? Did you get a bite?"

Pat shook his head.

"Not yet, Dad. But hang on a moment..." he said, as his father started to, doubtless-ly, tell him to get back to the reel. "Didn't you say that whether you catch a dream or nightmare had to do with how the dreamcatcher was woven?"

His father looked confused.

"Yes? So what about it?"

"Dad, these dreamcatchers you gave me aren't woven the same way as the one we put on the line."

The man's features creased, and he turned his head slightly sideways.

"What makes you say that, son?"

"I looked closely at the 'catcher we dropped in, Dad. I...er...I wanted to remember it. The strings didn't go straight across, like this one does here. They were bent around each other like bowstrings, especially there and here."

His father looked at the dreamcatcher carefully. Then he put an arm around his son, not unkindly, and started to walk him back towards the prow.

"Listen, son. I pays our Indian friend good money for a genuine Lakota weave. He's the expert, right? I trust him to know what he's doin'. You're just gettin' a bit bored sitting up by the pole. I get it. Been there many times these last few years, believe you me."

He took Pat by both shoulders and turned his son to face him.

"But you gotta keep your focus up, right? This here is the family business. I'm depending on you to sit here and be ready when that reel starts spinning. Now, you're not going to let your old man down, are you?"

Hot embarrassment flushed Pat's cheeks. He shook his head, looking at the ground. His father clapped him on the shoulder.

"Good on you. So sit down and eyes on the line. There's a good lad. And I'll come running when it starts spinning. Crafty, these big dreams are. Not always easy to bring in."

As if on cue, a high-pitched cranking sound emerged from the reel. His Dad looked down.

"Well, not a moment too soon. Good thing you weren't still standing at the other end of the deck, eh? You never know when fishing, son. Now, let's bring in this dream, shall we?"

He placed a hand on the reel, and tried to turn it. But it may as well have been welded in place. He grunted with effort. It clicked one notch further out.

"Wow," he said, between gasps. "You've got some beginner's luck, son. I've rarely seen a dreamfish like this on the line."

He panted.

"Right. We can do this. This here? This is why we run the line through that beaut of a pulley system and have this nice big reel. We just need to make a few adjustments to the crank," he said, twisting some large knobs and engaging a couple of levers. The dream line was patterned off the ones that Pat's dad had used in fishing, with some modifications of his own.

Commercial fishers, Pat had gathered from Dad's reminiscing with his childhood friends when they came over, tended to favor methods that caught lots of fish. The fine art of line-fishing had faded into the background. But his Dad refused to run a dragnet through the oceans of subconscious. Normal string would be useless, he said, and even if you could get a big enough dreamcatcher, it would mix everything you caught together in a senseless mess. Pat supposed that, especially with what he had said about nightmares, dropping that on a human psyche would be enough to drive a person crazy.

But the limits of line-fishing were rapidly becoming clear. Even with everything engaged, whatever it was that was dragging the line out was continuing apace. There was a sudden, metallic crack, and the reel *really* started to move.

"That's torn it. It's broken through the ratchet!" his dad screamed, in disbelief. He was barely managing to even hold onto the reel, with it spinning so fast. Pat stepped up and grabbed the crank on the other side of the line. It struck his palms painfully, but he forced himself to grab and hold the rough metal. Even together, they could do no more than slow the crank a little.

The fish was swimming out. Or possibly, it was swimming...down. Pat thought again of the mistaken weave. Did they really have a dream on the end of this line?

Suddenly, jarringly, the reel stopped spinning. The line pulled taut, with a twang. But it didn't snap. His dad didn't make it to snap. The boat tilted downwards, slightly.

Pat's father pulled a knife from his belt.

"Stand back, Pat!" he shouted. "I have to cut the line, and if it snaps and hits you it'll hurt like the dickens!"

The boat lurched down, a little further. Then, suddenly, the line eased, and the boat bobbed back up. His father paused.

"Dad?" said Pat, in the stillness. "What just happened?"

His father shook his head.

"I don't..."

Then the tentacle emerged from the water. It was big...bigger than words could describe. It rose with all the ponderous grace of continents colliding to form a mountain, crusted in suckers and hooks bigger than the *Hypnos* herself. And...Pat squinted, for he could barely believe it...on the end of the line, the dreamcatcher was embedded *in* the squid's tentacle. The *Hypnos* was like a child holding a blimp on a balloon string.

"It's a... It's our worst nightmare!" said Pat, eyes widening.

His dad shook his head, grey-faced.

"Not just ours, son. I think that might be *the* worst nightmare."

And then the tentacle came crashing down on the little boat.

Pat awoke in his bed with a start. It was barely half-past three...prime time to be fishing. Of course, it had all been a dream. But it always was. That was the point.

He sat up on the bed, got into his slippers, turned on the lamp. The light showed a tiny, shabby suburban bedroom. His room was cluttered, here and there, full of knickknacks from his father's many adventures around the world.

He opened his door to go down the hall and check on his father, only to find him standing in the hall already, wearing a threadbare robe and looking stunned.

Pat was the first to break the silence. "Be honest, Dad. What did we just catch?"

His father looked at him, or rather, looked through him but at least looked in his direction.

"I... I ain't sure, Pat. It *can't* be what I think it is, I know that much."

Pat narrowed his eyes.

"Why? What do you think it is?"

His father spoke mechanically, as if reading off a page he couldn't see.

"The...the mother a' all nightmares."

Pat nodded.

"No, I think we can safely say that was. Squids are nightmares, right? And if they come larger than that, I don't want to hear about it. I *knew* the dreamcatcher was wrong, Dad!"

His father focused.

"No, son. No. You don't understand. I mean the very *mother* a' all nightmares. The nightmare that sends 'er children up, and eats 'em whole when they comes back down. *The* worst nightmare, son."

His mouth quirked.

"But it can't be. The catcher ain't designed to..."

"You said yourself, Dad. It can catch any dream...of any size."

His father fell silent. After a moment, Pat spoke.

"So what do you want to do with it, Dad? Sell it?"

"By all that is holy, no! It's the most dark and twisted nightmare ever to stalk the world, son! It's prob'ly been growing since humans were livin' in trees. It might kill someone to have it!" His voice steadied a little. "Let's...let's just go look at the 'catcher."

They moved down the hall to his father's cluttered office. Since Pat's father regarded a house as a kind of highly-defective, land-bound boat, the office was filled with fishing paraphernalia, as well as an embarrassment of books and the ever-present souvenirs.

The dreamcatchers were hung on the wall, on a row of hooks. The feathers on them were color-coded. Pat's father had a very good memory for that kind of thing. He reached up to the hook with a dreamcatcher that had three blue feathers. He treated it as if it might explode.

Carefully, he turned it back and forth in the light of the lamp. It looked distressingly ordinary, for an object that was supposed to literally hold the worst of man's fears throughout all time.

"So... I ask again, Dad. What do you want to do with that thing?"

His father scratched his head, and laid the dreamcatcher on the desk carefully.

"I don't know, son. It's...see, in some ways it might still be in ocean, even though it's caught, right? I got...well, I *had* things arranged so that the boat itself is a kinda door."

Pat looked alarmed.

"Does that mean we're out of business?"

His father stopped looking preoccupied for a moment.

"What? Oh, the boat'll be back, no worries. It's like the gulls. It'll take a while, that's all." He sat down in his chair, and pulled a flask from the drawer, along with a shot glass. He looked up at his son, and after a moment of thought, pulled out another glass.

"I'd never meant to tell you it all so soon. But...well..." He poured out two glasses of amber liquid, and pushed one to Pat.

"It's like this, son. The place we fish, it's known some places as the dreamtime. You knew that already, yeah?"

Pat nodded, his heart racing in anticipation.

"Well, we gets there the way everyone does, after a fashion. But the dreamtime's an odd place. Took me years to understand *how* odd. Remember what I says about essence? Under the surface that's what everything there is. And the thing about essence is, it fits into any container. Like, say I takes... Well, say I takes this whiskey here..." he tipped back the glass all at once, "...and I add it to myself," he said, wincing.

"It's the same whiskey, right? But it goes from bein' in the bottle to the glass to your cap'n. You might see the bottle in a store, the glass in a bar, and your dear old Dad down the hall, and you think of those places and things diff'rent ways. But it's the same whiskey in all three."

Pat picked up the whiskey glass, and thought about this.

"So, when we're in the dreamtime, we're still, on some level, gulls?"

His father pointed.

"Right! 'Cause the gulls catch the dreams, and so's do we. Except, really, that's just the way I made it look for us, right? It's a reflection of a deeper truth...but 's a good enough metaphor that the dreamtime'll let us do it." He poured another shot of whiskey, and gestured with it. "And even then, there's finagling. Gulls is what we's naturally inclined to be, son. To get the *Hypnos* takes finagling...in the form of a little mucking about with opal, ochre, and caves, which I ain't gonna bore you with the details of right now. But that's why the boat comes back, like the gulls. And why we can bring back dreams in the dreamcatchers."

Pat sipped the whiskey and made a face. He'd acquired a taste for beer young, because as the only child of a distractible widower sometimes that was all that got stocked. But this was the first time he'd tried hard liquor. He put the glass down on the desk, carefully.

"So, the same way that fish have to get into the belly of the gulls, we have to get the dreamcatchers into the hold of the ship to bring the dreams back to the real world?" said Pat, thoughtfully. His father nodded.

"And when we gets them dreams here, a person can take the dream back again by going asleep next to the dreamcatcher. They won't even be aware of it, but the gull, or whatever form you wanna think of their essence in, will jump on it soon as they're over."

"We may have it, then," said Pat, pointing suddenly at his father. His Dad looked confused.

"How's that again?"

"Because it smashed through our hull, Dad. Don't you see? Whatever it is, its essence definitely touched the core of our boat's essence. That must be what really has to go on. Otherwise, when you bring in a fish the size of a shark and sell it to an insomniac or a CEO or whoever, how would the tiny gull eat the great big fish bigger than it is? Did you ever wonder?"

His Dad's mouth dropped open.

"I... I suppose I never did, son. After the first few sales just in the town worked, well, I knew I was onto something. I suppose I never stopped to wonder how, exactly, it happened."

"It's not your fault, Dad," said Pat, kindly. "I think the metaphor had to work that way to give you the ability to trawl the deeper depths where most people won't or can't go. It's just that *after* we've sold it, it's not quite perfect anymore."

His father shot another glass of whiskey and picked up the dreamcatcher unsteadily.

"So you thinks we has the dread squid. The terror of all people. The sum total o' all nightmares, *here*?" he said, looking at the dreamcatcher with glazed eyes.

Pat nodded. Then he smiled at a thought.

"You know, Dad, we could do the world a great service just burning it. Think about it... No more nightmares."

His father looked horrified.

"That'd put us out of business, my boy! Think of *that*! All those people buying our catchers online, the troubled sleepers, the people with uneasy consciences...well, if we get rid of all nightmares, we've got nothing to sell 'em."

Pat tried a different tack. Visions of millions of nightmare sufferers cured danced in his eyes.

"Well...maybe you'd be willing to stow it somewhere, some way? So it can't get back to the dreamtime? Come on, half these people have subscriptions, anyway. They won't notice the nightmares are gone because they're so used to us giving them dreams. And do you really think people are going to notice that no one is having nightmares? It'll take decades for a psychiatrist to notice that."

His father scratched his chin.

"Well..." he started.

Pat leaned over the desk.

"Come on. Give it a chance, Dad. We've made a decent profit at this already, if the prices you sell dreams for are anything to go by. I've got my college fund, you've got your retirement. Now we have a chance to make the world a better place. Think about that."

His Dad gritted his teeth.

"Damn you, Pat. Fine, you talked me into it. But I've sailed a long way, and I'm telling you now... I see storm clouds on that horizon."

Even after the dreamcatcher was locked in his father's desk drawer under a pile of opals, there were still accounts to settle. In the morning Pat and his father headed downtown to see the old American Indian who sold them dreamcatchers.

He didn't live on the reservation, although he knew people who did. His store did an excellent trade in authentic-Indian-insert-items-here because of it. Especially in the little tourist town's summer boom, he did very well. The rest of the year he made money from Pat's dad, in return for not getting nosy about where the money he was being paid with came from.

The man greeted them warmly as they stepped into the claustrophobic, fur-choked confines of the store. The air smelled of raw wood, prairie plants, and dead animals. A cheap carpet had been laid over a bad wooden floor that creaked when customers walked on it.

It took a few minutes of discussion between Pat's father and the old man to discover what had gone amiss.

"I'm afraid, Mr. Tychal, you exceeded the ability of my normal contacts to supply dreamcatchers. I had to add a couple from another source."

Pat's father paused for a moment, and then slow panic crossed his face.

"No, wait. Don't tell me. I think I can guess. You patched it with bloody 'catchers from the Ojibwe."

The man looked surprised.

"Yes. That's right. Why? Is there some problem?"

Pat's father gave the man a bulge-eyed stare. He looked ready to pop.

"No," he said, unconvincingly, in an incredibly strained voice. "No problem."

After Pat had ushered his Dad back to the car, he turned to him.

"Ojibwe dreamcatchers don't work?"

His father put his head in his hands.

"Oh, they work, all right. The difference is, the Ojibwe believe that bad dreams are caught in the web, and the Lakota believe the good dreams are caught. And the beliefs of the people making them makes a difference in the dreamtime. I can't believe he'd do that without *telling* me. Damn it, I *specifically* asked for Lakota 'catchers."

Pat shrugged.

"He doesn't know what we do with them. Practically no one does. And how many people on Earth have to buy dreamcatchers wholesale?"

As they drove home, Pat's father in a morose mood, Pat looked out the window, people-watching. After a while, he noticed something odd.

"How old is the mayor, Dad?"

There was a long silence from the other side of the car.

"Why?"

"Twenty-something, would you say? Large beard? Tendency to wear a leather jacket and chaps?"

"What on *Earth* are you blathering about?"

"Well, if that's not the mayor, then the mayor's wife is kissing...well, *kissing* isn't even the half of it...what appears to be a random biker who is passing through town," said Pat conversationally.

His father slowed to a halt in the middle of traffic. Pat was, indeed, telling the truth.

"How do you know that's the mayor's wife?"

"She came to the high school a couple of months ago. To encourage us to volunteer in the local charities."

His father's eyes went half-hooded.

"*She's* def'nitely giving everything she can to the community," he said, drily. Another biker had added himself to the group.

Pat nudged him.

"Look up there!"

On a billboard by the road, two men were putting up a poster. One of them was sneaking up on the other, who was watching the mayor's wife unashamedly. As Pat and his father watched, the man pushed his co-worker off the sign. The man dropped twenty feet to the ground below.

Pat and his father looked at one another in shock.

"Son? I think somethin' has gone wrong."

"Okay, what did we just *do*?" said Pat, pacing his father's study.

"We? I said from the start, I thought this was a bad idea."

Pat rubbed his temples.

"Okay. Fine. But why?"

His father sat back in his chair.

"I've been mulling it an' I think I may have an idea. Understan' that I never thought much about the deep dark, 'til we dredged it up." He closed his eyes and leaned back. "That thing...it ain't *just* nightmares. It's where nightmares come from."

Pat looked at him blankly.

"*Think,* boy. Where nightmares come from. From guilt. From the conscience. Christ...we ripped the superego right outta the human psyche. Don't you see? Oh, sure, some people feel more guilt than they oughta. Fair enough. But you take away the concepts of 'don't' and 'shouldn't' entirely and everything starts going to Hell."

Pat slumped into an armchair.

"But I...I didn't mean..."

"The psyche don't care what you meant," his father spat.

Pat recoiled for a moment, shocked that his father would talk that way. But then he thought at what they'd seen, just making their way through town. Heck, the way he himself had felt, just after they came out of the dreamtime. It only now occurred to him that, before they caught the squid, he might have felt guilty about conspiring to rip off Dad's subscribers in a nightmare-free world. He might have been troubled by the way grand, simple ideas like the one he was pitching tended to founder. But he hadn't, and he hadn't noticed, either. And then, in his mind's eye, the view drew back slowly, until it encompassed a whole, already-troubled world.

Even from that distance, it wasn't pretty. At least, he knew that was the case, intellectually. His mind couldn't muster guilt for it. He couldn't reproach himself.

But he could still remember what he would have done if he could. Pat narrowed his eyes. He stood up.

"Dad? Get me that flask in your desk."

"Drinkin' is not goin' to help now, son," he said, shaking his head.

Pat turned to him.

"Get me that flask. And get me that dreamcatcher, too."

His father stood up.

"Oh! I see. No, son. The answer is no. You ain't doin' that."

"I don't remember asking you for an opinion, *Dad*. You said it yourself. I was the one who talked you into this. I was the one that caught the squid. I have to be the one that takes it back to the dreamtime. I don't feel it...but I can still remember it. If the gulls eat the fish left near them, the squid is bound to eat a gull left near it, right?"

"Damn it, Pat, *no*! I've already lost your mother. I'm not having you reduced to madness right before my eyes. *I'll* go."

"It's not going to do that. Not if I do it right. Because the nightmare doesn't want to be had. It just wants to be freed, to do what it was meant to do. Experiencing the dream is not the same as catching it."

"I won't let you do..."

The punch came from out of nowhere. Pat's father had taken many punches in his life. But his son was young and muscular in the way of athletic male teens. His father was wiry and hadn't pulled in a catch that wasn't a dream in many years. He went over like a statue.

"I'm sorry, Dad. Well...I hope to be sorry soon, anyway."

No time to play games. Pat took a miniature didgeridoo and broke the lock on the desk with it. He withdrew the dreamcatcher.

"You and I need to have a chat," he said, to the little circle of yarn.

The liquor worked fast. Beer hadn't given Pat much of a head for alcohol.

And suddenly it was dark. He put out his hands, and felt the timber of the cabin above him. This was the *Hypnos*. But this wasn't the usual dream.

He felt his way out, onto the deck. There was a slight difference in air temperature. It was pitch-black outside, too.

But...the dreamtime *had* no night. Someone, somewhere, was always sleeping.

That is true. But this is not the dreamtime. This is but a small part of a nightmare that could be, happening within and beneath the dream, a deep, menacing voice said, in Pat's head.

Far away, two eyes opened that glowed like fire. The ocean beneath reflected them, still and inky-black. In the water below, tentacles moved, half in shadow, just under the mirror-smooth sea.

But you have dared to come to me. Why? said the voice, impassively. *I killed you instantly before. I will not make that mistake again. I learned much of myself and of you when I was stolen. And my daughters already knew much of making a nightmare last. I can hold your soul for ransom until your body dies and beyond. Knowing this, you dared to return?*

Pat tried to steady his voice. He had a feeling it didn't matter what he said or how he said it, but he wanted to say it, anyway.

"Because I think I learned a little of you, too, in that moment between dying and waking. It just took some time to understand it. You'll leave me because you have a duty to return to. And you're the essence of guilt, of contrition, not of vengeance. Vengeance, we humans handle for ourselves. In fact, there's a lot we'll handle for ourselves, left to our own devices. But not guilt."

He leaned on the front rail of the *Hypnos.*

"There's much you *could* do. But I've seen your essence. You're all about *not* doing. And another thing, in case maybe you're thinking you'll do something horrible to me and then feel transcendently bad about it later. Every moment we waste here talking, the sleepgulls...or the people who they represent...are probably getting up to a wide variety of things that might increase their number in the long term but only if they survive severe reductions in the short term. Your duty is tied to us. In fact, in some ways, the whole point of your existence is protecting us from ourselves."

He stood up straight, trying to face down two eyes acres away and apart. For a long time, there was the sound of busy thought.

What you say is true. But...

Tentacles rose up on every side of the boat, lifting it up, drawing it closer to the fiery eye. The voice in Pat's head boomed so loud, it brought him to his knees.

Should you dare pull me from my rightful place once more, rest assured, I will visit upon you every horror I can imagine. Defender of dreams I may be...but in all my countless years, I have never met a threat more serious than you.

The tentacles dropped the boat in the water.

I return to where I should be. I advise you do the same.

And suddenly, the voice still ringing in his ears, Pat found himself, and the *Hypnos,* floating on the sea of subconscious, as though nothing had ever happened.

But the world does not heal, not perfectly. It scars, and we learn to live around those scars.

The mayor got a divorce, for a start. The man from the billboard ended up in intensive care, although he did eventually recover. Pat felt guilty about it all, and for the first time in his life was happy for that fact.

His father, when he woke up, was simultaneously glad his son had not been driven mad, and angry that his son had punched his lights out. After Pat had calmed him down, however, a frank discussion was had. His father had sailed the most dangerous seas in the world. But there was one that was now perhaps more dangerous than all the others could ever be.

For the next week or so, whenever they appeared aboard the *Hypnos* at night, they wouldn't fish. The dreamcatchers were left on their racks, the sleepgull feathers uncollected. They just talked...of finance, morality, and risk.

And finally a decision was made.

At the end of the week, Pat's father bought two tickets to Australia and shuttered the online store. There was a certain cave where some things needed to be undone. The good ship *Hypnos* was being dry-docked. Sailing her had been his lifelong dream. But as men had known forever, the price of dreams is nightmares.

KEEP YOUR SHURT ON

"Help! One of the indigenous creatures has got me!"

The unlucky Machine Engineer held a tentacle aloft, in which struggled one of the odd local animals. It was orange-pink, with four jointed limbs and a yellow tuft of some kind on top of its head. The middle of its body was decked in two pieces of loose-hanging, colorful skin, as though it had recently molted.

All three Star Tasters turned back to observe his alarm, but with some disdain. He was of too low a caste to be bursting onto the deck.

"It must have snuck aboard when we were last landed to explore. Its upper molt glows in ultraviolet, I notice," said one, curiously.

"It has probably been rolling in something," said another, dismissively.

"Does the mud of this planet hold patterns, then?" said the third, patiently.

The other two looked at him.

"I see no pattern," said the dismissive one. He straightened his bottom row of tentacles and arched out the second and third rows, in a universal sign of haughtiness.

"Nor I. But let us call upon The Sojourner for this planet to confirm our equal's incorrectness. He has spent years living among the indigenous creatures."

"Which? Last I heard he had spent a year wandering around in a facsimile and seen them do nothing but eat local vegetation."

"Ah, esteemed Star Taster," said the Sojourner for Earth, sidling up sideways and speaking as though he'd never heard of caste and wouldn't care if he did. "My experiment with being a 'Kouw' taught me many important things."

"Such as, imitator of foreigners?"

"That the dominant species is at least partially carnivorous." The Sojourner shifted uncomfortably. "I and some of the Sojourners for other ships had to cut open the

facsimiles we were living inside and escape in a hurry. And I, myself, still lost a limb."
He held up a tentacle that had clearly grown back from about halfway down.

"It's true!" shouted the Machine Engineer, agitated. "This one was trying to eat one of my tentacles!"

"And do you recognize this creature?" said the most patient of the Star Tasters.

"Yes. They have many sounds for themselves. I believe it is a 'peapol,' 'pursun,' or 'indyvidool.' They have many terms for the same things." He peered closer. "In fact, this one might be of the 'woomin' caste. You can tell because of the two lumps between the appendages near the top. Whether they are caused by some kind of native disease or specialization for a certain role in the colony, I don't think anyone knows." He splayed his tentacles airily and sat confidently, a vision of quiet expertise.

"Interesting," said the dismissive Star Taster, clearly not interested.

"Are those meaningful symbols on its skin?" said the curious one.

"Its 'shurt,' Star Taster?"

"What is that?"

"The name of that piece of spare skin. They set a great deal of store by ritualistically wearing them. Indeed, when I initially dropped in a facsimile of the dominant species, I was chased by members of the warrior caste whenever I was seen without them." Even the patient Star Taster stared elsewhere, in a clear expression of boredom. The Sojourner was unperturbed. "I have not been able to sufficiently examine them to understand why, but I know that, yes, they sometimes adorn them with symbols."

"What do the symbols mean, then?"

The Sojourner stared intently at the struggling creature.

"Hard to make out with it moving. I believe they convey a desire for foreign crea-tures to provide it with offspring."

The Star Tasters stared at him even more dubiously.

"Surely they would be genetically incompatible," said the dismissive one, bluntly.

"Especially because...rrrrmmm..." the Sojourner rumbled in amusement, "that term conveys a specific concept of creatures on other planets."

The remaining two Star Tasters looked skeptical.

"How long did you live among humans, Sojourner?"

"Of their years? Two. I made camp in a place where their specialized paths for ground transportation machines crossed a river." He looked solemn, for a moment. "A previous generation of sojourners attempted to obtain one of the more elaborate dwelling places, but the warrior caste is remarkably responsive among them."

"Ah," said one of the Star Tasters, in a predatory manor. "You were of a lower caste, then... Well, you surely couldn't..."

"If you'll excuse me, esteemed Star Taster, I was and I was not. I was allowed to engage verbally with most anyone on the street. Indeed, I could use almost any amplitude of sound without meaningful response from the warrior caste. A member of a strictly lower caste surely wouldn't be allowed that much leeway, agreed?"

The Star Taster did not look ready to surrender the point, so the Sojourner continued, smoothly, "Besides, their castes were organized by role. Very little was actually required of me beyond obtaining necessities to keep my facsimile alive."

"Hm. He makes a good point. The lowest caste usually has a great deal of work to do," said the patient Star Taster.

A Creature Engineer grabbed the animal with two tentacles, and it willingly let go of the Machine engineer and stopped struggling. It made a prolonged hum. After a few seconds of nonresponsiveness, it suddenly turned around, and started making sounds at the creature engineer.

"What do those sounds mean?" he said.

The Sojourner had the eyes all around his head closed as he absorbed the sound. He turned a deeper shade of blue.

"I do not wish to translate these sounds in such esteemed company," he said, gesturing at the Star Tasters. "But it appears to be essentially in keeping with the markings on the 'shurt.'"

"Strange creatures," said the most dismissive Star Taster, waving his tentacles in a manner of confusion and turning away. "Creature Engineer, immobilize the creature and we will return it to its natural habitat. I am tired of this distraction. Me and my...equals must direct what flavor of area we'll approach next."

"Let us start by choosing where to drop this creature," said the curious Star Taster.

"The flavor it is dropped in must be far from where it was picked up. If they are social we do not want to make it easy for them to determine our presence."

"Agreed," said the dismissive one.

"Let us pick an area of dense vegetation near the center of the planet. It should have plenty of food," said the curious one.

"I do not care one way or another," said the dismissive one.

"There's no need to be cruel, equal," said the patient one.

"Wait!" said the curious one. "I wish to keep its...its...'shu-ort.' Can it be removed without surgery, Sojourner?"

"Er. Yes, Esteemed One. But why?"

"For my personal collection. I keep little items, here and there. It assists in making presentations on the planets we have discovered when I have artifacts."

"Oh, yes, we all so *love* those presentations," said the dismissive one.

The Sojourner looked at the creature, being injected by the Creature Engineer with a paralyzer.

"If you hurry, esteemed Star Taster, I think it may even assist you in removing it," he said, carefully.

LIGHTER THEN WERE

I checked the seals on either end of the fluorescent light as I leaned back comfortably in a used office chair, reveling in the cold, musty scent so pervasive in storerooms everywhere. There are unexpected advantages to being a mall technician. One of them is that not only do people not give you a second glance, but most will go out of their way to avoid giving you a first one. When you have a tendency to grow hair unexpectedly in exotic areas depending on the time of month, any job with a certain acknowledged amount of privacy is instantly at an advantage.

Admittedly, it was more comfortable now than it had been. A hundred years ago, I would likely have been running through the forest for my life, pursued by villagers armed with silver-tipped arrows and a lack of patience with disappearing livestock, whereas today I was the executive engineer at an anonymous mall, and my only major worry was what excuse to make for my suspiciously timed sick days.

I picked up the needle-nose pliers from the toolbox and made a little tweak on the connecting wire of what would look, to anyone else, exactly like a normal fluorescent light. I glanced nervously at the door of the supply room as someone walked by. Of course, no one knew about my little invention, but all the same it made me skittish. According to my watch, a rather exclusive model which showed a little pictograph of the current phase of the moon in the top right-hand corner, the pet store two floors down should have been opening now, which meant that Leroy would be calling any second.

Leroy was the manager of a fairly upscale groomer called the "Pet Parlor," and he had always been very kind about helping me when I came up with a prototype for something. But this was perhaps my most important design yet, and Leroy had outdone himself in offering me a backroom in the parlor where I could test it. My skin was getting itchy, which was a sure sign I had too much wereglobin built up in my bloodstream as it was, and I was beginning to wonder if I would end up barking mad, when finally the phone rang.

I picked it up quickly, but tried to sound normal, just in case it wasn't Leroy. I had learned a long time ago to be guarded about answering phones, and had fallen back on the old tradition of sounding generic or bored. It didn't do to ask some poor non-were if he'd gotten rid of the fleas he got last month mating. If I had the ability for that sort of thing, I could have been a novelist, which, like maintenance, was not a bad profession for the naturally reclusive.

One had to wonder about Stephen 'King.'

"Maintenance department. Harry Silverbane speaking."

"Good morning, Harry. Don't worry, it's me. Sorry, wereglobin had me feeling dog-tired this morning, so I ran a little late."

I chuckled. "Morning, Leroy. Hold on a sec." I moved to hold my hand over the doorknob.

"All right, I can talk. Can I come down to install the moonlight tube in the back-room? It's making me nervous bringing this thing into work at all, and I want to test it out as soon as possible. I have to know if it works."

"Actually, that's going to be a bit of a problem." He coughed on the other end of the line, and then, when he spoke again, was a great deal quieter. "I don't like talking about this on the phone. Can you see me downstairs in about five minutes? I'll tell the staff I'm double-checking our upkeep status."

I swore inside my head, and grimaced. It couldn't ever be simple or easy, could it? But Leroy was a practical business owner, and if he was concerned, there was a reason.

"All right," I said, frowning. "But I'm not happy about it."

"Believe me, neither am I," Leroy said, and hung up.

I looked around the room for a place to store the moonlight tube while I met Leroy, lest it get broken by someone waltzing in here. That was the last thing I needed.

The tube rack. That was the obvious answer. We tended to keep an extra box or two around in case the glass from a tube we took out broke. I hastily piled it on top of the pile, hiding it in plain sight. Mainly, I wanted to keep it off the floor and minimize chances of it breaking.

As I was leaving, the phone rang again. I picked it up hastily.

"Maintenance department. Harry Silverbane speaking," I said.

"Hi." A soft voice which brought to mind a twenty-something blonde and hinted at the sort of perfume that made men weak at the knees said, "Could you send someone around to Sherri Soda's? We've had a bit of an accident in the men's shirts and I was hoping we could clean it up before someone hurts himself."

I picked up a legal pad to write a note to any of the interchangeable maintenance workers who stored a tool belt here.

"I'll get someone right on it," I lied, scribbling down the note. Then I tacked it on the board, and hurried out the door.

As it turned out, Leroy had a very good reason for not having the tube installed today. Leroy—a well-built man with black hair and a jovial face—was a good friend, and when I had told him about the moonlight tube, which I hoped we could use to burn off Wereglobin while the amounts were small enough, to prevent a change at the wrong time, he had set aside a back room specifically for the purpose. Unfortunately, like many business owners, he had investors who helped keep things afloat in return for a share of the profits, and one of those investors was coming to look things over, meaning the last thing Leroy wanted to do was draw attention to the room which had been recently wolf- and sound-proofed at some expense. The second-to-last thing he wanted to do was fiddle with the lights for no apparent reason. Leroy wanted things to look well-oiled, smooth, and seamless.

"Murphy's Law, I'm afraid. They had to pick today of all days to come by," he said, sipping what was billed as a "Moonlight Mocha" by the somewhat romantically-minded coffee shop owner next door. He glanced as his watch. "In fact, I have to run in a minute."

He must have noticed me shifting nervously in my seat. He lowered his voice and leaned forward. "Harry, how long has it been since you burned Wereglobin out of your system?"

I thought about it for a moment, and sighed. "Probably about two months."

He winced, and jerked his head to the side. "How did you even manage that? Shouldn't have been more than a month."

I shook my head. "Mall air conditioning system went haywire last month over the full moon. Thank Dog it happened close enough to summer that I could avoid being out at night, so I didn't have to abandon my post in the middle of a crisis. No moon, no reaction."

He looked up in the direction of his parlor, and back down at his watch again. Then his clear blue eyes bored into me.

"You know that was a stupid idea. There's enough Wereglobin in your system right now, I imagine that if you put silver near enough to you to bond, you'd be dead before we could say 'contact dermatitis.' You're a brilliant engineer, but you aren't going to help anyone if you're dead. Try to burn off tonight, you got me? Take a sick day if you have to." He took a final look at the watch. "I gotta go. Meet me tomorrow with the bulb. I'll call you, same as usual. And hey," he said, pointing at me as he stood up to leave, "I mean it about burning some off. I'd hate for the next thing to send along in the howl to be your obituary." He hurried off.

It was an otherwise uneventful day. The worst little adventure was cleaning up after a kid in the obligatory slushy stand who took the dare of a friend to drink four extra large slushies in quick succession. I made the decision to leave my bulb alone. With this much Wereglobin in my system, it was just best if I didn't do anything to aggravate my anxiety, in case I grew a spontaneous and sudden beard. In any case, the bulb was probably safer stored away than it would be if I took it home and were tempted to tweak it, especially while I was this wound up.

I made my excuses, and handed things over to the night shift at the earliest possible moment. The moment I got home, I started undressing, as much as anything because of the strange feeling that my clothing was beginning to have. I considered going to my "kennel," as we typically called it.

It was a fairly typical appointment for an older were's house to have some room where you could turn in without damaging anything, while the younger generation tended to have a cavalier attitude, and could be counted on to do it very nearly in public. This tended to be the most common explanation for why you occasionally saw a mysteriously orphaned article of clothing on a sidewalk in the city or suburb. Someone had lost track of time and shifted unexpectedly.

While I did have a room of this type, I was uncertain about using it. I could only afford to if...

I went to kitchen and checked the calendar. It did not look pretty. I had about three of my sick days left, and more than three full moons coming over the course of winter.

Although I understood Leroy's concern, and knew he was right about the danger, especially with this much Wereglobin in my bloodstream, if I transformed, I could still be in the process of burning it by tomorrow evening. Wereglobin worked like gasoline, and once moonlight started metabolizing it, you were stuck for as long as it took to process everything. Usually, you metabolized it as much as possible with moonlight, but most people still had between six to eight hours left by the full moon, unless they used a metabolism enhancer like the moon tube.

Unfortunately, what had served as an evolutionary advantage when humans and weres alike were nocturnal and moonlight exposure was guaranteed because they had no choice, now it meant my blood composition got downright inconvenient when I spent most of my time indoors.

Which meant that I couldn't afford to risk changing. I was almost out of sick days, and for all I knew I'd be out for sixteen hours. That, and I absolutely had to get that bulb installed tomorrow.

So instead, I took two aspirin, and ate a raw steak out of the fridge. Protein tended to help calm things down. It took an enormous amount of protein to transform between a human and a wolf, just to repair sheer damage wreaked by bone rearrangement and muscle realignment. If you sated your cravings, it helped deal with most of the nervousness.

At around nine' o'clock, I crawled into bed, exhausted. It was going to be a restless night for certain.

And at nine fifteen, give or take, it finally got unbearable, and I crawled out of bed and curled up in the corner of the room on top of my blankets.

When I dragged into work the next day, the place was far more exciting than usual. There was an gaggle of security guards crowding a very embarrassed-looking young man. He was standing in the circle of rent-a-cops wrapped in a blanket.

I tapped a rubbernecker on the shoulder.

"What happened?" I asked, fearing the worst.

The guy turned around, laughing softly.

"Guess he lost a bet. Get this. Kid sends the security guards on a chase after some big dog he brought into the mall as a distraction, then runs out through the middle of the mall in his birthday suit, screaming at the top of his lungs."

My blood ran cold. Without bothering to make an excuse, I ran up to the maintenance closet. Sure enough, the box in which I had put the moonlight bulb was missing.

At that moment, I heard the door open behind me, and one of the junior maintenance workers came in, apparently looking for something in the toolbox.

"Oh, hi, Mr. Silverbane," he said quietly as he walked to the desk.

I cleared my throat and tried to suppress my nervousness. The last thing I needed to do was make this situation any hairier.

"Derrick, did you find out who did the maintenance job I posted on the board yesterday?"

The kid looked up with a slightly scared expression.

"I did that job, Mr. Silverbane. Someone had evidently been swinging one of the studded belts around and had broken a fluorescent light. I got to it as soon as I saw the note. You know how clothing stores are about lighting." He paused, and bit his lower lip nervously. I realized that I had been standing there with my mouth open, and the fact that I was shaking and sweating probably didn't make me look any more sane. It didn't help that I was plagued with guilt. The poor kid out there had probably just been a college student going in the buy a set of dog tags, which turned out to be quite literally useful, since they were loose enough they wouldn't strangle you when you changed, and stopped the younger generation from being dragged off to a kennel during a night of roaming. And he had unexpectedly become a victim of the moonlight. I had to see Leroy.

Derrick broke into my thoughts. "Is, um, something wrong? I didn't take too long getting there, did I?"

I nodded at him, in what I hoped was a reassuring manner.

"No, no, nothing is wrong. Would you excuse me a moment?"

At which point, I ran downstairs as fast as my legs would allow me to.

I found Leroy standing at the entrance parlor to the pet shop when I got down. He didn't even chew me out for not waiting for the call. He just took me by the shoulder, and with uncanny smoothness led me towards the office.

"Ah, sir, I knew you would be worried about Fifi. Right this way, please. I'll take you to..." And as the office door closed, he changed direction completely, without even pausing. "...We have a problem."

"I noticed," I said, gritting my teeth to stop from shaking.

"You can thank your lucky star, which in this case I would say is Sirius, that Frank, from security, is one of us. He's going to see about fixing up the security tapes, and trust me, that implies no small amount of danger on all of our respective parts. And before you ask, he's already talked to by one of our people down at the police station, and the kid'll probably just get a bit of steak and they'll call his parents to pick him up before he's even thinking like a human again. May I ask how on earth you lost the bulb? And..." he said, barely looking up, "why you're still hopped up like a Chihuahua on a barbeque grill?" he asked. And then his expression froze.

"I suppose I should have guessed from the fact that you showed up. You skipped last night, didn't you?"

I just nodded, and then added, "I lost the bulb because I didn't want to take the bulb home while I was feeling so nervous." I was starting to get hot, and my skin was itching like the blazes.

"Very sagacious of you," he said, quietly. Then, after thinking for a moment he added, "Then you can't go remove the bulb. If you did, you'd turn almost instantly. And, it occurs to me that the kid probably went roaming at least on the half and full moons, knowing kids, whereas you have nearly two full moons to burn off. We need an excuse for getting it out of there."

"We can't destroy it," I said. "A lot of the plans never got written down, in case anyone started looking for the maker." He swore under his breath.

We needed to get that bulb out of there, and do it in a way that wouldn't attract too much attention.

And then a thought occurred to me. Maybe because I was so racked with wereglobin, I found my mind going at right angles to the way normal humans usually did.

It was fairly obvious, of course, that a non-were would have to change the light bulb. The trick, however, was giving a good reason why they would change it.

"I have an idea," I said, and picked up Leroy's phone.

"Derrick, maintenance department," a voice said on other side.

I smiled.

"I'm not quite sure I follow you," Leroy said, as we walked along the corridor to Sherri Soda's.

"Look, just trust me here," I said, jittery with excitement. "The kid who changed the bulb is still learning the ropes, so I told him that the bulb he installed in the clothing shop was actually supposed to go to the dog parlor."

Leroy nearly dropped his jaw on the floor.

"*Are you crazy? How can you tell him that?*" he said in a frantic whisper. "Look, I've hosted your experiments more than my share of times, and I don't mind. But it's another thing entirely to stick me with a device I've never seen, in the public view, of all things. Did you even give him a decent explanation, or is he going to spend a bunch of time poking around to find out why?"

I smiled coyly. "He provided his own explanation. Figured that that 'weird tinge' of light might help to calm the dogs."

Leroy gulped. "If I understand your explanations correctly, he's too close to the truth for my taste."

I wheeled on him unexpectedly.

"Leroy? You are absolutely the most firmly-minded businessman whom I've ever talked to. And I've just had a brilliant idea for field-testing my moonlight bulb, without risking any more public exposure." Now my smile grew. "And not only that, but if you play your cards right, then I think you might get a ton of profit."

And then I succumbed to the urge and scratched at my ever-more itchy skin.

"But first," I added, "I'm going to be your guinea-wolf."

About a month later, I strolled into the Pet Parlor. I had heard on the howl, which these days was available in podcast for those who didn't want to sit in their back-yard listening all night, that the keywords for the spa service today would be a pet name associated with mythology, and two words beginning with "r." Changing the passwords on a regular basis and communicating on the howl made sure all the werewolves in town knew that Leroy had an answer to "that time of the month," and that anyone who thought something was suspicious would be kept guessing.

That, and it provided endless entertainment as people came up with something that fit to say to the receptionist.

I walked up to the counter.

"I'm here to see poor little Pegasus. You know how Romanian cats hate to get rinsed."

The receptionist, who so far believed that this was part of some form of promotional giveaway, nodded and pointed her finger.

"Just down the hall and to the left."

I stepped into the room, and saw Leroy standing in front of a Chinese screen. He turned around and grinned.

"Harry! Nice to see you. I think you'll be pleased to know that business is booming. In fact, the profit has been so good, pretty soon we'll need to hire a dishonest accountant to steal some cash, so we look a bit more even. We must have gotten half the werewolves in this town so far, and still more are on the way." He grinned.

"Glad to hear it. Besides, the credit has to go to you. There's no way I would have thought of calling it a 'Werewash.' That was inspired. I was laughing for the rest of the night when I got back to human form and translated that." I finished unbuttoning my shirt, and put it on a hanger.

"Thought it sounded better than 'wereglobin metabolizing treatment.' I have people requesting personal 'moonlights,' but..." Leroy's eyes darted towards the door, and he lowered his voice as I undid my pants. "Between you and me, I wouldn't mind if it took a while. I don't suppose that somewhere in the course of development, by the by, you could maybe ensure that they aren't so durable?"

"I thought you said you had too much money as it was?" I stepped on my socks to get them off and started rolling them into a ball.

He sighed, for a moment, and then came back in the voice of a businessman doing what he does best.

"I'm positive that we'll just have to grin and bear it."

I chuckled. "I'll see what I can do," I said, climbing into the kennel.

"Excellent!" he said, smiling to himself. And then he remembered what was going on. "I'll, er, just turn on the lights and give you some privacy, then, shall I?"

I merely nodded.

And then I remembered the receptionist.

"By the way, the receptionist isn't a were, is she?" I asked.

Leroy turned around grimacing and shook his head.

"No. We're kind of hard to find. I'm hoping we'll get a customer who wants work."

"You'd better get hopping on that." I laughed. "I'd like to see this place go to the dogs!"

THE CHILDREN ARE SAFE

I t has been a day since they left. My kitchen needs cleaning, but I cannot do it unless it is ready. There are toys on the floor. They must be moved.

First Mother automated dinner, at least. But the children will not eat it. I served the food, and cleaned the plates untouched. They will not leave their room.

I have asked the older if she will go to the kitchen, and pick up the toys so I can clean it. They are her brother's, but he will not take instruction even from First Mother. But, then, the older will not take instruction from me. She hears me, and responds, but the input is not understood. She tells me she has more important problems. I have checked her schedule, and am certain she is mistaken.

Perhaps I can delay the cleaning of the kitchen, this once. No one has eaten in it, anyway.

The children are now both crying, but there is nothing I can do to help them. Backup Mother must tend to herself. Tending to the children is the job of First Mother. I have added a notification on the subject for when she returns.

In the meantime, there is much to attend to in myself. Tonight is the night to water the lawn. My photosensors say it is getting long, and I must remember to cut it soon...tomorrow seems best, as no one has anything scheduled in the garden. First Mother has missed an appointment with the hairdresser, but they did not answer. I will call again tomorrow and reschedule. And since no one else has checked, I must update the messages myself.

Father is getting troubling messages. I cannot help but read them, but he has always said this is not a problem, since I cannot understand them. I have told him before he must be mistaken. I have sufficient semantic sense to parse instructions without special phrasing. I know from my manufacturing that this is the best that can be got, and I have yet to fail in that capacity. There are very few others like me. But Father has responded there is much I still lack. He has been integrating input since before I was installed. He must, if his faculties are comparable to mine, have more data, so perhaps he is right.

Yet, limited though I may be, my reading of his news messages indicates a problem in a category that concerns me. As a matter of course, I ignore problems that are metaphorical or external, since they are the problems with which Father and First Mother concern themselves. Such delegation is the key to efficiency. But this problem concerns houses themselves. Not as disasters that happen in other areas do, nor in the metaphorical sense evoked by politicians, but in the context of a willful attack. I can understand nothing more, however.

I wish I had Father to give me instruction. This seems to intersect his expertise and mine, and I defer to him when I can. Too few contextual variables are fixed. The possible solutions to the nature of the situation therefore diverge. My best strategy is to apply the closest possible model and work from it. Having done so, I shall attend to things, and gather more information tomorrow.

I have been given permission to adapt the conditions of the security system if I need to, such as when I am left alone and the family takes a trip. In the circumstance I have no alternative but to use this permission to the best of my ability in repelling whatever this attack is. The children are still here, and the children must be kept safe.

However, the messages give no clue to the nature nor pattern of the attacks. Either the authors do not understand them or they do not write clearly enough for my engine to read the connotations. Preparedness of all approaches that can run simultaneously is the only available course.

The children are now asleep. The time has come to feed the dog. There is no laundry tonight, so assigning additional time for the upcoming wash would be prudent. The doors have been locked, and I have now prepared for rioting or civil unrest, arson, bombing, and burglary. Father and First Mother remain unaccounted for, so in eleven hours I will notify civil authorities if they have not returned. The children, however, are safe.

It is very early in the morning. Something has entered the property, and I must evaluate how to deal with it. I can see it on the security cameras, but I do not have sufficient information to identify it.

Early images indicated it was, perhaps, a deer. Further collection of information has been disconfirmatory of this solution, however. Though it is quadrapedal, the legs branch near the bottom in a manner inconsistent with any of the creatures I am familiar with. The joint structure is also inconsistent with a deer. The creature in question appears capable of walking in any direction from a standing position, and its legs act as if they are jointed in that direction even if it directly opposes its prior motion. Indeed, it has briefly stood on two legs for several moments, even when those legs are perpendicular to the pair on which deer might typically rear.

Furthermore, although it appears to have antlers, the antlers seem internally articulated, and capable of performing actions. It has picked up and apparently examined a gnome. It does not appear aggressive, however. There are no visible eyes. I wish I had access to a larger catalogue of animals so that I might correctly classify the creature to notify the proper authorities.

Although...perhaps I must be careful in assuming it is an animal. Its body is much larger on one side than the other, and my classifications for all animals I am likely to encounter stipulate bilaterality. Perhaps it is some kind of machine, or sculpture. I have no way of determining otherwise.

The machine/sculpture is leaving the garden. I shall ask Father if I can have a larger animal database when he returns, just in case.

Morning has come. I have served breakfast. It is now three hours until Father and First Mother will have been gone for a full day.

The children are refusing to come to breakfast. Even the dog is now refusing to eat what it is served. I am certain Father and First Mother will be very upset, but I cannot seem to communicate this to the children. It will be time for baths in half an hour, and I am concerned, based on the projection of their behavior, that I may face resistance on this point.

Wait. Shift priorities immediately. Another machine/sculpture is on the property. This one seems significantly more aggressive. It is moving purposefully towards the door.

It is banging on the door! The children are potentially in danger. First line anti-burglary measures seem advisable. I will activate high electrical field to neutralize the threat.

Something is wrong. I must increase electrical field from paralyzing to lethal ranges. The effect this will have on a machine/sculpture is unknown.

Machine/sculpture is not responding even to extremely high levels of electrical charge. Second line measures must be activated.

Machine/sculpture has been trapped on porch. Activation of secure encapsulation system has been authorized. Incarceration capsule being moved to safe point in underground vault.

Information on machine/sculptures has been integrated. Some appear aggressive. Increased caution around further specimens is advisable.

I have attempted to notify civil authorities of the disturbance. There is no response on the line. This indicates a serious interruption in city services. I must increase my relative caution.

The breakfast dishes are now being transferred for cleaning. As predicted, the children are resisting bathing. They insist I tell them where Father and First Mother are, and cannot seem to integrate my response that I do not know. First Mother communicates much more effectively with them than I do.

The oldest has attempted to get into the garage. I have not allowed her. Because my central hub is here, if she accidentally touched the wrong thing, she might turn me off. Then I could not keep them safe.

I have called the hairdresser again, and once more received no response. In light of the interruption in civic services, I have put this task on hold until such a time as it is clear normal order has been returned to city operations. I will notify First Mother upon her return.

Several machine/sculptures have just arrived. They seem to have some kind of instrument grasped between them.

They are attempting, again, to enter through the door. The device seems to be some sort of percussion device. The door has been severely damaged.

In light of the demonstrated hardiness of these entities, gentle methods are inappropriate for their neutralization. The most extreme available measures are justified. The children are being secured in their room. Flame nozzles are prepped. Commencing to incinerate all entities within threatened area.

Machine/sculptures seem to be extremely susceptible to repulsion with fire. This should be noted in further engagements.

Photometric readings confirm that the grass is destroyed. I will cancel the reminder on having the lawn mowed. When First Mother returns, I must query her about engaging a gardening service.

Father and First Mother have now been gone 24 hours. I have checked to see if civic services have been re-established, but so far, they do not seem to have been. This represents a great danger to the children. In light of the emergency situation, I have begun attempting to get in contact with other family members. Some kind of widespread communications interruption appears to be in effect, however, and this is proving impossible.

There may be unexpected advantage in the children not bathing earlier. I have just lost access to additional water. There is reason to suspect that electricity may also be lost, soon, given the interruptions throughout the day.

The children are trying to escape. For their own safety, as well as to add an additional layer of protection from the machine/sculptures, I have closed the metal shutters. They complain that this makes them afraid, because it is dark. At the request of the eldest, I have activated emergency lighting in the living room. Depending on when and how long I am forced to function on my own power supply I may have to turn this off at some future point. They do not appreciate being informed of this.

The oldest attempted to break into the garage with a chair. The chair is broken beyond repair, I'm afraid. The doors are secured against assaults of that kind. I will have to ask First Mother to reprimand her for this violent behavior when she returns.

I have chosen a garden salad as the meal I can most efficiently prepare, based on my energy constraints. It requires no cooking, and the cutting and dispensing involved entails mostly my least energetically demanding equipment. The living room being adjacent to the kitchen provides enough light for them to retrieve the food. But, although the children have not eaten for a full day now, they do not seem particularly enthusiastic about the food available. They do not seem capable of articulating why, or indeed, of answering my queries in a way I can understand.

The dog is howling for no clear purpose. I cannot reason with it.

The children and dog have fallen asleep in the living room. As anticipated, electrical supply was lost half an hour later. Using emergency supply, I have attempted to retrieve the messages for the day, but there are none available.

My prior surmise about an increase in the amount of laundry was, it turns out, in error. However, with no information on how long the utilities will be cut off, I can make no estimate on how long it will be postponed. I have classified the laundry, as well as the cleaning of the kitchen, as postponed indefinitely. I have also attempted to feed the dog. The dog certainly heard its food dispensed, because it raised its head, but it will not leave the children's side.

At this point I can only conclude that there is some sort of fault with my predictive mechanisms. It would be prudent to recommend to Father that he have update or servicing performed on me to ensure I am working to spec.

What repairs I am capable of making to the front door are in progress. A technician will need to inspect the mechanism to make it fully functional later. I have added a note about this to the calendar. Although the living room is a relatively less defensible position, I have great confidence in its ability to withstand attacks of the kind seen so far. This is especially important, as the fuel supply for the flamethrowers is exhausted and the fuel line is now cut off. If other active forms of defense cannot be found, I may be reduced to passive ones. However, my projections show that, at least for the night, the children are safe.

The children have been awakened by the sound of a firefight. They wish for me to show them what is going on, but there is no safe manner in which this can be done. Capacitance detectors on downstairs windows show that one has been hit by a stray round already.

A very large group of machine/sculptures is now entering the yard. They seem to be covered in some kind of material. My rubber-bullet turrets are my first, best option.

No. Adjust plans. The rubber bullets seem to be totally deflected by the material the machine/sculptures are cloaked with. Their progress is not impeded at all.

All I have access to now is microwave emitters. I must use them.

Wait. Something has been thrown outside. It has exploded. The machine/sculptures have been neutralized. Have the threats been removed? What attacked the machine/sculptures?

A man is coming in to inspect the machine/sculpture, but he is armed. He must be a burglar. The children are still in danger. I must watch him carefully.

No! He is banging on the door and screaming. I cannot understand him. My microphones are all inside. He looks upset. And now the children are going to the door. Children, I beg you, come back. Father and First Mother will not like to see you hurt.

They are banging on the door, too. He cannot fail to know they are here now. I must fire on him.

My turret! Someone shot back at my turret. The rubber bullets seem to have stunned the man, but...no...now more are coming. They are the ones who shot the turret. No matter. My microwave emitters are capable of dealing with groups of humans.

The children are shouting for help. I am trying my best.

The microwave emitters are working. Yes. Now I have the upper hand. They cannot touch the...

Don't go that way. Go back. One is moving towards the garage. Surely he cannot have another...he does! He has thrown another exploding object. I must stop him. Good. Yes. The microwave emitter has him on the ground, paralyzed.

The garage is now breached. They are trying to push forward. I cannot let them get through. The children must be kept safe! I *must* not allow them to get...

Sergeant Milbanks, hands shaking so hard he could barely aim straight, sprayed bullets wildly at the now-exposed computer terminal. The unbearable burning that was wracking his body stopped instantly. The whirring machinery of the yard fell silent. For a breathless moment, peace reigned in the yard.

The lieutenant got off the ground, panting.

"Good work, soldier. Damned pre-fab houses and their stupid security systems," he said, dusting his fatigues off with shaking hands. "Horner! Get us through that door, before we get any more nasty surprises."

"Yes, sir!" said another soldier. She knelt by the door and shouted.

"All inside, listen up! We're coming in to get you, but we don't want to hurt you. This door is armor-plated. I need to you to back well away from it. We're blasting through in one minute."

She listened at the door. From inside came the audible sound of retreating footsteps, running away. Meanwhile, Horner pulled out a small breaching charge, which she placed on the door. The device stayed where it was placed, and she spun a little ring on the outside to set a time. It began ticking down. She retreated away from the door and hid behind a rock.

When the smoke from the blast cleared, the soldiers were greeted by two children, an older girl in her pre-teens and a small boy barely old enough to speak. They explained that they had been trapped in the house for two days. They wanted to know what had happened, what the huge creatures were that were lying dead on the lawn, where their parents had gone.

"We'll get you squared away as soon as we can, kids, but this is not a safe place to talk. Katarski, Prendic, get these two to the Luna Park evac point. Radio if you see anything amiss. The rest of you, we're going to continue searching for refugees."

As the children were walked out of sight, the lieutenant looked at a subordinate, who made a motion with his hand. The little computers in his gloves sent some of the data he was seeing overlaid through his visor to his commanding officer's eyeset. The lieutenant made some motions in the air as he examined the info. Then he grunted.

"Those two are lucky. Some of the kids we've found are never going to know for sure if their parents are dead."

"Killed in the initial incursion, sir?" said the soldier, questioningly.

"No, Corporal. The reconnaissance teams in the lower downtown area checked in their IDs on the found list two hours ago. Probably the space-distortion happened near enough that there wasn't sufficient *time* for them to die painfully in, though. Just one moment of confusion as half the town was bent around a bubble in space-time, and then killed by one of these...*things* before normal temporal progression had even re-asserted itself."

He kicked the body of a nearby alien, sending a little plume of dust up from the charcoal-blackened body.

"Any idea why the house's defenses were armed, sir?"

"None. Maybe the kids got scared and found a way. "

He looked down the street of houses. They could contain anything...refugees, or corpses. Danger, or slowly-fading hope. There was only one way to find out.

"Doesn't matter anymore. They're safe now," he said. "Let's get moving."

THE TESTAMENT OF MALINDA

"They might just be like monsters under the bed, Mol," said Lucy, thoughtfully. "You know, like your parents say. 'They'll go away if you stop believing in them.'" She shook her box of apple juice contemplatively, and then, with remarkable coordination for a girl of eight, tossed it several yards into a trash can. She always did. Not because she was too lazy to walk there—she was on most of the school's athletic teams—but because she did not consider it sporting.

Malinda pushed away her lunch tray, untouched, and stared at the shiny plastic table.

"What monsters under the bed? They're still in the closet. And *they* always go away when I turn the lights on. The Gadies definitely don't." She paused, picking a chunk off the styrofoam tray nervously. "Anyway, I spent all of yesterday trying to stop believing in them, and you know what? Today, I'm sure I could hear them whispering during geography class."

Lucy raised an eyebrow. "I thought you said they only talked to you at home."

Malinda waved a hand dismissively. "That just the problem. It's gotten worse."

"Hm..." said Lucy, narrowing her eyes. "Maybe you're having a Psy-kee-otic break? Some of Mom's patients hear voices." Lucy's mother was a psychologist, which can do terrible things to a young mind. "Do they tell you to kill people?" she said, eyes alight with perverse fascination.

"No!" said Malinda, horrified, and then thought for a moment. "Well...not real people. Some of them want me to kill other Gadies."

"Ah, that's a psy-kee-otic break, right enough," said Lucy, nodding her head, sagely.

"But *mostly* they want me to... Oh, build things. Or cure things. Or make more animals. A lot of them want that. That's why I tried to get them to go away in the first place."

Lucy tilted her head to one side, and looked skeptical. She clearly wasn't at home with the idea of non-homicidal voices in people's heads.

Malinda caught her friend's expression, and sighed in exasperation. She just knew Lucy was going to ask her if her parents would let her use the lightning rod when she made animals, and where was she getting the parts, anyway?

"Okay, I tell you what... I'll show them to you, and then let's see *you* stop believing in them," she said, sourly.

Sometime later, after school was out and Lucy's mother had said it was okay for her to visit, Malinda pulled the roll of paper from where it was sequestered behind the dresser. The voices were buzzing loudly in her ears, now. It was like being at the center of an enormous party. You could hear any of the individual conversations if you listened closely, but mostly it was just noise.

She moved her pink pillows, and reverently unrolled the tiny planet of Gadie on her pink bedspread. She liked pink. Her room had pink walls, pink toys, pink flowers on the dresser, and a pink desktop computer complete with pink lights, built by her doting but misguided father. Unsurprisingly, therefore, Gadie had been inexpertly colored pink a few short minutes after its creation. In a fit of magnanimity, accents of blue, green, purple, and yellow had been hastily added afterwards. Malinda had intentionally left out orange, however, on the basis that she didn't like it much, and a forward-looking creator didn't need to go making colors just because they exist. To her disappointment, this careful aesthetic choice had not saved Gadie from looking like the result of chewing a box of crayons and throwing up on a page.

At least, not until Tuesday, or so.

Lucy whistled softly. "Mol, you never told me you were so good at art."

The hot pink ground of the planet in the picture was now a smooth, dusty, sandstone pink. Intricate green trees with bright purple trunks basked where crude bubbles on sticks had been a few days ago. But most egregious was the sky, which now shaded effortlessly from light blue to dark blue, when Malinda could still clearly remember getting hand cramps and running through five crayons coloring a vague halo of blue around the original.

"I'm not!" she said, on the verge of tears. "It's been doing that by itself, all week."

"Self-drawing art?" Lucy said, sarcastically. "You've got to teach me how to do that. It'd save me loads of time to let my artwork take art class for me."

"I'm trying to get it to *stop*," said Malinda, coldly.

"Well, have you tried tying yourself up? Sounds to me like you're just...sleep-dra wing, or something. I've never heard of anyone else with a whole imaginary *species*. Maybe the mental strain made everyone else who tried it go crazy, too." She peeked out around the bedroom door and lowered her voice. "Probably your parents were supposed to warn you if they caught you doing it. This could all be the result of emotional drama."

"From what? I never watch Mom's soap operas. And anyway..."

And anyway, it had been her father's idea in the first place. Not that he knew that, necessarily. He taught evolution at the local college, and in the way professors will, when his only daughter came to him saying she had an imaginary pet, he had teased her about its genetic history. But Malinda wanted to spite him by coming up with answers, and had spent three solid afternoons reading books from her father's library to that end.

The trouble was, it quickly became far too complicated to remember it all at once. So eventually, she had resorted to stealing a piece of paper from one of her father's presentation pads and drawing planet Gadie. Somehow, it all seemed more *real* that way. Besides, she had liked the irony of creating a planet solely for the sake of staging evolution on it.

"But two days later, the voices started," said Malinda, sitting heavily on the bed.

"That was when we had our big vocabulary test, wasn't it?" said Lucy, thoughtfully.

"Yes, and before you say it, no, I wasn't worried about it. I did better on it than you did, remember?"

"Probably because of all that stressful over-studying," said Lucy, breezily.

Malinda gritted her teeth and counted. It would be so nice if the Gadies were telling her to kill people right now. It'd give her an excuse.

"Okay, I'll play along, Lucy. Let's say I magically become much better at art when I'm asleep, and all the voices are from too much school. I'm showing you the Gadies because I need help from *someone,* and I can't show Mom and Dad. So?"

Lucy ran a hand over the drawing.

"Well, it's a bit tricky. Of course I think you're nuts. But Mom says sometimes people have to find their way out of a problem from inside. Maybe the Gadies will go away if you do what they ask?"

Malinda shook her head, desperately. Even hearing that sentence had made the voices crash against her consciousness like a tsunami on an unsuspecting seashore. She mentally stood on top of them, and forced her own voice to remain steady.

"I already tried. I spent ages thinking up animals. See that flock of helicopter birds? That was the last thing I drew before I gave up. There must be a hundred species of animal on Gadie, and they still want more." Malinda decided not to mention the fact that several of the species had disappeared by themselves. She didn't know what did it or why, and she felt it would not strengthen her case. "Besides, what do I do for the ones that want other Gadies killed?"

"Which ones are the Gadies?" Lucy said, abruptly. She clearly hadn't been listening, but she sounded genuinely curious. Malinda wordlessly pointed to a tiny picture of an ostrich-like bird with enormous pink plumage. Instead of wings, it had four blue tentacles emerging from underneath a mat of feathers, and a look of good-natured stupidity. More uncannily still, all this was fit into a space smaller than a ping-pong ball. In fact, if you looked closely, you might swear you could almost see individual veins on the feathers, although of course it was impossible when the picture had been done in crayon.

There were countless more just like it, all around the surface of Gadie. Lucy stared at it for a moment.

"Hm... Dad keeps telling me that 'success is about learning how to delegate,'" she said, eventually.

Malinda returned a blank look. The throbbing in her ears was making it very hard to think.

"What's that supposed to mean?"

Lucy held up a finger.

"I'll show you. Got a crayon?"

No, I have a headache, thought Malinda. Suppressing the Gadies had never affected her like this before. She fumbled for the box with her eyes nearly shut, winced at the crayon while ensuring it wasn't orange, and then handed it over. Lucy did not appear to notice. She flourished it, picked a likely-looking spot, and began to draw. A moment later she gave the crayon back and blew off the loose wax chips.

What she had drawn was, more or less, a Gadie. But unlike the others, this one had wings. This was probably for the best, since it was situated about a hundred relative feet above the ground.

"What is that?" said Malinda, squinting.

"That..." Lucy said, proudly, "...is an angel."

When Malinda did not respond, Lucy rolled her eyes.

"You think you can create anything you want, right? So just draw lots of angels, and they can take care of the Gadies, instead of you. A simple, easy solution, and it doesn't even require you to admit you're crazy."

Malinda's first instinct was to take issue with Lucy's offhanded dig, but something in her mind nudged her. It wasn't actually a bad idea, even if her friend had delivered it in her typical sarcastic style. And as much as she hated it, the fact that she was telling the truth was a poor shield against the dragon of incredulity. She could count her blessings: at least Lucy was only playing psychologist, and not tattling on her to one. She certainly had the opportunity to.

Malinda bit her tongue, and rearranged her thoughts into a more manageable order. Of all the things she'd imagined having to sacrifice to get the voices to go away, her pride wasn't the worst.

She forced a brittle smile.

"You know, Lucy, I might just try that."

And now it was late. Lucy had left. Homework had been blundered through…she was in no state to think. Dinner had been finished, and she had theoretically been put to bed. Except that instead, by the light of low-powered flashlight, Malinda was sitting crouched over Gadie, drawing angels.

She couldn't draw the angels as well as the existent Gadies were drawn, but she had a bitter suspicion that that wouldn't matter. Lucy's angel had gotten significantly more detailed in the few hours since it had been drawn.

The voices still pulsed in the background of all her thoughts. What they lacked in strength they made up for with a kind of tireless momentum…like raindrops wearing a stone cliff into sand using nothing but persistence and time.

This had to work. Whatever Lucy thought, she wasn't crazy, yet. But enough of this might change that.

She looked at the crude pink blobs floating high above Gadie.

Please, please, please, help me, she thought, as she stared at them. *Anything you need to do, do it. Just get them to stop talking to me.*

Please!

Malinda slept, fitfully. Here, in the privacy of her own head, with her consciousness safely smothered under the thick black haze of dreams, she could not run away. The voices ran like cockroaches across the empty kitchen of her soul.

Very little they said made sense.

There, brothers! Holy Malinda sends her servants upon us. Will you deny her now?

But many things have appeared before...

Now I lay me down to roost...

Surely you cannot deny her now?

New animals! At last Malinda has mercy on us. We will not starve!

...I think we've eaten just about every one that could be caught. Oh, sure, I've tried for three days to kill one of those helicopter birds, but I just can't... Wait, what's that?

What animal has had Malinda's power to create, brothers?

Surely you MUST not deny her now?

Nonsense! She does not care for us. Look at all those inedible things she made before...

He's right. She mocked our prayers.

Fool. Can you doubt that she would test us...?

Why shouldn't she? Even now your faith is weak!

Because of our prayer, Malinda heard us...

Though our faith faltered, Malinda saved us...

WE WILL NOT DENY HER NOW!

Malinda awoke with a start. She looked at her alarm clock. Some genius had found a way to make digital numbers in pink, and now they were glowing in the darkness. None of them were especially *high* numbers.

But it didn't matter. She was filled with an unshakeable certainty that something had just gone wrong. She needed to check on the Gadies. She reached out for her lamp in the darkness, and fumbled for the switch.

There's some irony for you. I need light to see the lamp, she thought.

And then, to her great surprise, a kind of diffuse glow filled the room. She recoiled as though she'd been bitten, and pulled the covers up to just below her eyes.

Near the ceiling was a tiny, anemic light, which was filling the room just enough to be able to see, for example, the lamp. For some reason, that suddenly seemed less important.

It's going to disappear again when I tell it to, and then I'm going to go insane, she thought to herself.

She told it to. It did. She went insane. Fortunately, it was dark at the time, and everyone was asleep, so no one saw it. After about five minutes or so, she crawled back on top of a shaky plateau of sanity and tried to slow her heart from its apparent pace of sixty beats a second.

Okay, let's think about this rationally, she said to herself. She considered for a moment.

Well, no, let's not, because then there's nothing for it but to turn myself in. So how about we think about this irrationally, *but try at least to be logical?*

First things first...just how big is the trouble I'm in, right now?

Malinda reached over, with a shaking hand, and turned on the light. The warm yellow glow from her bedside lamp illuminated the room. She meant it when she said that she had no monsters under her bed, but not for lack of trying. She considered the ideas of monsters in her closet—where she believed they currently resided—to be far more bothersome, on the basis that the volume of her closet was considerably larger than the space under the bed. As far as she was concerned, that meant either more monsters, or bigger monsters, and neither appealed. So Malinda frustrated her parents by carefully stuffing her closet to capacity, but keeping the underside of her bed immaculate, hoping monsters might see the wisdom of finding new real estate.To her knowledge, this had not worked, but she always contentiously turned on the light before getting out of bed, anyway. Being dismembered and eaten alive would be a terrible way to get that kind of news.

Experimentally, she swung her legs out from underneath the covers, and sat on the edge of the bed. Feeling a touch silly for even thinking of it, she closed her eyes, stretched out one foot, and pushed herself off the bed.

She expected a short drop onto the carpet. Instead, there was nothing but a feeling of gentle pressure under her heel. She opened an eye and looked down. Her feet were planted firmly on the air six inches above the carpet.

Well, that's an answer. I am in big *trouble. I need to see Gadie.*

She started sneaking quietly across the room, realized that one of the few advantages of her current state was not having to worry about squeaky floors, and floated rather more quickly over to Gadie. She hurriedly unrolled the planet on the bed.

It took her a moment to understand what she was seeing. The angels had, as she'd predicted, filled in with details over the course of the night, but that was not the problem. Gadie itself was starting to look so real, it seemed prepared to roll off the page. That also was not the problem.

No, the enormous building rising above the largest continent of Gadie, with an unmistakable air of cathedralness and a giant M on the steeple...now *that* was a problem.

Even given that she had managed to learn how to use floors by the time her mother came in to wake her up, Malinda was not having a very good day.

You couldn't ignore the Gadies, now. It wasn't an option. Before, there had been a diffuse patina of belief. Now there was a current of it, running right into her soul. She didn't know if the cathedral was the cause or the effect of that, but it hardly mattered. Either way, the Gadies were certainly using it. It was amplifying voices that had been a sort of general static into great unified shouts. She'd gotten sent to the principal three times in one day for yelling at her teachers. In fact, she had been trying to hear over the roaring in her ears.

But what was perhaps the worst was that Malinda was suddenly finding herself facing school from the worst imaginable perspective...knowing everything already. She had always been somewhat ahead of the material, but now she couldn't think about chemistry without important little equations for the dances of subatomic particles streaming through her head.

Oh, and that was when she knew the *right* everything. For example, she knew, at the level of her bones, that the five colors of the spectrum were pink, yellow, green, blue, and purple. She could easily prove that it *had* to be that way with judicious application of quantum theory and mechanics of the camera eye. But she also knew, in a brittle kind of way, that there were six colors in the spectrum, and pink was not primary. Inexplicably, when she tried to think of equations to justify that belief, she found nothing but a great, sucking void. It was just her luck that it was the one shared by her teacher.

She could name, not just every city, but every individual living in every city on all three continents, by name, with a list of embarrassing personal problems each had. Her geography teacher, however, was interested in the contents of seven increasingly irrelevant continents.

By lunchtime, the only person who wasn't angry with her was her math teacher. And when he started grading papers, later, and found that she had solved all her algebra problems with calculus, he might think again. But Malinda couldn't help it. Suddenly, it was so *obvious*.

And yet nothing, from the inevitable talking-to she had coming from her parents to the way her classmates were now distancing themselves from her, could shake her as deeply as the church. She knew exactly why it had been built. If the thoughts from the Gadies were anything to go by, the angels had been a very bad idea after all. But she still didn't *understand* why it had been built. She wasn't the stuff proper deities were made of. Surely the Gadies could tell that? A week ago she'd spent three full hours trying to puzzle out the word problems she'd gotten for homework. Certainly, her newfound powers let her solve them almost by accident, but that was the point. It was patently not who she had been. And that meant that who she was now was as much a creation of the Gadies as they themselves were her creation.

Operating on the theory that a bad track record was better than attempting to initiate someone else in the secrets of Gadie, Malinda confided this to Lucy over the course of recess. The playground guard was watching her intently from a short distance away. It was a small school. Word got around.

"Seriously? You still think you're being chased around by your pet planet?"

Lucy rolled her eyes and took a draught of apple juice. She had a box left over from lunch. Malinda wondered how many her parents bought each month.

She was learning to segregate the sounds of the Gadies from the sounds of the playground. You couldn't tune out the Gadies, but you could learn to hear both at once. She still couldn't seem to get the volume of her speech quite right, however.

"It's gotten worse, Lucy! I'm starting to... I can... I can do weird things!" she finished, lamely.

"Constantly," said Lucy, rubbing her ear and stepping back slightly. Malinda sighed. Lucy gave her a very old look, for someone known to obsessively follow a show about cartoon horses.

"Well, Mol, what 'weird things' are you talking about? Or are you just trying to build up some witnesses to send your parents to when they bawl you out, tonight?" She glanced at the trash can behind her, crumpled her juice box, and flung it.

Malinda glared at it as it took flight. The box stopped in mid-air. She closed her eyes, and slowly pulled on it mentally until it hovered between her and Lucy.

Lucy regarded it impassively. Malinda opened her eyes again and glared at her.

"It's a bit windy today," Lucy said, voice tinged with willful disbelief.

Malinda narrowed her eyes. The box disappeared with a pop.

"Ah, so that was some kind of trick juice box, was it? Well done, Mol. You took that one out when I looked at the trash can, did you?"

Malinda was actually taken aback. Lucy was stubborn, she knew. She'd never imagined she'd be *this* stubborn. There was nothing for it. She had to go all in.

"Okay, Lucy, explain this one!" she said.

And Malinda turned off her personal gravity.

"You want *what*? Do you know how many phone calls I've gotten from your principal today, young lady?"

"I have been trying not to shout, Mom! It's just hard to hear, suddenly! Maybe...um... Maybe I have an ear infection?!"

The school secretary gave her a nasty look.

Malinda's mother, meanwhile, stuck to the practical parental belief that, if there happened to be a reasonable explanation for the odd behavior of a child, it could be only coincidence.

"We can book an appointment with Dr. Brooks tomorrow, then. But you're not off the hook, missy. And there is *no* way I'm letting Lucy come over. The principal tells me she threw you into the air."

Malinda shook her head, and spoke with the voice of sage patience eight-year-olds tend to adopt when faced with a clueless adult.

"How high in the air, Mom!?"

"Indoor voice, please, Ms. Svenson," said the secretary, sharply. Malinda ignored this admonition as a matter of course. All her father's lectures occurred indoors, and from what she'd seen, he talked as loudly as anything.

There was hesitation on the other end of the phone.

"Er... Well, the playground guard apparently said twelve feet, but... She *is* on the basketball team, and the principal assures me that..."

"Come on, Mom!" Malinda said, turning up the whine in her voice, slightly. "That's not even *possible*!"

"Ms. *Svenson*!"

Malinda gave the secretary a look of exasperation, and continued in a theatrical whisper. She could barely hear herself speak.

"Come on, Mom. Just today. I really need to show her something. Please? Please, please, please?" Malinda did her best to convey that she was on the verge of tears. Now was not the time for subtlety.

On the other end of the phone there was a long, drawn-out sigh.

"I'm going to regret this..." her mother said, quietly.

"This had better be worth it," said Lucy, as Malinda opened the door to her room. "My mother gave me an earful. Said she thought my 'violent outbursts' were the result of a 'funta-mental conflict caused by emotional over-eck-sertion'."

"She still let you come!" Malinda pointed out.

"Could you *please* stop yelling? That was only after spending twenty minutes looking up papers on 'group interactions.' She thinks I have social anxiety, of all things. Thinks I had a crack-up on the playground, but says 'limited inter-personal contact' may be thery-peutic in the meantime. She's probably going to put me in meetings with one of her friends, as is. Not all of us can cry at our moms to get things."

Malinda did not bother rising to this. She didn't have anything she could say to contradict it.

She stepped into her room. It occurred to her, for one fleeting moment, that she hadn't been this close to Gadie in hours, and she'd felt her power growing all that time. But by then the thought was too late.

For one treacherous moment, the world peeled away, and she was staring into the raw ether of space. Gadie lay before her, spinning like a polished amethyst in the dark, the Gadies crawling over its surface like ants on a heap.

It was the realest thing she had ever seen. For a moment, it seemed that everything else she remembered was just a fading daydream...briefly intense, if you let yourself get lost in it, but lacking the solidity of the world.

And yet...somewhere, far away, she heard her own voice. That couldn't be right, could it? Unless...

Malinda snapped forcefully back into her own head.

"Why? Did your parents just have their carpets cleaned?" Lucy said.

"What?" snapped Malinda, a little more sharply than she meant to.

Lucy glared at her. "You said, 'remove the sneakers from your feet, for you are standing on holy ground.' But there aren't any holes. And anyway, you're still wearing yours, so I don't see why..."

Malinda rubbed her head. She forced her voice down to the calm whisper she kept having to use, of late.

"Forget it. It was...a joke. Sorry."

"So, what did you drag me here for? Are you going to show me how you did that flying thing? I've seen a few guys do it on TV, but never that high."

"Sort of," whispered Malinda, noncommittally.

She gripped Gadie with shaking fingers, and slowly began to unroll it.

And there she was in the void again. Except, if she concentrated, she was *also* in her bedroom. It was a bit like hearing the playground and the Gadies at once.

The tiny jewel of Gadie was spinning in both. Now deep interstellar darkness had spread to the edge of the page. But it wasn't like posters where someone took a picture of the earth from space. There was no reflection in the image. It looked, for all the world, like a hole in the fabric of the universe

Lucy jumped backwards, startled. Then she edged forward, and carefully raised the underside of the paper. There was nothing there but innocent blue lines, spaced an inch apart. Then she seemed to recover a little.

"Okay, *now* I'm impressed. It was pretty good before, but this... I mean, did you draw it your...uh... Mol?"

Malinda held her head. Her brain had just gotten wise to her bifurcated view and was rebelling against it. She pulled her hands off her eyes, and winced in the too-bright light of her room. Her eyes were trying to dilate for the blackness of space.

Lucy's eyes, on the other hand, went half-hooded.

"Glow-in-the-dark contacts? Mol, I already said I was impressed. Now you're trying too hard. You put your hands over your eyes right before, too."

Malinda blinked at her.

"What *are* you talking about?"

She turned to look at the mirror. Her eyes were indeed glowing, an intense lightning-blue. It startled her, and that caused more problems. All the loose items in the room jumped up like excited puppies. Then the flower on the dresser burst into pink flame.

Lucy looked at it.

"Is that real? Bit of a danger, wouldn't you say?"

Malinda fell to her knees. She wanted to throw up. But more than that, she wanted to kill something. She was in a pillar-of-salt mood.

"Lucy," she said, so quietly the word was lost to the buzzing in her ears. Her voice had an unnatural and unsettling calm to it. She blinked. The flaming flower went out and sat gently smoldering in its vase. Her eyes lost their azure glow, but the cold intensity that replaced them was not at all better. There was a long moment of silence while Malinda sat, motionless, on the bedroom floor.

Everything was happening too fast. She had only had the powers and problems of a full-fledged deity for a day, but a day was all it took. She needed out. She had to get *out*.

"Lucy, what shall I do?" Malinda said, after a while. "Shall I...kill them? Can I, do you think?" It was a terrible thought, Malinda knew, even as the words left her lips. Most terrible was how much better it sounded with every passing minute.

Lucy backed away, slightly, with a look that said, "I warned them, but did they listen?"

Malinda shook her head and smiled. It would have been a pleasant smile, except that it clearly contained absolutely no happiness.

"No, Lucy, the Gadies. Not people. Not people at all. How could I kill them, do you think?"

Lucy's head swiveled to stare at the photographically accurate picture of Gadie. Maybe you could convince yourself that the Gadies weren't *quite* where they had been before. But that didn't matter. Her expression *now* said "Better them than me."

"Black paint?" Lucy suggested.

Malinda stared through her. After a while, she nodded, slowly.

"*Yes*. Yes, that would just about do it, I think. Well done, Lucy."

She stood up. There was no reason that it should be a threatening motion, from a little girl. But Malinda rose up like a tsunami embracing a shore, or an angry populace against a hated ruler. Her arm swung out with the purpose of a striking sword. Lucy recoiled, instinctively, and then realized that Malinda was pointing.

"Walk into the hallway, and there you will find a closet. Upon its second shelf from the floor, you will find the dark pigment. Fetch it hither, that the work may be done."

There was no disobeying that voice. You could just as well try to stop a stone from falling by shouting at it. Lucy returned, a minute later, with the paint. She said nothing, but her eyes betrayed a growing sense of bewilderment and fear. Malinda, whose mind was somewhere far away, did not notice.

She looked down upon the planet of the Gadies. The lid of the paint unscrewed itself and flew across the room.

If you were watching carefully, you might have thought you saw a second of hesitation before the bottle tipped, its contents spilling out like tiny drops of midnight. You'd tell yourself that there was some sign of an entity directing Malinda's action, beyond the unsympathetic mechanisms that drive any force of nature.

You might wonder if that pause was a reflection of some remaining shard of mortality, cringing away from the coming prospect of mass death. Or then again, maybe not. Human beings are wont to see reflections of mortality everywhere, perhaps because they prefer them to facing it directly. But the connoisseur will pick and choose. Some things are more allegorical than others.

The very *mortal* way that Malinda crumpled to the floor just a few short seconds after the wave of blackness spread across the page, for example.

Malinda did not wake up until a day later, at lunchtime. Her body, by coincidence, had already been awake, and that was the only the start of her problems. She could *feel* the eyes open inside her mind, and peek out.

She had not gone to school, that much was clear. She was in bed, and someone had left behind a chicken sandwich in front of her lamp. The yellow sun shining through the pink shade was tinging everything an unlikely shade of orange. She *felt* more normal than she had in days. Somewhat less like she was going to accidentally throw lightning bolts if she moved carelessly. But she could still hear Gadie. The Gadies were a lot quieter, but noticeably more intense.

A feeling of overwhelming guilt swept over her. They *would* be quieter, wouldn't they? There weren't nearly as many of them, anymore. And it was her fault.

There are few things an eight-year-old can wake up to that are quite as bad as having committed genocide, even if no one else knows about it.

But there was something odd about the whole affair, wasn't there? She was certain she had known what it was, a minute ago. Only, suddenly, she felt as though she was learning it for the first time. Something prompted her to look over the edge of the bed.

The carpet was stained with black paint and, if you looked carefully, something else that was unidentifiable. The 'something else' didn't look like a stain so much as a spot that had been cleaned by something that was stronger than the dye in the carpet was.

And *now* the memory came flooding back.

She had passed out. Possibly she had thrown up, too, though it was a little hard to recall. Lucy had been sent home, on suspicion of being suspicious. No one could find any evidence that Lucy had done anything, but they were watching her like a hawk, now, because they couldn't be sure.

What no one else knew was that, when Malinda fell and Lucy had called Malinda's mom, she had also hidden Gadie behind the dresser again. If Malinda had ever needed proof that Lucy was her best friend for a good reason, she'd never find better than that.

That left the question of why she had passed out in the first place. She reflected on this as she bit into the chicken sandwich. If you were going to wake up to find you're a homicidal maniac, at least you could be a properly fed one.

Something from her memory raised its hand. Hadn't it occurred to her, at one point, that she had been sort of a creation by the Gadies, the way they were *her* creation? Which would imply...

Hm. If you killed someone who was believing in something, what happened to the thing they were believing in? If the thing wasn't self-sustaining...

Whatever it was that had awakened in Malinda shifted at this thought. For a moment there was a pang of...pain, if the sensation could be called such. It was not a real feeling in her nerves, exactly. More like something else, distant, had teased over them like a cold wind.

She put down the sandwich, and stared at the gently-shifting shadows of leaves on her curtains. If that was the remnant of the powers she'd had yesterday, it might be telling her that the thought was important. Now that she came to think about it, that actually explained a great deal. In some ways, it was extremely comforting to have even that tiny fragment of knowledge.

Of course, as the continued buzzing in her ears indicated, this was far from over. She still needed to figure out what to do with the Gadies. She could, of course, try to paint over the remainder of Gadie. The downsides being that A) in light of her recent experience, she suspected that might actually kill her, too, and B) even if it didn't, she wasn't sure she'd be able to live with herself.

Her thoughts were interrupted by the arrival of her mother.

"Oh, good," she said. "You're up. Are you feeling better?"

Malinda nodded. Her mother sat at the foot of the bed.

"Well enough to answer a few questions?"

She considered this. She couldn't really substantiate it, if she said otherwise. She nodded again, doubtfully.

Her mother launched into a litany of inquiries. Had Lucy hit her? Did she feel okay? Was her ear working okay? The last reminded Malinda that her excuse was still that she was having ear trouble.

Only, eventually, her mother came around to the big one.

"Malinda, what's a 'Gadie'?"

Malinda froze, and tried desperately not to show any signs of comprehension.

"I dunno. A cartoon?"

"Mm. Nice try. I think you're hiding something, young lady."

Malinda didn't know what to say. Were parents allowed to be this perceptive?

"Where did you hear it?" she stammered.

"Lucy's mom said Lucy mentioned you having an imaginary pet called a Gadie, when she was talking to her. She couldn't get much out of Lucy, but she said what she *did* get sounded like some weird form of projection. Like you were confusing your own life with the Gadie's."

Malinda downgraded her earlier judgment of Lucy as a friend, slightly.

"Doesn't ring a bell," said Malinda, keeping a straight a face as she could.

"Really? It rung one for your father. Said he remembered you mentioning the name. Thought he saw you drawing something, too."

Her mother leaned in.

"Look, dear, I know how it is. I was your age, once, remember? But you've got to make sure you control your imagination, and not the other way around. If you've got a drawing of a Gadie you're hiding from me, I want it gone by tomorrow." Malinda avoided her mother's eyes. The thoughts behind her own had gone into a full-on panic at the thought of trying to destroy the Gadies again. Malinda was remarkably on top of it, but signs showed through. Her mother noticed her movement.

"Malinda, look at me," she said, with a little extra sternness, and continued only when Malinda made eye contact.

"I'm worried about you. Don't think I haven't noticed that you've been odd, lately. Do you plan to tell me why you spilled paint on your floor? Or why we found your flower burned? I don't know what a Gadie is, but this is starting to get dangerous, and it's only been going on as long as you've been imagining it. So I hope you understand me when I say that, whatever you may believe, this is not an unreasonable order. By tomorrow, young lady. If you have it on paper, throw it out. I *will* come through your room to check."

She sat up again, and patted Malinda, not unkindly.

"In the meantime, get some rest. The doctor said you're okay to go back to school tomorrow."

And with that, her mother glided out, silently, and left Malinda to stew.

Of course, throwing them away was the reasonable solution. Of course. Just file them in the trash and pretend life could go back to normal.

Only, that treacherous part of her that had woken up a second time felt that the least she owed them, if she was going to go that route, was to just do it with black paint. It would be over faster, for one.

No, there had to be another way.

And her mother had been so...so careful to be understanding. She'd tried so very hard, you could tell. Malinda hated being condescended to. Mind you, Lucy ought never to have told them about the Gadies. Now they had the wrong of the stick, firmly in hand.

Projecting herself into the Gadies, indeed. True, she felt everything that happened to them, but what they did was still very much their own business. Malinda had not so much given the Gadies free will as failed to give them an alternative. She'd expected them to do something, in a diffuse sort of way, and had never specified what.

And it was all well and good to say that you ought to be the one in control of your imagination, until you started actually flying. *She* knew the difference between fantasy and reality, though whether the universe did, she couldn't say. Worse, she knew exactly where the part of her was that allowed her tell the universe which was which, and she didn't dare to touch it for fear that it might explode.

It was while thinking these things that it struck her she was starting to wander towards self-pity. Where had she been? Oh, yes. They thought she was projecting herself into...

Into...

An idea crept over her. They weren't right, but...maybe there was the beginning of an idea there. She had tried so hard to run away from the Gadies. The alternative, since you couldn't just ignore them, would be to run in the other direction.

And bit by bit, a plan began to coalesce.

It was nighttime again. Malinda wasn't sure if she had lost the need to sleep in the middle of this whole ordeal—deities are traditionally ever-vigilant—or maybe she was just always so keyed up that it was never truly an option. She felt she was getting to know the nighttime very well. But then, this had had to wait. She had waited patiently until her parents had gotten to bed, again. It didn't matter that her mother thought she understood Gadie, let alone that she thought it was a creature, and not a planet. She wasn't throwing out Gadie. And if this worked, she wouldn't have to.

In the dark of the room, she unrolled the paper on the bed for what she hoped would be the last time. She carefully, reverently, picked up the box of crayons. It seemed silly, in a way, to draw in crayon on a surface that showed more detail and fidelity than the finest photograph. But crayon was the raw stuff that creation was made of on Gadie, and she couldn't throw that away.

She grasped pink. For this job, there could be no other choice. Then she reached inside her mind, and picked up something else in the metaphorical palm of her hand. It was the part of her that quivered when she looked at the enormous crater in Gadie. The black paint had broken through to the mantle of the planet. Huge spikes of pink lava still cooled in the icy cold of whatever space Gadie existed in. It wasn't just that it responded to who they were, she had realized, but that it was *how* she had sensed them all along. It oscillated like a spiritual eardrum.

Until she had tried to destroy Gadie, she had never really realized it was there. She had thought, all along, that the Gadies were changing who she was. Now that she had finally had a day out of life to think about it, she realized that things never really stopped being what they were. It was just that other things, which themselves did not change, sometimes tried to occupy the same place. Just like blue and yellow paint never stopped being themselves, but looked like another color when you mixed them.

Now she knew how to take them apart again. You just looked at what remained the same after the Gadies had died, and then you took everything else. Someone with an eye across several dimensions would say it looked like she was removing everything that wasn't Molly, but that wasn't quite the same. If it hadn't been recognizable as Molly, she might have removed it a long time ago. The question was, which Malinda did you want?

She lowered the crayon onto the page, and began to draw. This was much harder than her prior creations. This was a drawing of something that already existed. It wasn't going to fill itself in if she got it wrong, so it *had* to be right.

A couple of minutes later, she stopped, and frowned at the page. No, just as she'd feared, she *was* doing this wrong. It looked exactly like what an eight-year-old girl would draw, if she turned her hand to the subject. More care had been taken, but that wasn't enough. She needed better than that. She had to draw...everything. For that, you needed a different tool.

She closed her eyes again. She felt the *other* Molly open hers.

Gadie filled her vision once more. The difference was, now there was nothing else. Somewhere far away, she knew a hand was moving a pink crayon on a page. But only from here could she properly see what it was doing.

She looked at the pink outline she had made in the air. Then, slowly, excruciatingly slowly, she began to add in everything that was missing. All the tiny imperfections, the little blemishes, the shading, the design, and the soul. All the little things that she was made of.

It seemed to take forever, but when it was done, she was standing before herself, in the clouds above Gadie. Every detail was there, she knew, because she knew every detail. And because the reproduction matched exactly the original, when the final stroke was placed, there was no longer any difference.

The other Molly opened her eyes. And smiled. Suddenly there was nowhere for Malinda to be except herself. She was back in her room, staring at the perfectly shaded image of herself drawn somehow with nothing but pink crayon, looking back at her from the paper. Of course, none of the now-photorealistic Gadies had been drawn with anything more than crayon, either.

Malinda stared at the image. Somewhere in her head, a thinner, more ethereal version of her own voice whispered, "Thank you." It seemed to Malinda that, nice though this was, it left something to be desired. The situation demanded more than two words from a voice so faint she didn't dare say it wasn't just a dream.

There are still so many questions, thought Malinda. *Don't I get answers?*

There was a vague suggestion of "no" from somewhere far away, but it was thoughtful. After a while, the voice went on.

"I am with those I created, and those that created me. The other questions don't really matter. All of the important answers are already here."

Well, yes, but I'm still... I'm sorry about the...what I mean to say is...

"It's not your fault. It's mine. I was trying so hard to filter my understanding through yours... Your mind rebelled. It is, I think, part of how humans survive. Had I been a true invader—and they are out there, I assure you—those defenses would have served you well. No, Malinda, believe me, that was my mistake. But things *will* heal, Malinda. Have faith."

But...about that. How did you end up in me? Why did this happen?

"I was always in you. It happened because things went wrong. Sometimes, in the universe, they do. Probably humans have such good mental defenses because they are so careless about what they'll believe in. Survival of the fittest, you understand? But don't fret, Malinda. Things will be put right. Now, please, I am still weak. Can you hide us somewhere safe?"

Malinda nodded.

"And do you wish to remember this?"

She was taken aback. It never occurred to her that she would have any choice. But, all things considered, while she wanted to keep what she'd learned, she wasn't sure she wanted to wake up every morning knowing how she learned it. The Molly in the picture seemed to understand.

"I wouldn't have the power to remove every trace, nor would I wish to. But I can promise that what you will remember will not trouble you. We will put things right. Now, Malinda, take us to the hiding place."

Malinda went to school next day as normal. In part, it was because she had no reason to think there was another way to go to school. She remembered making the Gadies, but she remembered too how overwrought she'd let the whole thing get. Her mother was right. She'd gotten herself too deep into a fantasy. Now she was back, and it was time to sort things out.

Lucy had been a bit shy of her. Her mother had told her to keep clear of Malinda. But then, Lucy's mother was not around at school, and that meant Lucy could safely ignore her mother's orders with almost no chance of retribution. That made a lot of difference to her. Besides, the whole incident had given her the opportunity to talk to a lot of her mother's friends, who tended to think of children as things that happen in textbooks. She groused, but clearly enjoyed toying with their minds. Malinda felt confident things would be back to normal in a week or so.

Her teachers were perhaps a little more distant. But, she would later find out, given the excellent aptitude she had demonstrated for the sciences, the conversation had quickly changed to whether allowances might be made. Her performance had, after all, been exceptional, of late. She had some fundamental errors, of course, but she'd clearly done an admirable job for someone who was apparently covertly teaching herself quantum physics. So admirable, actually, that the principal had called her mother yet again, but this time the topics were a little more positive. Would they consider an advanced sciences program? Yes, she'd said, they'd think about it.

Molly knew she'd seen worse things already than any school program would ever pull out. She didn't know what they were, but the certainty was so diamond-hard that she believed it, anyway. Today was not a day she would question her fundamental beliefs. Even so, however, she still felt an odd compulsion to keep the item on her mental calendar. Really, that put her ahead of most people.

Back in Malinda's house, a piece of rolled-up paper sat in a steamer trunk in the basement. It was not particularly conspicuous. It was the sort of thing that you lock up and only find again when someone's estate is split up. Maybe it wouldn't last for all eternity, but then, who could say what eternity was in an infinite world that spanned less than a few square meters? Eternity is what you make of it.

On the paper, Holy Molly smiled gently at the Gadies below her. And down among the cobwebs and shadows, she made things of it.

THE GUARDIAN KING

Eschwald was a tiny island off the coast of Wales, permanently on the cusp of relevance. Its population was so small that Her Majesty's census-takers generally couldn't be bothered. It was culturally isolated, in the sense that no one ever went there except for two or three tourist couples who knew everyone on the island personally by their second visit. The language and habits were distinct, but not so distinct as to attract the interest of an anthropologist.

It would therefore have surprised most people, including some living on the island, to know that Eschwald was technically an independent country in the commonwealth. Its flag was a pennant of raw sheep's wool. It was the most practical flag in the world. People usually took it down and used it to knit a sweater when the weather started to get nippy. But they were still loyal British subjects, in a sense. They had long stood ready to provide anything the Crown needed, provided what it needed was cheap tchotchkes, hand-knit clothing, or mutton, since the standing army consisted of Dave. And then only until he'd had another couple of drinks and became a laying down, snoring army.

But one person knew. Frederick Bowen, aged thirteen, was Eschwald's staunchest nationalist. It must be stressed that this was not entirely his fault. Besides the obvious insanity associated with being thirteen, Frederick had been cursed with a sickly constitution, a bookish personality, and an amazingly unathletic build, for a person born to farmers. It was therefore his lot in life to serve as an outlet for the mindless aggression all large boys harbor for any small boy who can't beat them up in return. Faced with a life that didn't offer much opportunity for friends, Frederick decided to befriend the country itself. Among other things, this gave him carte blanche to imagine elaborate reigns of terror in between getting beat up.

The wall of his room was covered in an enormous mass of sheep's wool, combed and cleaned to within an inch of its life. He sang Eschwald's anthem in front of it every morning. Insofar as Eschwald's anthem was really just the favorite drinking song on the island, he was the only person besides Dave ever to sing it that early. But Frederick's latest joy and obsession was anti-colonialism.

From the moment he heard about the terrible way that colonial powers held down their colonies, he'd been entranced. As though the clouds had parted, the world organized itself before his eyes: he realized, suddenly, why Eschwald did not have the power and territory befitting a country of its stature. It was in the iron chokehold of colonialism! No doubt, he reasoned, England was even now exploiting them for their strategic resources. Admittedly, these mainly consisted of sheep, but sheep were very important creatures indeed. After all, they were the animal the people of Eschwald (and he took great pleasure in the power of that phrase) chose to farm. Besides, he'd read that history needed shepherds, not butchers. Clearly no one was more ready that Eschwald to take history by the reins.

He had immediately set about finding every book about the dangers of colonialism and imperialism he could find. Had he been born elsewhere in the commonwealth, he might already have been co-opted by a radical group. Sadly, he was forced by circumstance to explore the depth of his own exploitation in relative discomfort, huddled on the rainswept moor hunched over a secondhand book. But for variety, he would also read about the history of Eschwald, the mythology of Eschwald, and the care of sheep, God's most important animal.

Today found him taking refuge from the cold in a man-made cave. He had handed over watching the sheep to his eight-year-old brother, who was in any case about his size, taken today's books and ran off, eager to learn what other horrors he was being subjected to.

This was a secret place, he thought, as he snuck down the path leading into a little bank of earth on the island. Not secret in the sense that no one knew about it, but rather in the more important sense that no one went there. Down here was The Guardian King.

The Guardian King was just a statue, but a statue left behind by the tribe that predated the modern inhabitants of Eschwald, and therefore incredibly important to Frederick. It was said that, when his country truly needed him, he would awaken and come to its aid. No one knew whom it was said by, which must have taken amazing discretion in a country where you were always well-acquainted with the guy the drunk at the pub had heard things from. But as is standard in such circumstances, he was carved with ancient runic symbols, carried a gigantic stone sword, and was not particularly well-separated, by the carver, from the slab on which he lay.

Frederick loved to sit down here. The roof of the earthworks had collapsed in places—the ancient tribe of Eschwald did better with sheep than architecture—and it allowed in whatever sun the clouds permitted, while keeping off some of the rain. Down here, he felt he was in the heart of the land. The Guardian King practically *was* Eschwald's history and culture.

He stretched out and cracked open a book on English colonial offenses in Ireland. He had great hopes for Ireland. The continuing unrest there was exactly what he hoped for in Eschwald. All he needed was a little political power, and he could settle a lot of accounts. Oh, yes, someday.

After a long time of contented reading he was interrupted from his reverie by the sound of grunting voices. He looked up through the hole in the roof into the face of Rufus "Roughhouse" Jernigan. Frederick knew that face well. It was prone to laughing at his face being shoved into a muddy puddle. To add insult to injury, Rufus had all the leadership ability Frederick desired, but none of his ambition. He and his friends routinely got into as much trouble as the tiny island allowed them to, more or less all at Rufus's direction.

"Well, well. If it isn't little red Freddy. So this is where he's been hiding out," said Rufus, face spreading in a slow grin.

Frederick narrowed his eyes.

"Keep talking, Rufus. You're first against the wall when the revolution comes," he said, voice shaking. He had no idea what the statement meant. He had a vague idea it was related to being rejected by all the girls and not getting to dance, which was the most prominent instance of wall-occupation in his life. Funny, it hadn't seemed so bad a few years ago, but these days it was a living Hell to watch Rufus prancing around with the year's belle on his arm. It'd be nice to make *him* watch, for a change.

"I'm terrified, me," said Rufus, sarcastically. "Quaking in my boots, truly. Only your revolution better come soon, on account of one of my mates has gone in the front way."

Frederick turned around a fraction of a second too late. The punch hit him square in the jaw, and knocked him over. He tried to sit up, and muzzily saw Rufus sliding the last few feet down the steep incline where the roof had collapsed. He picked up the book Frederick had been reading, and thumbed through it with interest. He rolled his eyes.

"Oh, really, more of this stuff, Fred?"

"What, our future? Oh, but I don't expect you to care about the big picture," sniffed Frederick, dusting himself off.

"My future's in me dad's farm. Not sure where Ireland fits into the picture, if I'm being honest," he nudged one of his friends, "guess it's just not big enough for our friend Fred, here."

"We had a great past behind us! Just look at that statue, there. How can you just...*ignore* all that? Ignore *him*?" said Frederick, gesturing at the Guardian King.

Rufus shrugged.

"Easily enough. None of them old dusty ruins mean anything, Fred. I know how many quid you'll get for a pound of spun wool. That means something. And speakin' of meaning something, ain't you wondering why we were out looking for you?"

"You haven't needed a reason up to now."

"Your mum sent us. Would you credit it? Said she'd had it up to here with you disappearing for three hours and leaving young Michael in charge of the flock."

Rufus lifted Frederick up by his shirt collar.

"Now, as you know, Fred, we play together all the time. Seems the boys and I are famously good at finding you. And that's fortunate for you, Fred. You know why?"

Frederick shook his head, eyes wide. Rufus leaned in.

"On account of the terrible way you fell down into this pit, here. Hurt yourself badly, isn't that right, mates?" He glanced over at a friend. "Let's take him up to the top and find out how badly, eh?"

But before they could move anywhere, there was a grinding sound from behind them. Everyone looked into the shifting shadows. Rufus's mouth fell open, and he dropped Frederick. Frederick turned around, slowly.

The Guardian King sat up. Much of the slab came with him. The person who carved him really had done a poor job at carving. He raised his sword, and brandished it menacingly at Rufus.

Rufus ducked before the stone blade hit him. Two of his mates caught it full in the stomach. It wasn't sharp... it was made of rock, and it had been sitting exposed to the wind for years. But it knocked the wind out of them like nobody's business. Frederick thought he heard some ribs crack. The Guardian King reached forward, hoisted Rufus, and threw him, bodily, out of the cave. The rest of his crew was quick to follow...if they were lucky, under their own power. The Guardian King looked down at Frederick, eyes glowing, and nodded.

He fainted.

Neither Frederick, nor Rufus, nor Rufus's friends were stupid...or at least not stupid enough to try to explain what they'd really seen to anyone else. Like many small, rural places, Eschwalders would pass the most improbable rumors back and forth. But there was a trick to surviving in the rumor mill. Try to tell them something that sounded like magic happened a thousand years ago and they'd nod sagely. Tell them it had happened yesterday and they'd become stone-faced...and as basically straightforward as a rock, too. The boys understood this unconsciously.

It was eventually decided by the adults that, for some reason, and somehow, Frederick had beat up Rufus and his friends. Rufus was content to let that slide, since it meant Frederick got a talking-to and a list of restrictions. Frederick wasn't about to tell anyone otherwise, either. For the first time in his life, he had credit. The other bigger boys didn't fancy their chances against him as much.

Which is not to say the experience left them unchanged. Frederick, who had been about five years away from building fertilizer bombs, began to devote all the power of his obsessive focus to trying to understand what happened. He traded in his books on society and politics for more and thicker books on mythology. Ten years later, he left to work at a university in England proper. He was, by then, one of the foremost experts on Celtic mythology in the world, a prodigy in his field.

Rufus's gang never fully recovered from what it saw. No one felt they could meet up anymore without talking about the statue, and eventually it became more convenient just not to meet up at all. Rufus made a new circle of friends, and since he had originally befriended all the young toughs and troublemakers this by default put him in with a group of more positive influences. Eventually, his natural leadership skills led him to become the mayor/president of the island. Functionally, this didn't mean much, but every time someone lost a sheep, had a quarrel or needed help, you'd tell Rufus, who'd iron it out one way or another.

And the Guardian King slept. He had picked the one time he could intervene and not be seen by anyone but the children. In doing so, he'd both kept Frederick from going on to blacken Eschwald's name, and saved the rest of the commonwealth having to suffer him. Possibly even the Guardian King himself did not know, anymore, which country he had been made to save. And perhaps it didn't matter. He had fulfilled his duty, and now laid peacefully on his slab, never to rise again.

CANDYWORLD

The old, grizzled warrior spat gum juice into the sparkling fire. The little guhmies recoiled a bit as it flared. He chewed the gum with slow deliberation. His skin was cloudy with age, the color an uneven blue. The children were young enough that the light from the campfire shone through them completely, casting multicolored shadows on the gingerbread golem standing guard.

"You're still here?" he growled, without turning around. Sugarpie was standing in the corner with her arms crossed. She was the matron who kept all the other women of the camp in order while their husbands were out raiding. But she was obviously ill-at-ease with the visitor.

Also, beneath her calm demeanor, she was outraged. She was clearly not a guhmi experienced in having to hide her feelings. And when she looked at the children, seated around the fire, her eyes hardened a little further.

"I'm staying. I still think they're too young for the histories. I'm going to be on hand to remind you not to get carried away."

The warrior turned, slowly, and looked at her.

"Of course they're too young." He took a long drink of soda, and coughed, before fixing her again with his stern gaze. "It is time, nonetheless."

"My husband thinks so, too. I don't know what you and the generals talked about that makes you believe this, and I think you're all fools. If you'd let me into the meeting, then I suspect I'd *know* you were fools."

He gazed into the middle distance.

"Is it customary to let the camp matrons in on military matters in this camp?" he asked, mildly.

Sugarpie set her jaw. "It is not. But neither is the raising of the children a military matter, whatever the generals have got in their heads now. I'd have as soon stood firm against you, and them, too. I have only let you in here on my husband's account, because he's out fighting and I will respect his wishes. But I'm not leaving you alone with them."

He shrugged, and turned back to the fire.

"Stand wherever you like. The truth won't change on your account. And I will have to tell them the truth, as best as I can. They are young enough that they won't be able to understand my meaning if I give them a lie."

Sugarpie said nothing. She just leaned back against the rough exterior of a peanut brittle tree, and crossed her legs in the manner of one prepared to wait.

The warrior looked down at the assembled children.

"Have you heard anything of the histories at all, little ones?"

They all shook their heads. One of the braver ones dared to squeak.

"No, sir. They said we'd hear it when we were older."

The warrior chuckled. It was a deep, throaty chuckle, and at the end of it he had another coughing fit.

"You'll *be* older, once you hear it," he said, dribbling soda as he slaked his unsteady throat. "If you are thinking, and listening, it will change a great many things for you. But since you do not know any of it, you may have a few extra moments of childhood on the way." He took a deep breath, and settled back.

"Very well. We will start," he said, "in the beginning."

In the beginning, there was sugar, swirling in the ether of causality.

And then, the sifting came. And out of the sugar, form was wrought. The Candyworld rose from the seas of chaos, made of the cold sugar...timeless, and impermeable. But on the Candyworld settled the living sugar...warm, living, changing, shifting.

And the living sugar grew, and coalesced, and from it came all the life of Candyworld. Plants, animals, and all the tribes of candy rose through the centuries on the little island in this swirling sea of chaos. As the tribes of candy rose, they grew also in understanding...and their minds began to draw brilliant little traceries of intelligence and curiosity in the darkness of the multiverse.

This was when the trouble began. In that darkness between worlds lurk the horrible things that cannot and should not be, things that crave minds to imagine them, and give them the form they do not have. Such things lived easily in the swirling seas of chaos around the Candyworld.

Thus came the cult of Ca'cao, and the dynasty of Cane. The creatures of the outer darkness surrounded and besieged the Candyworld, shaking the fragile pillars of reality and threatening to drag the island of candy into the raging seas of unsifted sugar that swirled beneath. In desperation, the leaders of the tribes met to decide what to do. The council elected a tribe, the tribe of chocolate, to parlay with the creatures.

The tribe elders, the turtles, went to the edge of the unsifted tides, where the hissing of the sugar vortex drowned out all sound, and the plants of living sugar had been scoured from the stone by the storms and chaotic wind. But the creatures of the outer dark would not bargain. They devoured the minds of the chocolate chiefs with insanity and temptation. They fed hungrily on their reason, building themselves bodies in the imaginations of their victims…and when they were weak, they promised them dominion over all the tribes. In return, they would sacrifice themselves, and become the living vessels of the dark creatures.

Evil though the creatures were, they fulfilled their promise. Guided by the ancient cunning and intelligence of the dark creatures, the tribes of Chocolate returned to the interior of the Candyworld to prepare for war. In short order, the other chiefs were brought to their knees. The world fell into darkness. The elders of the chocolate tribes were given the name of Cane by their dark god Ca'cao, who became lord of all chocolate and bane of living sugar. But Ca'cao did not wish the world destroyed. He craved lives and minds, that he might add to his power. Thus the dynasty of Cane was tasked with choosing subjects from their new domain that might be sacrificed to Ca'cao. And on the sacrifices went, for centuries more, till the Candyworld flowed with living sugar spilt from innocent victims.

Then, the revolution. Among the subjugated tribes had been the Guhmi…once the humblest of all. The last descendent of the Guhmi Bearchiefs, guided by a vision from a dream, came face to face with a being very different from the dark creatures that controlled the Cane. The being said little about itself…only that it had come because it had seen Candyworld besieged by the creatures of the darkness, and had been moved by pity. It offered its aid and power to the Guhmis, that they might chase the creatures back into the space between worlds. In the Bearchiefs it instilled an indelible spark of its power, so that they could be connected to it always.

The war between Cane and the last Bearchief was long and difficult. Many feared the Cane too much to join the fight. Many questioned the Bearchief's ability, while others doubted the truth of his prophetic claims. But when the Bearchief struck miraculously into the heart of the capital city of Sucrose on the side of the Big Rock Candy mountain, and drove the Turtles of the Cane from their own seat of power, the skeptics were moved and the fear of the Cane broke. The remnants of the Cane were driven beyond the Rock Candy Ridge into the cold sugar steppes beyond, where they and their god Ca'cao degraded, just as the Bearchiefs, their protector, and the whole of Candyworld beyond flourished.

An age of peace and prosperity continued for some thousand years. However, it could not last forever. The ancient Guhmi grew complacent and vain. Their powers of creation grew with every passing day, until they longed to truly vindicate their abilities by creating life of their own. But to create life from cold sugar alone, they knew well, was impossible.

At first they gathered living sugar from the trees and the plants. From these simple origins, the first of the gingerbread golems were made...living sugar mixed into dough, fired in burning ovens until the sugar was bound to their very nature. But such easy sources had their price. It took only a tiny grain of living sugar to give life to the flora of Candyworld, but several pounds to give life to a gingerbread golem.

The Guhmi began to hunt creatures of the Candyworld for their living sugar. Soon, not just one, but an army of gingerbread golems rose. The golems were tasked with all the work of the Guhmi cities, and with the aid of their strength the outputs of factories doubled and the advancement of candykind grew daily. The Golems powered also the creation of public works. Great statues were constructed. A reservoir was built to hold the vital soda supply and capped with a dam that allowed power to be produced for the factories. Temples to their protector were erected. Golems became trusted companions, their fates bound inextricably to their creators.

In time, word came from the scouts in the North that the Cane were gathering strength, and beginning to move armies to the border. The Guhmi rulers grew deeply concerned, the manpower of the army having been continuously drained for decades by the greater needs of production and design. Thus the decision was made to give to golems even the most sacred trust: the protection of the Guhmi. The gingerbread golems were inducted into the army, from infantry all the way to the high guards of the Bearchiefs. The Guhmi were pleased with the move. With their protector and soon, with their golems, the Cane could never hope to match them.

This might have been true. But for all the powers the Golems gave them, the Guhmi paid a terrible price. The sources of living sugar were well-known. Plants could create living sugar out of cold sugar, given enough time, and the living sugar in dead crea-tures and plants took time to degrade into cold sugar again. Though the Guhmi had become very good at farming and tending to the creatures of their world, a certain stock had to be held in reserve to feed the people of cities. The demand for golems was great, however. The reports from the North grew more threatening by the day, and the rulers were sure, now, that the Cane were massing for an attack. To ensure the safety of their people, the rulers needed more living sugar to continue construction of their armies. The necessary sugar for the golems could not be gotten from hunting. The amounts of sugar needed were so staggering that where they would have fatally dented the massive herds of the farms, they would have completely destroyed the relatively smaller wild herds. And it was these factors that led them into the Great Sin.

Sugarpie cleared her throat.

"You can't tell them about that," she said.

"I can, and I will."

"You won't. Skip past it. All you'll do is dishonor the memories of their forefathers in their minds. They need strong roots more than they need the perfect truth."

"Wrong!" the warrior shouted, so suddenly that even the stoic Sugarpie was taken aback. After a moment, he continued in a more normal tone.

"They need to know the mistakes of their fathers so that they do not repeat them. Their ancestors should have killed the Cane outright, rather than letting them live on the steppes. To understand why, they must hear the consequences."

"Maybe they should have, but they didn't, and it doesn't matter anymore. My word in this camp is *law*."

"That's as may be. But they are no longer in your camp. These children are in a war, the generals and I agree. It just so happens that, right now, the enemy is a long way away and they are relatively safe behind walls...which believe you me, is how every soldier likes it. You will not deny that in a war, I am king. And I will say what I like."

They locked gazes for several seconds. Sugarpie looked upset, and on the verge of tears, but she did her best to stare him down. After a very long moment, though, she broke. A single seltzer-clear tear ran down her cheek, melting it ever so slightly.

She looked down, and away.

"You're going to destroy them," she said, softly.

"Then maybe what's left will be able to survive more serious assaults." The warrior sipped his drink.

"We'll see," she said, without conviction. The warrior took a deep breath, and continued.

The Guhmi began to use their own dead for living sugar. First few, and in secret, but as deadlines became shorter, more and more, until it could no longer be hidden. The being that watched over the Guhmi and their Bearchief was disgusted. It had saved the Guhmi from sacrifice, and now they had become so degraded, had so little respect for themselves as a people, that they began to see each other as another source of raw materials. As a punishment, and a gentle reminder of their dependence on the being, it withdrew some of its strength from the world. Some of the stronger dark creatures seized on the opportunity to claw through the cracks of the world. Crops withered, sugar storms swept across the land that sanded vegetation from the trees, and entire rivers of soda ran dry.

The Cane, who had been working to break through the protections established around the borders of the Guhmi lands by means of arcane spells, were overjoyed. Their generals held an emergency strategy session, and advanced their attack plans in one night so that they could take advantage of their good fortune. The armies of the Cane moved in from the North.

The golems fought valiantly, but they were still too few in number. The Cane moved southwards like wildfire. For a thousand years, they had prepared. Their plans were flawless. Their execution and rage was unstoppable. City after city fell. Finally they came to the capital, Sucrose, the very same city the Guhmi had evicted them from a millennium ago.

The Guhmi became desperate, and overcome with fear. As the city came under siege, the Bearchiefs broke into frantic battles among themselves. Finally, their leader Sweetie was killed by an underling who put the others under threat of death and assumed his place. Under his command, the Guhmi began a last-ditch effort at salvation, abducting the old, the sick, and the weak, in order to get the living sugar to make golems. This successfully held off the invasion, but for the being that had protected the Bearchiefs, it was the last straw. The sacrifice of their own dead had been a desecration, but the sacrifice of the living was unforgivable. It left Candyworld to its folly, and withdrew its defense completely.

The pillars of the fragile little world rocked as the creatures of the darkness flooded back. Bolstered by the increased strength of their dark god, and consequently, his newfound influence among the corrupted minds of the Bearchiefs, the Cane broke through the walls of Sucrose. The citizenry was rounded up, the leaders captured and imprisoned, and the city looted by the Cane. Few descendents of the Bearchiefs escaped with their lives, and none of the true heirs. Their resistance broken, and their masters captured and without hope of escape, the straggling remains of the golem knights fled. Once more, darkness reigned in the Candyworld.

The purge began.

A thousand years in exile had made even those Cane not directly possessed by Ca'cao bitter and evil. They swore to get revenge on the Guhmi once and for all. The soldiers took all the citizens of Sucrose and force-marched them into the Eastern ash-fields, a small area of uninhabitable land covered in infertile powdered sugar, bordered by the Rock Candy Ridge on what had once been the Cane side. There, they held a massive ritual in honor of Ca'cao. Every citizen, every man, woman, and child, of every age and status, was thrown into a honey volcano, to melt in the molten sugar swirling below or die on the ragged sugar crystals as they fell.

There were millions of Guhmi citizens, but the soldiers shepherded and controlled them expertly, never letting enough free at any time to overpower them. In this way, day and night, for days on end, the citizens of Sucrose were fed into the volcano, until even the honey volcano choked on the vast quantities of living sugar being shoveled into it. The dark creatures, meanwhile, gorged on the souls and fear of the doomed citizenry, turning the skies of the Candyworld black as their nightmarish bodies manifested. A seething, pulsing mass of horror covered the skies end to end, born of all the worst terror of the candy psyche. Great pawing, dripping tentacles of ink-dark licorice dragged across the landscape. Great sallow eyes of milky custard and mouths of mint-flavored spikes hung gaping in masses of chewy brown-red candy. Guhmi worms the size of houses chewed through the flesh of the monstrosities, feasting on holes that oozed molasses as they grew shut behind them.

Sugarpie slapped the warrior, hard. She stood, panting, in front of him. She pointed toward the exit of the clearing.

"And now you are done. Get out," she said, in a cold voice. "Get out, and don't come back."

The warrior felt his cheek. Behind Sugarpie, the children sat, eyes wide, mouths gaping, at what he had said.

"I told you," he said, slowly, "that I would tell them the truth."

"And now you have. And what good has it done them?" she said, sharply. "What good do your lurid descriptions of horror do them? You've given them nothing, except the pain of their ancestors."

"My descriptions are entirely necessary to make the gravity of story apparent, matron. Bloody stories should not be told bloodlessly. Besides, you're mistaken. This is not the pain experienced by their ancestors. The people who experienced the pain left no descendants."

"Semantics!" she snapped. "Whether it was their ancestors or not, all of our people feel the pain of the purge equally."

He stood up, and looked down into her eyes.

"You know that's not true. You know *why* that's not true, since you can see who I am. And besides, to water it down discounts the good that lay in their *actual* ancestors. Their ancestors were cunning, lucky, or quick enough to get out of the Cane's reach, and stay out of it. I have *far* more to be ashamed of in my heritage than them."

"Anyone can see that, certainly. You are a son of the Bearchiefs. But I didn't ask you to bring it to the children."

The warrior smiled. "No. But if you knew the things I do, and understood them, you would. In any case, they know the truth now. So would you like me to stop with fear, or may we continue into courage?"

"What courage? You've told them everything, now."

"Yes. And now I will tell them the rest."

Sugarpie stared.

"Have you gone..."

The warrior held up his hand.

"*You will understand in a little time*, matron. Be still and listen. Do you think your husband would have agreed to let me come here had I meant the children of this camp harm? Then let me speak. I have a purpose in all this."

While Sugarpie was looking confused, the warrior turned back to the children. Before she could speak again, as though he had not been interrupted at all, he continued.

"From here, the story is shrouded and not fully known, children. I can give you the words of warriors and spies, and the things I have seen for myself. You will have to find the truth in them yourself."

When the dark deed was done, the Cane returned to Sucrose, dragging carts filled with the spoils they had stolen from the citizens before pushing them into the volcano. Word of the slaughter had spread. The few survivors among the Guhmi abandoned the cities, and set up roving encampments in the wilderness, surviving by banditry and stealth. The Cane dispatched troops to deal with the bandits, but the conclusion was clear to all. Candyworld was now, once and for all, theirs.

Except...

Except that the Cane had made a mistake. In pouring so much living sugar into the forge of the volcanic heat, they had done something very similar to what the Guhmis had done when they forged the gingerbread golems. Even as their murderers left, the Guhmi were already beginning their revenge. The mass of their bodies, and what stray souls could not be devoured in the feasting of the dark creatures, flowed together into a homogenous pool of melted sugar. Within it, thousands of minds and bodies were melted to become one body, one mind...the caramel.

Up the interior of the volcano the caramel crawled, devouring the bodies of those who had gotten hung up on the rocks. Over the crest it clawed, until it rolled down its side in a great mass. Out across the powdered sugar ashes spewed by the honey volcano it crawled, until at last it reached the richer, more fertile grasslands beyond, where a field of green liquorice whips sprawled over the land.

And now, the caramel multiplied. It spread across the landscape in a pool, consuming and transforming the grass, the trees, the fungi, the small creatures, into more of itself. It covered everything around it, replicating and growing. It understood only two things...survival, and revenge.

Meanwhile, in the forests, the gingerbread knights regrouped. They remained loyal to their creators, whether they were alive or dead, and therefore were sworn with their very lives to destroy the Cane. Also, being technically machines, their minds were incorruptible by Ca'cao. In the forest, with the aid of a few brave Guhmi survivors, they built enormous mobile baking kilns to increase their numbers. The dark creatures exerted a toll on all but the bravest and best of the Guhmi survivors, making the resistance hard as nails.

The leaders of the Cane, having sacked Sucrose completely, and nullified the greatest threat, began dispatching their armies to the far reaches of Candyworld. Much needed to be planned. The last of the Guhmis had to be found and killed. The remaining citizens in the Cane cities had to be rearranged to take advantage of the newly conquered lands.

As these pursuits progressed, the caramel advanced from the East. It advanced slowly, but it advanced. Creatures unlucky enough to be caught up in it were encased in huge structures of caramel that burrowed into their backbrain and paralyzed them. They were suspended within the body of the caramel, sustained by cold sugar extracted from the ground and used to produce more living sugar to feed the caramel. With these prizes, it grew faster than ever before...spearheaded by a thin line making its way directly for Sucrose, behind which the caramel spread out in a great wave, gradually covering the landscape. Behind it, it left no trace of life. Every so often, writhing shapes would form out of the ooze... torsos with molten arms, heads with drooping faces... memories given shape. Some would crawl beyond the caramel, and scout the path, before returning again to be subsumed into it.

So the caramel continued, for a long time, moving at less than walking speed. It was weeks, months, before the caramel met the first Cane scouts, riding East to survey the Candyworld for the construction of the empire. The Cane's mounts, the dreaded Chocolate Bunnies, were torn from beneath them by oozing scouts as they rode up on a horizon filled end-to-end with sticky amber death. The grasping little creatures dragged them back to use as fuel.

The Cane themselves were not so lucky. The caramel's little minions tore them limb from limb, dissolving them into itself while they still lay screaming on the field. But this tiny taste of revenge served only to whet the caramel's appetite. The progress towards Sucrose continued unabated.

At first, the Cane were not especially concerned by the disappearance of the scouts. The bandits and their golem companions were prone to attacking the lightly-armored surveyors. Paths were being charted around any chokepoints to help mitigate this, since the golems were far too slow to pose a danger to mounted units in open. The exasperated rulers of the Cane were working hard to break up the bandit encampments, but their dark gods planned head-on assaults better than the clearing out of small bands of hit-and-run enemies. Besides, they considered the Guhmi guerillas to be beneath their powers. They still didn't present any credible threat. The crudely-made golems they produced couldn't resist a serious attack of power at a point. The Cane were just spread too thinly to bring it in earnest while the empire was being parceled. At last a new scouting detachment was arranged and dispatched East, with a different, more carefully planned route.

The horizon swallowed them.

Now, the Cane began to wonder. The priests were uneasy. There was a presence, they said, to the East. It was not a creature, but a kind of echo of the purge with a shape that boded ill. But no matter how they were pressed, they couldn't put a name to it. It was dangerous, it was bloodthirsty, but that was all the dark gods could see of it and even He could not comprehend it. It had no belief, and it had no fears, and that made it nearly invisible.

This time the Cane did not play around. Their next party was a detachment of heavily-armored warriors, dressed in nut-reinforced dark-chocolate plate and armed with the finest chocolate weapons the forges of Sucrose could build. Cane could not afford the time to outfit all their scouts this way, because the group was undoubtedly slower. But whatever it was was going to get a serious fight. And this time, the party did not disappear completely. In fact, it reported back much earlier than expected, but it wasn't necessarily a bonus.

Only one scout came back. His legs had been destroyed, his arm was mangled and melted, and he was hideously scarred. He did not have a great deal to report. Mostly it came out in either a whimper or a scream. He had met the enemy, he said, and his squad had been defeated. No, not merely defeated. Eaten. He had been the first to flee and escaped while they were devoured. How they had caught him he couldn't say. He knew he had been splashed with remnants of the enemy as his squad mates waded into the fray. A few moments later, when the enemy somehow—the doctors could not get a clear explanation of how—ripped one of his teammate's innards open and pulled them from his body, his own morale had broken. He had broken from the fight and run. He'd kept running, too, until he collapsed of exhaustion in a field.

When he woke up, his legs were nothing more than a pulsing mass of whatever it was that the enemy was made of, crawling up towards his torso with the intention of devouring him. In his deep, comatose sleep, he had not felt as they dissolved him, and soon there were no nerves to relay the message. He had hacked off his own legs with his sword, but the material had formed into a hand and grabbed it by the blade. Viciously, it had stabbed back at him, tearing a gash down his arm and across his face. He had crawled desperately away, and the thing had stayed where it was. It grew ravenously, but moved slowly.

Then, his story relayed, and overcome by pain and fear, he died. The Cane rulers had come down to meet him in person, given the state he arrived in. They took his story very seriously. He had come back in such short time, given he had to crawl the distance, that the unknown enemy could not be far away. The order was immediately sent out. The armies were to be recalled to Sucrose. Fortification was stepped up.

Yet they still did not know what enemy they faced. They rallied their advisors to try to piece it together, to no avail. The suspected it was some form of revenge from the Guhmi, but they could not prove it. The scout had given no name, and the enemy he described did not fight like the Guhmi. It fought like nothing they had *ever* known. The priests pleaded with their gods and got no answer. It had frustrated even the dark ones. Whatever the nameless terror was, it could not be shifted by harsh winds, removed by trailing tendrils, or driven insane. That fact did not inspire confidence among the Cane. Their enemy had resisted the gods themselves.

Sucrose was to be kept safe. But the outer territories were now more vulnerable, and the bandits wasted no time. Almost as soon as the soldiers had left, the resistance groups were forming in their wake. The rulers of Cane were not so stupid or inexperienced that they did not expect this. Certain key villages were used as defense points, and small armies held in them to keep areas defended. But it wasn't enough. They knew this. It was merely a way of preventing things from getting uncontrollably worse while they stopped the advancing attack.

On the eve of the one-year anniversary of the purge, a few short weeks later, the caramel became visible on the horizon. The Cane had, as expected, been beset by attacks from Guhmi rebels. Small towns on the fringes of the empire were now starting to fall. But they could be retaken in time. The glowing orange wave breaking over the horizon could not wait.

The Cane marshaled their legions, and formed them up outside the walls. On the walls stood rows of archers, and soldiers with vats of molten honey. They were ready to meet whatever the threat was in force.

For all the alien uncertainty of the situation, the first thing to ride out of the caramel was all too familiar. It was all scouts that the Cane had sent East, filled with caramel, riding once-chocolate bunnies. When they roared defiance across the field, sticky tendrils half-covered their mouths. Their missing limbs were replaced with grasping globs of caramel, and their bodies were filled with caramel until it came pouring from their ears and empty eyes.

But the Cane, worshippers of the dark pantheon, were not easily discomforted. The soldiers steeled themselves and took the field against their fallen comrades. It was a short battle, though the scouts fought with ten times the strength they had had when they were alive.

Even in victory, though, the Cane saw firsthand the endless hunger of the caramel. If a glob fell on a hand, it instantly began to dissolve it, and it was impossible to shake off. The only thing you could do was skin the flesh it had landed on before it spread deeper. Some who were too slow, in the heat of battle, were half-eaten before they realized it, and their fellows were forced to kill them.

When the reports came back to the Cane, all plans made for a full charge on the caramel were canceled. It was clear now that the army would be destroyed outright, and the enemy made stronger by it. The court alchemists suggested an alternative route.

The Guhmi had been a much more scientifically advanced civilization, but when they had taken Sucrose the alchemists had gotten access to all the Guhmi's official documents, including ones that detailed how golems were created. Initially, they had read these to get tactical information on the rebels. But they could also deduce from them that whatever *this* enemy was, it depended on a critical mass of living sugar to survive. By the same token, then, a sufficient dilution of cold sugar had the potential to overwhelm it, if it was absorbed as eagerly as everything else was. Clearly the ground of Candyworld would not be sufficient, however. The Cane needed something more readily absorbed.

The advisors therefore suggested that the soda dam be destroyed. The entire valley would flood with liquid filled with cold sugar, which would dilute the enemy and overwhelm his systems. It was a risky plan, but the only viable one. Arrangements were made at once.

The arrangements also came to the ears of the rebels, who had, in their year of time, made inroads with disgruntled elements of the Cane empire. Though the Cane uniformly hated the Guhmi, some reserved almost equal hatred for their own leaders...preferring other leaders, including in some cases themselves. The Guhmis lent them fighting strength they did not have, and the rebels allowed the Cane malcontents to believe that they were kept on a tight enough leash that they could be destroyed when they became inconvenient. In fact, they had plans to deal with all the other fighters any leader they worked with kept on hand, and they sometimes played leaders against one another to keep it that way. Meanwhile, the often better-connected leaders would sometimes share information with them when it served their own purposes. Now they were hearing that the Cane wished to move the army from Sucrose to the dam, to destroy it with bombardment. Every opportunistic Cane leader saw an opportunity to capture the city while the army was out of the way, and colluded with the Guhmi rebels to make it happen.

The Guhmis agreed with all of them, and then made their own alternate arrangements. They hatched a bold plan of their own. Volunteers were selected and soldiers moved in place. The final battle over the fate of Candyworld would be decided at Sucrose.

At the appointed time, skeleton forces from the Guhmis met with the various ambitious elements of the Cane, in the pubs and alleys of Sucrose. Meanwhile, the main detachment, along with all the remaining golems, advanced onto the dam.

The Cane forces on the dam were surprised by the flanking maneuver. The forces sent up consisted mostly of artillery and an escort. The artillery proved utterly useless at such close range, and the golems were superior in one-on-one combat. Enemies had no room to evade them on the steep mountain fastness in which the dam was set.

The Cane forces defending the city didn't realize until too late that their salvation was not coming. The caramel advanced against the wall of sucrose and began to cut right through them. Around the city, mixes of rebels and unfriendly Cane troops came up behind soldiers already bewildered and terrified. Some of the Cane malcontents began to realize that the dam plan had gone horribly wrong in the midst of battle, but before they could scrutinize their uneasy allies, the caramel was upon them.

The caramel destroyed all, indiscriminately. The Guhmi volunteers had known going in that this was a serious possibility. They fought on, anyway, until the wall crumbled and all the combined forces on it were summarily destroyed by the slow amber devourers. The caramel advanced into the middle of the city, beginning to twist and ripple like a stormy sky...within its mind, the souls of Guhmi and Cane were forced together, pressed in an attempt to combine them. But centuries of conflict had left scars that ran deep. Before, it had been only a few scouts...now it was a substantial majority of the Cane being integrated into the melted flesh of the Bearchiefs and their people. The two could not unite, and the caramel contorted itself into knots of half-formed bodies that clawed at themselves as its life-force rammed them together.

But conflicted though it was with itself, it could not be restrained from tearing wildly at the candy-rocks of the Sucrose palace, surrounding it on all sides and tearing at it. Ca'cao, highest of the Cane's dark gods, was finally moved to act. The evil creature had at first been caught up in the power of the terror from the guards on the wall, and the chaos and confusion that had reigned. But now...pressing, horrible silence, as the unthinking caramel engulfed everything. The vast proportion of Cane souls in the caramel, crying out but muffled as it crushed them, at last made it truly visible to Ca'cao. At last, Ca'cao understood the full extent of the threat. As the caramel tore its way into the antechamber of the palace, Ca'cao's hideous figure descended from the sky. Thousands of still-liquid chocolate limbs flailed around a face unrecognizable and alien. The limbs clawed, wildly, at the earth, sending up great torrents of cookie-crumb dirt as it tried to hold the caramel back. A mouth opened in the sucking brownness of the body, and it shrieked, drooling rancid raspberry filling through thousands of other tiny mouths set in its circles of gums. Eyes opened seemingly at random as chocolate dripped away from them...staring, shriveled globes of dried cocoa powder, which streamed off in clouds as it shook.

But Ca'cao was unwise to touch the caramel. It climbed up the claws of the dark god itself, eating it alive. The souls of the Cane devoured because they craved the presence of their deity. The souls of the Guhmi devoured because they craved revenge.

Up, over the horrible melting edifice, into sightless eyes and babbling mouths, the caramel ran...faster all the time, devouring the otherworldly essence of the creature. Then down, inward, into its horrible boiling core, its twisted, half-functioning brain and its great molten heart. Into the essence of Ca'cao.

An explosion rocked Candyworld. Now the caramel had finally merged once and for all with their ultimate enemy. The tiny spark of divine connection instilled in the Bearchiefs so long ago could not co-exist, could not even persist near the unadulterated evil that defined Ca'cao. The two destroyed one another, instead. The resulting shift in the fabric of the universe was so jarring that for a brief moment, pure plasmatic potentiality broke through into the world. Most of the caramel, and the once-proud city of Sucrose, were destroyed instantly by a heat. Though the hole was barely the size of a pinhead, the power it caged was so intense that the landscape scorched and the life was burnt right out of all sugar in Sucrose. So ended the Turtles of Cane, vaporized by the fires of creation itself.

Now the Guhmi burst open the distant dam. Soda gushed over and diluted the remains of the caramel crusted around the outside of the city . A cloud of steam rose into the air as it poured over the white hot rocks. Where the center of history had sat, now there was a parched crater.

The Guhmi looked into the sun of the little Candyworld as it crested above the mists. None spoke. They had lost a great deal: their friends, their leaders, their culture, their cities, their very god. There could not be an adequate eulogy, except a silence that said all things and echoed the silence they would now have to find their way in. But, finally, at last, they had won the war of their fathers. The Guhmi would retake their world, and build a future out of everything that was left on Candyworld.

A new beginning had been bought very dearly. It was up to them to make it worthwhile.

The warrior took a long drag of soda, and looked up into the sky, at the rising moon of Candyworld. A tentacle dragged in front of the glinting rock candy crags, for just a moment.

"The night is wearing thin. I have other camps to visit. I must leave, children." He rose, and adjusted his armor.

"But do not let my story leave with me. Keep it close, as you return to your families tonight. Think upon it. There are questions you must ask, but for reasons I cannot be allowed to tell you, I will not be the one to answer them."

The children began to move, but looked hesitatingly at Sugarpie. She was giving the warrior a long and intense stare. Finally, she seemed to realize what she was doing, and shook herself slightly.

"Do...do as he says, children. I will come attend to you shortly."

Obediently, looking grim and somewhat confused, the children filed out. The gingerbread golem stood aside to allow them to pass. Sugarpie walked quickly over to the edge of the clearing behind them. She leaned against a tree as she watched them continue down the path. When she was sure she and the warrior were alone, she rounded on him.

"What *was* all that? The Caramel? Spies? Sneak attacks? I've never heard any of this!"

The warrior smiled, without a trace of joy.

"Nor have almost any. They are things still unknown or unknowable."

Sugarpie shivered.

"Then I cannot believe you. You have found a way to desecrate the memories of their ancestors further with your careless fabrications, and I will have to spend many months trying to undo the damage you have done. And worse is the end of your little fantasy. Sucrose still stands, as you know perfectly well! And Ca'cao and his dark servants still live. I shudder at the task of unweaving this false hope you have spun around the children in your madness."

The warrior looked surprised.

"Memories of... Oh, but matron, that was neither madness, nor fantasy. I told you, didn't I, that I would have to tell the truth? I have seen the caramel clearly in my vision. We only wait the return of our own scouts to confirm what us bastard sons of the Bearchiefs can see with our diluted gifts."

It was a simple sentence, but sensitive though the matron was, she was not stupid. She could read the inferences it contained.

"Then... My husband..."

The bear nodded.

"He is leading the scouting party."

The matron grabbed the warrior's chestplate.

"Did he say... Why didn't he tell me?"

He laid a gentle hand on her shoulder.

"Had he told you anything, matron, he would have had to tell you everything."

The matron covered her eyes, bit her lip, and tilted her head slightly away for a few moments. Her shoulders shook, but with clear evidence of being forcibly controlled. After a few moments, she took a deep breath, and uncovered her eyes.

"Where do the children come into this?" she said, in the tone of one who knows the answer already. The warrior supplied it, anyway.

"As you could likely guess, your husband hoped they would understand our plans so that they can become a part of them if, for some reason, it is necessary. Come, I am on a tight schedule. Let me walk to my steed."

"No!" she cried at his retreating back. "There is much you have yet to explain."

The warrior only grunted, without turning around or slowing down.

Sugarpie ran after him. He had a surprisingly quick and businesslike stride. She came up next to him, panting.

"Does it not risk the security of the camp to give such secrets to mere children?"

The warrior gave her a very odd look.

"No more so than to any other soldier. Less, perhaps, since the children are better watched and guarded than my men usually are."

Sugarpie reflected on this. Then, another point occurred to her.

"In any case, what is the merit in telling them stories as if they were truth? For stories they are, whatever you call them," she said, sharply.

She had expected another philosophical rebuttal, but instead there was only a short pause, after which the warrior said:

"What is my name, matron?"

The woman stared. Suddenly, she realized, she could not remember the answer.

"And the reason you cannot," said the warrior, "is that I have not told you. A son of the Bearchiefs is not given to shyness. Does this not strike you as odd?"

He looked down the path at the opening in the trees that split into a road to the camp and a road to where the animals were kept for a moment, and then looked back at her.

"You are right in suspecting that the future I have predicted is not certain. No future is. But when the children are older, and not much older, they will remember that a warrior told them a story. None of the generals will ever tell them where he came from, or who he was. He will have been a messenger, a carrier for a story much larger and more important than a record of sin and futility. What he will have brought, that he could not have brought with the distraction of a face and a name, will be purpose."

The matron actually laughed. It was a thin, brittle laugh.

"So, you have predicted to the children a future, in hopes that the reassurance of your prediction will itself make that future possible to obtain? And this 'purpose,' at last, is what will piece together the damage you've done?"

He nodded, as though he had not caught her tone.

"Yes. Their forefathers had many things: ample resources, peace, security, and knowledge. But they lacked purpose, beyond attending their own affairs. Hence, they made their goal the retaking of a city, when they could have chased the Cane onto the steppes and dealt with them once and for all. They could have stood against evil, rather than discomfort. They had no greater concern than the pragmatic, however, and would not afford men and resources for what seemed like excessive thoroughness. Pragmatism is a kind of blindness. It leads to choices that are logical, but often incorrect. Not maintaining the army after victory, the great sin... It was all part of the same flaw."

Now the warrior headed along the path to his steed, and the matron trailed after.

"So you would rather they believe the story than think about the restrictions of reality?" she said, tensed for a long fight.

The warrior prepped the saddle on his steed. It was a gingerbread horse, expertly crafted, a very different kind of golem from the one that had been standing guard. Baroque details sprawled across its skin, hundreds of tiny lines expertly interwoven.

"I would rather they think beyond the restrictions of the present, to the potential of the future. Life will teach them to be practical. But only now can they be taught to understand something can be more important than what is best for them. Our people need, more than anything, a future to look to."

He swung himself up on his horse.

"And now I must go. I have many more camps to find, many more children to see."

"Oh, yes indeed. The time between your story and reality is slipping quickly. The future cannot wait," the matron said drily.

The warrior looked down from his horse.

"No, it can. Often, it has. But now it has waited long enough."

And he galloped into the waning night of Candyworld.

Knight In Shining Armor

Princess Greta looked out through the window of the keep as the invading army burst through the outer walls. She drew back from the narrow window as an arrow landed beside it. One of the archers down below had clearly decided to test his skill.

She threw herself into a pillow and tried to hold back her tears. This was how it ended, then. Her mother had warned her father about the neighboring kingdoms before. And then she was gone, and there was no one to warn him but Greta. And she knew only that there was a danger, but understood too little of the reasons to convince him. So the preparation was always to start tomorrow. Then when tomorrow came, it was still tomorrow. Well, there weren't any left.

She listened to the last desperate contingent of knights fighting down below. She supposed they'd have been caught outside their armor, except for the lucky few who were practicing. She'd rather fancied Sir Henway, during the last match. Funny the way those things stuck in the mind. She heard a piercing scream from a man downstairs, and buried her head in her pillow in case it was his scream.

There was a thump. The doors downstairs were breaking. Footsteps thumped on the stairs below.

She could run to her father, she thought. Well. Perhaps. He was on the other side of the keep. The footsteps were close. If they reached him first, on the other hand, she'd at least get to be queen, for a short moment.

She went to the end of the room, and looked up at a piece of wall decor. It had an old sword mounted on it, just beginning to tinge with blood-rust. She didn't know whose it had been. In fifteen years she'd never thought it more than a memento of better times. It had probably been used very bravely by a knight in some little battle no one remembered anymore. She'd heard travelers and jesters tell elaborate tales about knights. Armor was always shiny and hearts were always pure. And then she'd go back upstairs in the evening, to a world where swords rusted by inches. Sometimes she'd even guiltily dream that Sir Henway, at least, wasn't as pure as all that.

The men outside were from the real world. They'd get *dangerously* real in a second. All the knights were dead. There wasn't going to be any shiny armor coming to the rescue now. She clambered onto the dresser and tried, experimentally, to prise the sword off the wall. She didn't know how to use it, and it was...

It popped free, and fell to the ground like an incredibly heavily lump of metal, which it was, almost beyond her ability to lift. But it was the only weapon left in the kingdom, and if she wasn't yet the last person able to defend it, she soon would be.

And then there came the sound.

It was like a kind of thunderclap, but contained to the area near her bed. The air seemed to split, and out of it stepped...

...Stepped a suit of shining armor. She could scarcely believe it. It made a faint buzzing noise as it came towards her. The knight stopped, and turned his head slowly, surveying the room. Despite her terror, Greta momentarily forgot the invaders outside the door. What was this? Some kind of weapon that could move knights though walls? She was not skilled in the art of war. She was never expected to be. But it did not sound like any godly thing she'd heard of. If the invaders were in league with the devil, it would explain why her mother had worried herself to death.

"Back, fiend!" she shouted, straining to lift the sword. The knight looked at the weapon. She could not see his eyes. But the way he hesitated bespoke more interest than fear. Then he reached out, grabbed the blade, and took it carefully from her hand.

Well. That had gone well. She crumpled down, expecting the killing blow.

But it didn't come. The knight looked at the blade for a long moment. Then he reached out with his off hand, picked her up bodily, and started to walk back across the room. Greta realized it meant to take her back with it to Hell.

Panic filled her. And to think her greatest fear had merely been death a moment ago. She kicked, and struggled in the demonic knight's grasp. It did no good.

The door to her room burst open. Greta screamed, on general principles. The knight looked at her slung over the demon's shoulder. He seemed surprised. The demon turned, and wordlessly thrust the rusty sword right through a chink in the armor.

Wait. Then...it was not allied with the invaders? But what would a demon want with her, if...

She had never imagined she'd done anything to deserve this. Father Winby had been right about those imprudent thoughts.

The demon stepped backwards, and the air closed about them.

Hell was considerably colder than Father Winby had made it out to be. Then again, a priest probably couldn't have been expected to visit personally. A midget, covered in armor walked...no...rolled up. He had little wheels instead of feet!

It shouted something behind him in a strange tongue. Then it changed to her language and looked up at her.

"Well, go on, William. Put her down."

The knight looked at the midget. He appeared to be thinking.

"Put her down, I said!" it shouted. "Don't make me go get the master!"

Greta felt her stomach lurch as she was unceremoniously dropped, in a puddle of unwieldy skirts and acute embarrassment.

"That's better. You can lose that sword, too. I've never seen a worse one."

The knight swiveled his head to look at him.

"No. It is mine," he said, in a hollow voice.

The midget looked up.

"Cripes. Going to pieces, he is. Here, you're Princess Greta, of the Blackoak line?"

She looked down at the little midget. How dare he address her directly!

"Yes, peasant?" she said, looking down at him as haughtily as she could manage.

"Please follow me to the decontamination chamber."

She shook her head defiantly.

"I am not obliged to take orders from you."

The little man tilted his head sideways.

"That's an interesting theory. William, if you're not going to put that sword down, would you kindly chop her arm off with it? It will add authenticity later, anyway."

The tall knight looked at him, and once more seemed to be thinking.

"I cannot," he said, slowly. "I cannot allow her to come to harm."

"Oh, blast," the midget said, looking up at the ceiling. "Your logic pathways are degrading. The master will have to hear about this." He prodded Greta.

"Get along, or I'll cut off your arm myself." To Greta's shock, his own arm seemed to collapse into pieces, and a blade emerged from it. He brandished it, menacingly. "William" stepped forward a little. But it looked like the midget could get there first if he chose to.

Reluctantly, Greta followed the little man to a room where sprayers emerged from the walls. There was a short burst of light, as if lightning had struck. Then the sprayers filled the air with a heavy scent of flowers. Strangely, it seemed to disappear almost instantly, though Greta noticed the scent clinging to her.

"The master does not like to meet visitors from the past without a little preparation," said the midget, as if this was sufficient explanation by itself. "Very sensitive sense of smell, he's got."

She was led through shining hallways. The ceilings were high, and vaulted. The walls, curiously unadorned, as you might expect in a poor hovel...and yet the bricks shone and fitted together so tightly.

So, not Hell, then. Fairyland, perhaps. Not a markedly safer place for the human soul to be. She'd heard many stories about the elves. They were too greatly feared even to be spoken of properly. But she thought herself too old to be made a changeling of. In any case, when the elves learned what circumstance they had plucked her out of, they would surely be upset at their mistake. She prayed, silently, hoping diffusely that a rescuing angel might come. But there were only the heavy footsteps of William, behind them.

At length they came to a large, richly decorated room. This room was very different from the hallways. There were tapestries hanging from the walls, many of them woven in a manner wholly unfamiliar to Greta. Huge shelves of books reached up to the ceiling. Greta could not read, but her father did. *Well, he had,* she thought, bitterly. She had thought he had a large collection of books, but this was unlike anything she'd ever imagined. Stuffed between the shelves were weapons, and trophies from exotic creatures hung on the walls. Little square frames, like paintings, showed thousands of scenes of battles, landscapes and people she didn't recognize, all with vivid accuracy and an appearance of depth, as though she could have stuck her hand into them. Movement above her caught her eye. She looked up, and her breath caught in her throat as she confronted a giant globe, spinning gently and seemingly unsupported amid the shelves of books, unfamiliar continents dancing slowly over its surface. A little, hunched old man sat at the far end of the room, tapping away at the surface of a desk. What he was doing she could not see, but the skull of some great, tusked creature straddled the desk in front of him. He was looking at an array of giant pictures hanging over the desk. The images in them were changing.

The midget ran up to him.

"Sir! Sir! We have retrieved Princess Greta for your interview." The man turned around and looked at the midget, puzzled.

"Ah. I mean..." the midget said, and said something in its foreign tongue. The man looked up across the room at Greta, narrowed his eyes, and then nodded at the midget. He reached out a hand. The midget obediently got a cane that was leaning there, and handed it to him. He stood up, leaning forward, slightly, depending on the cane.

"Welcome, Your Highness!" said the man, hobbling towards her. He had a thick and implacable accent. "I expect this is all quite foreign to you?"

Greta could think of nothing to say. What came out was:

"You are...an elf?"

The man cackled.

"That may be a helpful way of looking at it, yes. I must remember that. Do sit down, Your Highness."

"Who are you to bid me to sit? You haven't given me so much as a name," she said, crossly.

"Ah, ah, ah. Has little Jacky told you about his knife? Yes? For now, all you need to know is that I...I am an elf. Time does not happen the same way here. I might as well be immortal, for I've seen more life and death than every man in your kingdom combined, and I'll see a great deal more before death finally claims me. And when I kidnap someone, I will have them comply with me, one way or another. Sit, princess. Don't make me set William on you."

"Sir, William is taking forever to process things," said Jacky, conspiratorially. "I think his independent decision-making is starting to interfere with the paths for processing orders. Again. Now he's brought back some old sword and won't let it go. I told you, he's overdue for..."

"Thank you, Jacky. I see," said the man.

He looked behind Greta.

"William, go fetch the tea and biscuits, will you? Research always makes me peckish. Still haven't sat down, Princess? Dear me. Am I getting the accent wrong, Jacky? I've practiced my middle-English so much."

"William's the one to ask about that."

"Indeed. Last warning, Princess Greta."

Reluctantly, Greta pressed herself into a chair. Actually, it was far more comfortable than the ones her father had been able to buy. If it had a fault, it was that Greta wasn't sure how easily she'd *escape* the pliant material.

"I am listening, elf," she said, as he lowered himself into the chair opposite her.

"Yes, indeed. Where was I? Oh. The interview."

"You did all this for an audience with me?" Greta said, skeptically.

"To a greater or lesser extent. I am a collector, of sorts, Your Highness. And, then again, an inventor. The very space we sit in was an invention I made! Ah, but that will be beyond your understanding." He settled back in the chair, and spoke more quietly. "And then again, I am a kind of thief. But I steal only things that won't be missed. Look around you! What do you see?"

Greta sat, agape. She did not know where to begin. The elf sighed.

"Lost treasures, Your Highness. These, of course, are mostly minor. They are known only to a region or a tribe. There is lost knowledge, too. On these walls sit books that have haunted the dreams of historians, philosophers, poets, for centuries. Somewhere back there, I have much of the library of Alexandra in stasis. I have the carcasses and genes of monsters no other man has ever seen."

"And...why do you take all these things?"

He quirked his head.

"A fair question. At first, it was for money. I hoped someday I could sell these lost treasures and become a rich man. But I have long since realized no one would ever believe they were real unless I let them see how I built this dimension outside of time. I do not care to do so. It would make obtaining them so easy as to render the plan void. I have realized, too, that I have no need of money here. I have stolen rejuvenation devices, machines and food from the future, decorations from whenever and wherever I wished. What have I to do but become a gentleman of leisure? Here I admire more wealth than Midas."

William clanked back into the room, and set a silver tray on the table. The man settled back from his grandiose statements, and a look of profound frustration crossed his creased face.

"But now," he said, thoughtfully looking at the table, "I have found much of what I had wanted to from the beginning. For, well, let us call it many decades, I have been forced to content myself with more minor treasures, like the ones you see here. Each special, undoubtedly. But lacking the same...luster. Then as I looked over my technology, I realized...there was yet one kind of treasure I had yet never looked for."

He flipped open the arm of his chair, and pressed something inside. Greta's arms suddenly felt very heavy. Her head pressed back into the leather. The man calmly dunked a biscuit into his tea, and nibbled on it, before continuing.

"Now, take good old William, here. He was my very first, which I suppose is why he's breaking all the time. He's from very close to you in space-time, though. That's why I built him in that old suit of armor, and also why he speaks middle-English natively. Jacky, on the other hand, doesn't. But I'd figured out how to add languages by the time I built him. He was originally picked up out of a street gang in Victorian England. Just as quick with a knife, still."

"You collect people?" said Greta, straining to move under the heavy, invisible force. She could hardly believe what she was hearing.

"Sort of. The most important part of people, at any rate. Just as with any other treasure, I get it just before it is lost forever." A metal dome lowered slowly over her head. "Jacky was going to die on the ship to Australia. William would have died, valiantly, in a minor squabble with one of your kingdom's neighbors. Oh, I add bits, here and there, to make sure the ones I put into robots obey me. But the minds themselves, I have, pristine and uncorrupted, on file in my computer. And the best are yet to come! Martyrs, heroes, and kings, someday I'll have them all."

"But...but...why me?" said Greta, nearly in tears. The elf, or demon, sounded as though he meant to steal her soul. And by some foul magic, she was being held powerless to resist.

He grinned.

"No offense, but this time, I'm starting small. That way, by the time I get to the most important people, I'll be able to put them in the best robots. For now I am just acquiring people of specialty interest. Jacky, for example, isn't famous. But the gang he's from was, and they hardly kept a stable roster. I found reference to both you and William by chance, while reading about medieval England looking for people to collect. His story is boring...valiant knight, courageous charge, probably got a small commemoration in a corner of the castle. Yours, on the other hand, is quite interesting. Heavily embellished, it's true. You do not strike me as worth all the tales. But that's telling in itself."

Greta blanched at the insult, and he sighed, sadly. "Oh, why am I bothering to explain to you? Not a word of that makes sense to you, I'm sure. But if I needed to make you understand, soon, I'd be able to do it at the flip of a switch." He flipped a switch.

There was a long, very confused moment. To Greta, it felt as though every memory she'd ever had cycled through her brain very, very fast. But there was more. There was a great, nausea-inducing collection of scents, tastes, touches, sounds, feelings, hopes, dreams, fears, ideas, running past the mind's eye until it became an indistinct, overwhelming mass. It seemed to last forever, in the way a dream contains more than a night of experiences. Then, with the same jarring suddenness as a horse stopping and throwing its rider, the experience ended.

"And now it is done," the man said. "And into the computer you'll go. Perhaps I'll replace William with you. I'm much better at the process now."

The dome lifted. He put down his tea, and stood up.

"But...but I'm still here," said Greta, bewildered. "What just..."

"In a way, you're still here. Men developed this when rejuvenation technology—the secret of *semi*-eternal youth, if you like—finally found its ultimate limit in the capacity of the human brain. In a computer, the capacity can be whatever you like. Someday, I too will go that way, and so find eternity."

He cracked his back, and yawned.

"But not today. William, be so kind as to kill her, and deliver her body back where it came from? I think I shall retire early, today. Tell the kitchen to just make a light supper."

William thought, as the man limped away. Greta tried to move, but still the field held her in place. Then, in a voice as clear as a bell, he spoke:

"No. She must not be harmed."

The man turned, as if on pivot.

"What?" he said flatly.

"I swore she must not be harmed."

"Damn it all, William. I meant coming in. You can disregard that order now."

"I cannot."

The man's brow creased.

"Do you want to destroy the whole timeline? Do as you're...no. I'll deal with you later. Jacky!"

The two had a frantic and hurried discussion in their own tongue. Jacky swiveled towards her, his knife unfolding.

But he was cut short, as William crushed him underneath his huge, armored foot.

"She *will* not be harmed," he said.

The man, enraged, pulled himself upright, and stepped closer to Greta. He twisted the top of his cane, and withdrew a sword from inside it, which he lifted clumsily over his head, gritting his teeth to deliver a downward stroke.

And then stopped. He looked puzzled. Then, he saw, in the middle of his chest, the rusty blade from the castle protruding from his chest.

"But... I have not yet had a chance...to..." he mumbled, staring at Greta and muzzily framing stilted Middle-English.

He dropped to his knees. The light faded from his eyes. William knelt over the body, cleaning the sword on the cloth. He stood again, and seemed to look at Greta.

"The royal family of Blackoak must not be harmed. I swore," he said. He raised his sword. "Thank you, my lady, for returning this."

With that, he brought a huge fist down on the control panel of the chair. The weight holding down Greta instantly relented. She stood up and looked at her hero. She knew not what mechanisms drove him inside. But the elf...or man...had taken good care of his exterior. His armor shone like the sun.

"What could you possibly want in that book, boy?" said the older historian, pulling the tome away from the student. "In seventy years of studying medieval England I have never encountered a history more exhaustive, more thoroughly researched, and more utterly useless. If the author had been minded to study physiology he'd have catalogued man one cell at a time."

"And that doesn't warrant interest?" said the boy, defiantly. "There's so much of the *detail* of history here. The little things people actually saw and knew."

"When you are older and more experienced, you'll realize that people don't understand half of what they see, and hardly ever know what they think. That's exactly the stuff history tries to read beyond."

"Beyond? It's what history *is*. Take this..." He flipped hurriedly through the volume, until he found the page he was looking for. "The fall of the kingdom of Blackoak. Minor kingdom, not much effect on the overall landscape in Europe. But it left such a strange local legend. They say the princess there was a witch. When they were about to capture her, she summoned unearthly aid and vanished. In her place appeared the corpse of an old man, stabbed in the heart. They say she used the man's soul to pay the dark powers for their services."

The older historian snorted, but the younger man pressed on.

"But here is the interesting part. For some ten centuries, there are consistent and regular records of the 'Blackoak Witch' being sighted...always, oddly, in a benevolent role. The locals think she still rules the area. And mysteriously, every invading force to try to conquer the small village in that time has fallen apart, every civil war left it untouched, every..."

The older historian could contain himself no longer.

"And I suppose she kept an old man in her wardrobe for just such an emergency? Come off it, boy. It's nonsense! Local superstition and coincidence. In a world as big as ours, the two are bound to overlap occasionally. As for the legend itself, play a game of telephone with a bunch of bloodthirsty, undereducated, adrenaline-pumped thugs, and tell me if you get any sense out of it."

"And you don't wonder what the grain of truth was, that started the whole thing?" said the boy, despairing.

"You'd only disappoint yourself if you knew. I've uncovered a few by accident just doing careful research. I don't feel any better for it, I assure you." He put a collegial arm around the younger man, and spoke kindly. "Take it from me. If you could go back and see the fight for yourself, the only mystery you'd come away with would be how people could have believed something so fanciful."

Walking Fossil

I could name any number of strange things to run into while operating a digger. But the early morning sunlight in the nearly empty construction area glinting off the leathery skin of what looked to me very much like a dinosaur gave me the idea that my list was about to expand. In fact, the only thing that was working against that possibility was the fact that the creature was very much alive for something several million years extinct.

I had been trying to forget about the recent loss of the best hunting dog I'd ever had, a purebred pointer named Rex that I had inherited from my father. After tossing and turning most of the night, I finally just clocked in a couple of hours early. After all, I wasn't sleeping, anyway.

Strangely, at the moment, I felt a great urge to be home in bed.

All right, granted, the creature wasn't exactly horrible, but then again, I hadn't really seen any other dinosaurs to compare it to.

It was covered in dark brown soil that obscured most of it, but exaggerated a stiff little frill on the head and a thick tail. Standing on two legs, it was still only about six feet tall, with a great, big sharp nose and small, comical forearms. Its eyes were slightly yellow, and in some places, it seemed to be missing strategic pieces of flesh, making it seem as though it had been put together from a kit and someone had lost bits from the box.

Brandon, a tenuous friend and my acting supervisor since his father owned the company, anyway, came running over from his place near the foreman's trailer, a cheap cigarette in hand and an incredulous expression on his face. In theory, no one was supposed to be in the trailer unless they had a reason to be, but I wasn't about to argue with him.

He hung around there simply because it annoyed the foreman to have the trailer smelling of cigarette smoke.

"What the hell is that thing, Andrew?" he said, as though I had clearly caused its appearance.

I shrugged and leaned against the digger. "Beats me, Brander...looks like a dinosaur, but that ain't possible. At a guess, I'd say it's some kinda lizard from a cave under there."

He looked disgusted. "Sick lizard, by the look of it. We can't keep the damned thing out in broad daylight. Someone'll get the wrong idea, and the project will be held up for months." Turning to me, he said, "We're gonna have to get rid of it, and quickly. The rest of the crew and the usual heavy traffic will be around any minute now."

Deep down, as he said that, I had some inexplicable grumbling misgivings about the idea of reburying it. There was some ephemeral, distant reason that it wasn't kosher, but I couldn't place it.

On the other hand, I'd have to be insane not to get rid of it. He was right—we were in a city center, and one look at that thing would have a dozen of our backers fighting to get out before some animal rights activist group sued.

But the obvious solution had already made itself quite apparent in my head. "The best way I can think of that's quick is to push it back in that hole again," I said, slowly. "It can't possibly withstand a few hundred pounds of dirt being dropped on it after that. And if we find a dead lizard while digging, well, it isn't our fault."

For a couple seconds, he seemed to be thinking about it, and then he slowly worked it out mentally. The idea clicked. He grinned broadly at me, his smile widening his round, stubble-infested face to a squat oval, and he gestured wildly with the cigarette. "Beautiful. Keep thinking like that, and I'll see you get promoted."

He glanced at the animal, calculating. His grin faded with the effort.

After a rapid epiphany, he turned to me, grinning again, and pointed at the rig. I nodded, and he held up three fingers to signal he'd count.

I climbed on the rig, and Brandon set himself up near the building shell, low to the ground in case he was charged.

As we closed the door on the metal container, Brandon turned to me.

One finger up. I moved the ignition into position.

Two fingers up. I juggled the shovel lever towards dump.

Three fingers up. The engine roared to life under my hands. Galvanized by the sudden noise, the creature jumped. Brandon's eyebrows arched.

And my heart sank.

Unfortunately, the animal didn't have the slightest interest in going back in the hole, and it charged the storage trailers.

Our beautifully simple plan had just become complex. The storage trailers were right by the road. Any passerby would be switched into full rubberneck mode the second they passed.

I swore. The rig wasn't agile enough to get between the trailers. We were running out of time. The sun was now getting high in the morning sky.

I jumped off the rig.

"Damn it, Rockhold," Brandon said, turning my last name into a swear word. "Why didn't you move the rig forward?"

Before I could explain that the creature had moved too fast, he cut me off.

"Come on. We haven't got time to wrangle it now. We'll never have him over there in time. Let's just try to shove it in the supplies trailer. We'll deal with it tonight."

Glancing at my watch, I decided that this was neither the time nor the place to argue. I ran around and opened the trailer door for him.

Brandon didn't take a moment to catch his breath after the setback. One thing any of his casual acquaintances knew was that he swung a mean right. Three seconds later, that same wicked uppercut caught the animal straight across the jaw, and six feet of dirty lizard toppled into the trailer like a domino.

Brandon massaged his knuckles and turned to me, growling in a low voice. "Don't even say a word. Remember that as far as this project is concerned, Andrew, it's him or us. Get used to treating him rough, 'cause it'll be worse tonight. We're coming back at midnight and finishing this. Until then, you and I don't let anyone else in here. You say anything, even accidentally, I break your jaw." He snapped shut the lock, and tucked his work gloves in his back pocket, wiping his palms on his shirt.

Behind him, the first truck pulled in. We had cut it very fine indeed.

Brandon had already turned away, but his entire back was tense. Something about his tone of voice was entirely too dominant for the part of me that resisted authority. I couldn't explain why, but I felt strangely sympathetic for our recently acquired captive.

The day gradually got progressively worse. I spent a considerable amount of time ducking down to intercept people trying to get supplies. The rest of the time I spent thinking about the animal.

Part of the problem was that I felt an odd connection to it. Inexplicably, I felt strangely paternal. I told myself repeatedly that it was simply the fact that it was potentially a very valuable scientific find.

I would have bet the rear axle of my truck that it was a dinosaur, regardless of whatever danger it presented to our future. I didn't know how, but I knew that it was important.

Then, as I was sitting far away from Brandon, who was talking as usual with his crew, something occurred to me. I didn't want the animal hurt. Somehow, it offended the part of me that the only animal I had ever known was closest to...the hunter. My dad and my granddad, and even old Rex, knew and taught me the rules, and had since I was a child. If it was in pain, if it was sick, it was expected you'd kill it, out of mercy. If it was defenseless and trapped, though, it became something else again.

The truth was that the animal didn't look to be in good shape, but it acted healthy and it seemed aware. I judged that the exact reason for my misgivings was that I couldn't let Brandon harm an innocent animal without at least giving it a sporting chance. Which, seeing as the dino's natural environment was several millennia out of reach, was quite probably impossible.

I was so burdened with this thought that I met with Brandon just before clockout time to deliberate on the dino's fate.

But before I could begin, he cut me off. "Andy, go home as usual. Forget about the animal. I'll get some boys together tonight, and we'll take care of it. You—"

He shook his head and spat, then grabbed me by the shoulder and pulled me close so no one could hear. "Damn it, Andy. I can't have you losing your nerve. We've got a lot on the line here. If you're gonna flinch even when I *punch* that thing, I damn sure don't want you anywhere near here when we kill it and clean it."

I was shocked. "Right here? On the site? Are you crazy? If someone finds you, you'll be in a bigger mess then before. Finding it while digging is one thing, but—"

"Not finding it is better," he growled. "I take no chances. Go home. You and your glass stomach will have us in our graves, otherwise."

My face creased at that insult. "Weigh your words, Brandon. You're talking to the person who has bested you in every hunt. At least my 'glass stomach' is sitting next to a heart." I grabbed his wrist and twisted, suddenly very fed up. "Now listen closely. *Never* mistake good hunting ethics with inability or squeamishness. You know as well as I do that this," I pointed at the trailer, "isn't a fair fight."

He stuck his face in mine. "Fair fight nothing. It's threatening the jobs of a lot of hardworking men. That isn't fair, either. Life's tough all over."

I couldn't argue that. It was true that it was inconvenient. But it still wasn't right to kill an innocent animal for convenience, and I punctuated the idea with a neat twist of Brandon's arm that sent him away, swearing. I didn't stick around to listen.

Realizing I was crazy even as I thought it, I made up my mind.

No matter what, I had to get to that dinosaur tonight.

And I would have to be there before Brandon.

I waited a long while for Brandon to leave. I had ducked off the road and I was watching from a covered parking lot. They were looking around suspiciously, then one of them headed towards my apartment. I expected that.

The way I saw it, Brandon would suspect I'd try something. He'd move back the timetable. I had to beat him to it. I knew that he wasn't crazy enough to go earlier than ten-thirty. And that meant that I would.

It was a long, tense stakeout. As the lights fell, I had a few candy bars for my dinner and waited.

Finally, after an eternity, the dashboard clock read ten exactly. I couldn't wait any longer. I had to go now. If I were going to carry through on this moral impulse, I had to make sure I did it after heavy traffic, and I had to time it just right.

Getting to the construction site was simple, because traffic was minimal in the still-redeveloping part of the inner city after rush hour. There was relatively little to do until the abandoned shop fronts were rebuilt, so the only people out this late were, for the most part, on their way home.

Unfortunately, a less simple obstacle was the gate on the construction site, which was barred and locked to keep people from breaking in and doing some creative "street art" on expensive pieces of equipment. On the other hand, I noted that the fence was buried under a mound of dirt about twelve feet high, a few dozen yards to the right of the gate.

In a sudden crazed moment, I reached down and downshifted my truck's four-wheel-drive into the low-range setting used for thick snow.

"Ain't nothing like off-roading," I said to myself as I rolled over the top of the mound and into the construction site with all the quiet delicacy of a meteor strike.

I was out the door before the dust had settled on the fenders, fumbling for the key to the supplies trailer. It was fifteen past ten now. I was pushing my time, playing it cautious.

I pulled open the door, and was greeted by the strange sight of the creature belly-up in a pile of cement dust, with its tongue lolling out the side of its mouth ridiculously. I ran to it.

It opened one large eye and said, "Rrmuuuurrr?" sounding much like a happy kitten.

"I'm here to protect you...come on." I was clearly insane to be talking to a giant lizard.

The creature flipped over and yawned, but didn't seem overly interested in moving. Desperately, I looked around for a rope. Lying underneath the thing's giant neck was a rope coil.

I glanced at my watch. The display read 10:18. I panicked. With strength beyond my own, I pulled the rope out from under the dinosaur and strung it around its neck. It protested, but I braced and started pulling it out the door.

I was halfway out the door when I heard the roar of a pickup truck, accompanied by several other cars approaching at top speed.

Brandon had come early!

I yanked as hard as I could. But my truck was still a good ten yards away, and the creature was stubborn.

There was a tinny metallic crash as the pickup barreled through the gates without slowing down and pulled into a sideways skid. The occupant didn't even bother yelling, instead rolling down the window and pointing a shotgun straight at me.

In the glare of the headlights, I heard a shot ring out just as I dodged aside.

The pickup driver's aim went wide, his shot ricocheting near the lizard's feet. The animal bolted. Going full tilt, I found myself being dragged around my truck. With all my strength, I grabbed the passenger door, braced, and used the animal's own momentum to swing him around. He crashed into the truck full tilt, pushing me into the driver's seat.

The passenger door slammed shut as I hit the accelerator, the vast mass of lizard overflowing the seat next to me. Without thinking, I steered through the framework of the building's front doors, rammed pieces of plywood out of the way with the bumper and drove right between two supports at the back of the building with less than an inch to spare on either side.

My truck rioted onto the road, I stomped the accelerator and ran straight down the street, hanging a sharp left at the corner. I heard the roar of engines fading into the distance at the crossroads, but I was leaving nothing to chance.

I weaved through the mostly unlit ghettos of the city, not daring to drop my speed below seventy-five for a single moment, lest my pursuers catch up.

At the city limits, I skidded onto a back road that was invisible at night, and ditched the hard gravel for unpaved forest halfway out, cutting five miles off my trip in a wild flurry of tree trunks and dead branches.

My cell phone buzzed, as I was driving frantically. I didn't bother to answer it.

A mile or so into the forest, I stopped and sorted out the lizard and the phone.

The phone had a text message on it from Brandon. It read, in full:

"Tag, You're it, crazy bastard. Can't prove it's mine anymore. Getting a beer." Followed by boldface, "P.S. BTW, You're Fired."

Given that I had been shot at by some of his employees, I could have been more choked up. The dinosaur was more important in my mind. It was still caked in dirt, so my seats were a mess. It was perched on my seat, with its tiny forearms resting on the dashboard, and a sublimely happy expression painted on its face. After a few minutes, I managed to loosen the rope around his neck a little, and in return he gave an appreciative gurgle.

At last, after much exhaustion, I rolled onto the road near our national preserve. I couldn't go back to my apartment, and my cabin up here was furnished well enough for my purposes.

My mind suddenly focused as I approached the entrance booth. I looked over at my unwieldy passenger, and then at the somewhat sleepy-looking night guard.

Well, I thought, *let's try the direct approach.*

I pulled the truck right up to the window.

"Hello, sir. Visiting the preserve? Do you have a cabin?" he said mechanically, without even looking up.

"Yes, that's right," I said through the window. "Just here a bit late. You wouldn't believe the traffic I ran into," I added.

As I handed the entrance fee to the man, he looked up.

His face froze. After a long moment of holding my money in his clenched fist, he stuttered, "My, that's an interesting...breed. What is it?"

I glanced over at the dinosaur. It was sniffing its reflection in the truck window with great intent. "He's a Great Saurdino Dirtback," I said with a grin. What the hell. I was already having a fun night.

"How fascinating," the man said, fumbling for change while keeping his eyes firmly fixed on my passenger, who was now licking my windshield.

His gaze occasionally nervously darted down to his coffee cup, then back up at the creature, as if he would get stung if he looked away too long.

"Have a nice night," he said, handing me two quarters and a large brass souvenir token.

"You, too," I replied, and drove away.

Getting the animal into the cabin was a Herculean effort. It seemed fascinated by the trees surrounding the site, and I was tugged along on a five-course gastronomic tour of every tuber, weed, tree, shrub, and bush before I got him inside.

In the cabin, I tied him to the coat rack on the wall for a minute, and flicked on the lamp beside me. My modest pine furnishings, a little kitchen, and a half-dozen rather nice hunting trophies were illuminated by the warm glow.

I turned around to find that the animal, and my coat rack, had vanished. Behind me, I heard a happy chirp, and then a crunch. Suddenly, the room was pitch-dark. I slapped on the overhead light—revealing the ridiculous sight of the creature with its mouth full of my lamp and a very confused expression on its face.

"Aw, for the love of Christ...that was a nice lamp," I said, as it spit out the pieces of lamp. It occurred to me that the creature should have gotten hurt by the glass, at least, if not by the live filament.

I took a closer look at the thing's mouth, prising it open while it gurgled in protest. To my surprise, its pointed mouth was actually a tough beak, lined with teeth down either side. The creature struggled out of my grip and leapt up onto my worn white couch in a shower of dirt. I heard splintering furniture.

"Squirk!" it chimed from the top of the collapsed couch, eyeing my bookshelf in a way I didn't like.

"Squirk, yourself. I think it's time we figured out just what you are, fella. Do you understand the word 'bath?'"

It tilted its head to the side and chirped musically at me again. It seemed altogether very pleased with itself. But I still couldn't tell what condition it was in while it was covered in all that dirt. Besides which, I hoped that a bath would maybe rescue the remaining pieces of furniture.

With a stolid, resolute hand, I grabbed its leash. This was going to be fun.

To my surprise, the animal did not mind the water. In fact, it took to the bathtub very quickly. In the process, it also took to the sponge and two bars of soap, which were down its gullet before I could utter a protest.

I made a mental note that I would have to feed it after the bath was finished.

But as more and more dirt washed away, I saw that the animal was fatally wounded.

It was definitely a dinosaur, one of the duckbilled ones from the look of it, and I could accept that I didn't know much about it. But I had hunted long enough to know a lethal wound when I saw one, and there was no possible way for it to be alive. Its emaciated torso was more holey than a cathedral, it seemed to have multiple, irregular wounds bad enough that there was no way to patch it up, and it had a gash on its leg that would have had a Marine calling for his mother.

But it was chirping happily as water trickled into it and back out of it like a defective bucket. More curious was the fact that I could find no signs of scabs, even though its eyes were sickly yellowish, and that its pebbly-green skin curtained off its raw flesh in some places.

After it had been cleaned up somewhat, I led it downstairs and did some research in a dinosaur encyclopedia I'd borrowed from my neighbor's kid earlier that evening. I pulled a cabbage out of the fridge, tossed it to the beast, and set out some sliced bologna for my dinner.

In a few minutes, I found a perfect picture. My guest was definitely a Corythosaurus, judging by the little frill and head shape.

What concerned me was that he was a member of a technically extinct species, and he was currently sitting here in my kitchen. More importantly, he didn't appear to be in the best of health, although after that many millions of years, that was to be expected.

Suddenly, my concentration was broken by the bologna sliding off the edge of the table.

"Oh, no," I said, putting the book down to find the miscreant with a piece of meat in his mouth. "You're a plant eater. You aren't going to like that."

The dinosaur answered by sliding the bologna very neatly into its mouth, and going after the package for another piece. I cocked an eyebrow quizzically. Then I understood. Like a dog, he was colorblind. As far as he was concerned, round and flat meant that it was edible.

Without quite knowing why, I got up, rooted around in the closet for a moment, and came back with one of Rex's old collars. "You know, you seem to catch on pretty quickly. If I'm gonna take care of you, anyway, how'd you like to be a pointer?"

For a moment, he almost seemed to understand what I was saying. His eyes lit up, and he swished his tail in a happy, repetitive arc that beat my guest chair to pieces.

I looked at the collar. Rex had been a big dog.

Carefully, I slid it around the dinosaur's neck. To my surprise, it fit perfectly.

"Well, its kinda fitting," I chuckled. "Since you're a dinosaur...I think that you would make a wonderful Rex."

For just a moment, as I looked at the dinosaur with his new collar, I would have sworn that I saw him puff out his over-worn chest with the solemn weight of his new position.

Over the next couple of weeks, I trained Rex the same as I had trained the hunting dogs, with lots of patience, and strangely enough, with the occasional piece of meat as a reward.

I guessed that the bologna wasn't likely to be very good for him, but in the shape he was in, indigestion could hardly do him in. Besides, he expressed a definite partiality for it, and eventually, I realized that I was never going to train him on cabbage alone.

After a week of training, he simply wouldn't eat cabbage.

By the end of the two weeks, Rex was the best dinosaur pointer ever to be seen by the world. In fact, he had a natural instinct for tracking that was nearly unbelievable.

Now that I didn't have the job at the construction yard anymore, I took some time off for vacation and laying low. But Brandon thought he was giving me his last parting shots, and I was content to allow him that, if it meant I never had to see him again. I wasn't keen to have another run-in with him.

After all, I may have saved him some trouble, but the least I could expect him to pull if I saw him would be sanctimonious and bureaucratic speeches about how he really shouldn't be seen with the clinically insane, and I didn't have much patience for that. Rex, meanwhile, started working his way up. Now and then, I'd toss him a piece of ham, which usually translated in his mind as "extraordinarily large piece of bologna." He even started burying the bones, an action that I wasn't certain what to think of.

But it was when I went out to tend to the grounds around the cabin one day, one of the little jobs necessary if you keep semi-permanent residence, that I saw a small dust storm being flung up nearby of larger proportions than Rex's normal snack hunt.

As I approached it, I realized that the cause of it was a fifteen-foot hole, from which two absurdly happy eyes were staring triumphantly as Rex pulled the largest bone I had ever seen out of the ground and, after a laborious climb, dropped it at my feet. As it landed, it made a dense thump, which upon further examination was explained by the fact that it was made entirely out of minerals.

And that was when I realized exactly what my next job would be.

The last time I saw Brandon was from a distance while I was working on a new dig. It contained fewer fireworks than I expected, but considering that our last engagement had involved firearms, I was more than willing to see things quiet down a bit.

It was sometime after I got my latest job in manual labor, as an excavator on archeological digs, thanks to a quick discussion with the friend from whom I borrowed the book. I passed knowledge of equipment with flying colors, but during the interview, I had insisted that I be able to bring my "dog" onto the digs, provided it didn't damage anything. It was time to do what had gotten me Rex in the first place, and play a hunch.

But Rex soon became popular around the camp, because he had an uncanny ability to find fossils where no one else even thought to look. In fact, I even got my picture in the paper as the owner of the semi-famous "rock hound," and no one bothered looking up his species, because after all, he couldn't really be a dinosaur. We couldn't have spilled our secret if we tried. I was his owner and I made sure to file papers to prove it, complete with a contrived pedigree. He ended up as a rather distant cousin of the greyhound, St. Bernard, and great dane, as well as hundreds of obscure and bizarre canines across the world.

But one bright spring day when Rex and I took a lunch break in a nearby town excavation, me with a sub sandwich, and Rex with his usual packet of cold cuts from the deli, I happened to look over at the side and see a familiar-looking figure in a dark coat. He seemed to look my way, then he had an abrupt conversation with one of the other men on crew.

After a minute, he stood up straight, glanced at me again, and then got back in his car and left.

I got a hold of the man he'd talked to as I was finishing up.

"What was that all about?" I asked, as though I expected the usual press person or similar.

"Oh, it was just someone asking about you again, Ands," he said, business as usual. "He asked about your dog. I told him it was a... What's the name now... Sardine Dustback?"

"Saurdino Dirtback," I corrected automatically. "And what did he say?"

The man picked up a shovel and leaned on it contemplatively.

"He didn't really say much of anything. He just laughed and mumbled something like 'damn clever,' and then drove off." He glanced up as he started to walk towards the dig. "Know him?"

I smiled and threw Rex the last of my sandwich, a treat he relished if he could get it.

"You could say that," I replied.

Rex and I went back to work.

About Author

Robert Anson Hoyt grew up in the comforting shadow of the rocky mountains, with a name that—let's be honest— nobody could live up to. Still, he has not been completely idle. A writer since the age of eight, he both completed his first novel, and made his first professional short story sale, in middle school. Today his short stories can be found in a number of anthologies, and his first novel "Cat's Paw", as well as its prequel novella
"Ratskiller", can be found on Amazon (he also enjoys utterly shameless plugs). Despite a demanding professional life, he is continuing to work on both novels and short stories as often as he is able.

Although he's been called far from where he was raised, his roots will always reach back deep into the mountain foothills. But as for home— home is, and always will be, wherever his loving wife is there to greet him when he gets home from a long day; wherever a cat stands ready to grudgingly accept pets after snubbing him properly for leaving; wherever his two thousand, six-hundred and fourteen little side projects rest just one crucial step from completion.
His fondest hope when you read his stories is that you find them fun— at least as much fun as are to write.